Moonlight, Wine & Stakes

Lynn Warren

Raves for *Moonlight, Wine & Stakes*

"Funny, sexy, pithy, and so hot that you'll need an icy shower, *Moonlight, Wine & Stakes* is a rare pleasure and an exciting read. **Lynn Warren** hits the sweet spot in this smoking hot, Buffy-ish romp through a Vegas like you've never known. Elliot is the best kind of hero; he's confident, sensuous, sophisticated and the perfect foil for Eden's kick-ass spirit. Maya shines as supporting cast in this blackly funny slayer story – she's the advice-giving, quirky criminologist and best friend to Eden. Complete with some of the best sex scenes I've ever read, *Moonlight, Wine & Stakes* delivers some hot and heavy mattress dancing. Elliot and Eden make their own brand of wizardry in this lusty and luscious offering by **Lynn Warren**; I know you'll love this Recommended Read! 5 Angels." –Michelle, Fallen Angel Reviews

"This action-packed vampire slayer novel is filled with humorous connotations and enough sexual tension to keep my focus right until the end. ... The secondary characters, from the pushy butler to the wimpy redheaded vampire, inserted humor into the plot while maintaining the suspenseful plot. Overall, I greatly enjoyed reading this quick and exciting novel and look forward to future book releases by the talented Ms. Warren." –Francesca Hayne, Just Erotic Romance Reviews

"Moonlight, Wine & Stakes is a very intriguing read filled with kick-ass, non-stop action that will have you caught up in a whirlwind until the very end. ... Eden and Elliot are two robust and compelling characters ... If you are in the mood for a thrilling story that is jammed-packed with passion and suspense, then Moonlight, Wine & Stakes is just what the doctor ordered! 4 Hearts" –Contessa, The Romance Studio

"Ms. Warren has crafted a tale filled with adventure and colorful characters. The story line is intricately interwoven with love and desire. I enjoyed every word of this wonderful book…This one …will most definitely be placed on my prized book shelf. Thank you, Ms. Warren!" –Sue F., Coffee Time Romance

"MOONLIGHT, WINE, & Stakes ... is filled with romance, dusting of vampires, spells, and vanquishing of demons. One thing's for sure, Las Vegas will never be the same for anyone! ... I'm ready to spin the wheel, play the slot machines and produce some magic of my own. I highly recommend that you read this book, you'll enjoy the tale as much as I have." –Connie Spears, Romance Junkies

Triskelion Publishing
15327 W. Becker Lane
Surprise, AZ 85379 USA

Printing History
First e Published by Triskelion Publishing
First e publishing August 2005
First printing by Triskelion Publishing
First paperback printing June 2006
ISBN 1-933471-65-4

Ebook and cover design Triskelion Publishing
Layout by Michelle Rouillard

CHAPTER ONE

"Hi there! Is this an invitation only type of party or can anyone crash?"

Until that instant, Eden hadn't made a sound. Now, she ground the heel of her boot into the gravel walkway. The marble along the cemetery cast in a bluish glow from the moon, Eden curled her lip.

Cemeteries were so lame.

You'd think the undead could manage something a little more original. Occasionally. Periodically. Just something to jazz things up a bit and maybe throw a curve into things, the whole thing got boring after a while.

Big scary cemetery with its creepy mausoleums and gothic ironwork drew the undead like a party with a full keg.

Tonight there was a group. Eden tilted her head and examined them. Dressed in black with lots of silver jewelry, a recent favorite of vamps, with dyed black hair and an artificial pallor, Eden shifted her weight and strode closer.

"Oh for God's sake!" She could smell the waxy makeup from here. Goths. A lash of irritation struck her spine. It was a Wednesday and she'd had a hell of a "hump day" at work. Just what she needed, Undead Groupies. She honestly couldn't wrap her mind around the fascination of teenagers toying with vampirism. Really, a sick little hobby and these kids had no idea how easy they made it.

"Okay, let's go. Clear out. At the very least, you're trespassing."

"Yeah?" A very tall, skinny boy stepped up. "And I say you're not our mother." He licked what Eden really hoped wasn't blood off his fingers.

"A damn good thing too." Eden dropped the duffle bag she carried with her at the side of her feet. She wouldn't need the contents for this crowd. Scattered around the entrance to the mausoleum were empty beer cans and a bag of chips on the stairs. Eden merely shook her head. "I think it'd be a great idea if you took this little party to a different venue."

"Whatever." A girl that couldn't be more than fourteen twisted a gold stud in her left nostril. What a joy she must be at home. "'sides, the party's just getting started."

Eden drew her cell phone off the clip on her belt. "Okay, here's how we're going to do this. You kids are going to pick up your crap sans the beer and get the hell out of here."

"Or what?" The skinny one sneered.

"Or I'll call the cops and they can sort it out and explain it all to your parents." Even in the moonlight, the sardonic lift of Eden's dark brow became visible.

Another boy, stockier than the first, sat on the

white marble steps watching. "Why don't you take your ass out of here and we won't have to hurt you?" He wiped at a smear of blood on his chin.

"You and what army?" Crap. She hadn't meant to come off confrontational. Snotty teenagers shouldn't tick her off enough to start anything, but she worked late tonight and got into a pissing match with her boss. Besides, the teenagers would lose and she knew it.

He stood up and grinned pointing over her shoulder. "That one."

She felt it on some deep corporeal level. Eden could almost smell them. How creepy was that? Did it bring her closer to their kind or further distinguish Eden as one of the good guys? Given time, she'd worry about that but not right now.

They came out from behind the trees melding across the shadows. Gliding along the perfectly manicured grass, the trio hypnotized the Goths with their immortal beauty.

Eden recognized the men. Built like a defensive linemen, with wild red hair that spiked at odd lengths and angles and a close shaved goat. "Titan, gee, what an unpleasant surprise."

"Eden, hey, how's tricks?"

Stuffy, oppressive air clung to the trio with the vague scent of old dirt mingled with rot. The summer night was already bone dry and dusty without the vamps. Eden rocked back on her heels blowing the stink out of her lungs.

Titan stopped about eight feet a way. He

gestured elegantly at the other man. "You know Ringo."

Ringo was a ferret with a receding hairline. Boney assed, little weasel, he'd sell his mother for a drop of blood. "Yeah, I know Ringo. Surprised you two are still hanging out together."

"Well, you know how things are. It's safer than being alone." Titan shrugged. "You haven't met Dominique."

Eden acknowledged the exotic brunette with a tilt of her head. Titan's tastes had certainly improved since the last time they'd run into one another. "What are you doing here, Titan?"

"Here in the cemetery or here in Las Vegas?" A sharp, brilliant smile appeared accentuated by ruthless canines.

Eden put her hands on her waist and shifted her hips. "Let's start with the easy one first. What are you doing in this cemetery at this time of night?"

Titan put his palms out. "That's the best part. You see, *they* invited us."

Initiates.

For God's sake! Damn teenagers thinking they were immortal. They used their pretty, silver jewelry to lure Vampires out like a swarm of magpies. Well, if she'd come to this little party any later, her Goth's would never sleep again and they sure as hell wouldn't get any older.

Eden sighed. She supposed that idea might appeal. Funny, she didn't think that pathological brutality and mind-control were particularly sexy.

"Got nothing to say, bitch?" Ringo snarled, picking something out from under his grotesquely long fingernails with his teeth.

Never one to resist the temptation of a challenge, Eden smiled. "Ringo, I should've turned you to ash six months ago."

Ringo chewed on the nail like a toothpick. "I don't think you've got the balls to take me on."

He was so very wrong.

Her body moved fluid as water, fast as lightning jetting across the night sky. The Goths fell back stunned at the wicked speed Eden created.

Vampires had some outrageous attributes. Lightning speed, with reflexes so tuned jaguars appeared inept. They melded into the night encompassing all the creatures of darkness and the abilities. They didn't age but became more sinister, more complex killing machines with each passing decade.

A blur of motion and Eden gripped a pair of stakes in both hands. She twirled them between her fingers like a heavy metal drummer. "C'mon kids, who's up first?"

Titan stroked his beard. "You want to know why we came back?"

"I thought idle chatter was over."

He sniffed at the remark, but kept his distance. "I think the only one it's over for is you."

"So you went away and got brain damaged when you were gone." Eden stopped spinning the stakes. "Sorry to hear that, Titan. I can put you out of your misery, you know?"

"Ah Eden," his voice became soft and tender as if he was a dear old friend. "This time, my dear, you really do have a disadvantage."

Laughter exploded from Eden starting with a hoot and ending on a howl. She wiped tears from her eyes and sniffed. "You guys, I've got to hand it to you. Nothing better than a vamp with a sense of humor."

"Show her, darling." Dominique's voice was as exotic as her looks.

Eden held up the stakes. "Yeah Titan, show me what'cha got."

Wind chimes glimmered over the night, delicate as gossamer. Eden tilted her head trying to locate the source. Then she saw Titan sprinkle some sort of iridescent powder on the ground in front of them. The chimes seemed to come from the powder. How bizarre was that? Then she heard the words.

The language was old, very old. She didn't recognize it but as Titan whispered to her and she was struck by the beauty of those words. Eden tried to move but the words glided over spinning a web of silver strands. Weaving in and out, creating a blissful state, Eden stood helplessly enthralled as the spell took hold.

Was that a butterfly or a firefly? Eden blinked. A lacey fog covered her eyes making it difficult to see. The tiny threads cast a prism of color along her skin in the moonlight. She couldn't remember anything that pretty at night.

Eden inhaled and the air filling her lungs had the weight and consistency of syrup. She moved her arm as a test and the web stretched its silver threads holding tight. Her foot moved with the same resistance and Eden knew she had a problem.

Magic.

It was the first thing to come to mind and the absolutely worse thing that could occur. Eden knew she had no defense for magic. Damn it, she could feel the Vampires closing in on her and she was utterly helpless.

"Yooouu'vvve gotstobe kidddinngg meee." Her voice ran through the syrupy web in slow motion. The web shimmered around her as she shifted her weight still keeping her entangled.

Eden thought she'd just stepped into a scene from "The Matrix." While the Vampires and their wannabes closed in, she could only move in slow motion like a movie character. She heard their laughter, cold and taunting as Ringo approached.

"Let's see you get out of this one." He reared back and struck her across the jaw. Stinging pain ripped across her cheek, in normal speed. Think, think, think, how to undo this. She needed something anything before they knocked the snot out of her.

Eden didn't have long to wait. Ringo threw another punch into her midsection. Thank God, Elliot told her she ought to work on her abs. Ringo's punch didn't break her in half. She swung back rubber-armed and missed him by nine seconds.

Well, this was bad. How long did magic last anyway? A minute? Seven? Was she stuck like this until sunrise? "Whhaat kinda wooosssseey punch 's thhaat?" Her mind still worked, but the rest of her appeared caught in Jell-O.

Oh hell, wasn't this special? Her cell phone vibrated on her waistband and nearly leaped off her jeans like a freakin' frog. It fell at her feet well out of her range at the moment and she nearly sagged against the webbing in mock agony.

Sometimes Caller ID was the bane of human existence. Elliot Warwick, boss, self-appointed guardian, advisor and general British nag. Eden focused, trying to speak succinctly but she sounded smashed. "Nah nnnot now, 'lliot."

"Eden, for once in your life, just listen to me." Amazingly, his voice came crisply across to her and she forgot completely about the vamps and impending doom. "You have to disintegrate the spell, Eden. Those Vampires will tire toying with you eventually."

Nag, nag, nag and on occasion nursemaid and teacher, Elliot fulfilled a number of roles for Eden after the death of her parents.

Ringo made a grab for the phone and screamed in agony as it spiked him with current. The cell phone remained at Eden's ankles and she stretched a lopsided smile at Ringo.

"Unless you plan on letting these creatures end your life, you need to concentrate." Concern edged Elliot's rich accent and for the first time Eden was seriously frightened. Count to three and concentrate on removing the magic. Say this word, Eden. Once. Loudly. With force. Say *Chirack!* Say it now, Eden."

Eden drew in a sharp breath and expelled it slowly. "Chirack!" Clean, fresh power moved through her in a wild rush. The binding web fell away like children's glitter and Eden launched at Ringo.

Her booted foot connected solidly with Ringo's sternum driving him backward. Ringo fell backward off balance, stumbling in surprise. Eden risked a glance back at the Goths. Fear clouded their expressions, raw, open fear. "Run!" Eden shouted the warning and hoped like hell that they would heed the alarm. She didn't have any more time to consider them when Dominique came at her hard and fast.

The ultra exotic vamp swung her leg at her with a spinning kick. Eden dropped to a modified crouch with her arms out straight. Her palms flattened into the grass. Dominique kicked high and hard, aiming for Eden's chin. Eden pivoted and swung her leg into the planted foot of the Vampire's. Dominique crashed to the ground flat on her back. Eden got a good deal of satisfaction at the groan Dominique let out as she thudded onto the grass.

Ringo threw a right and Eden blocked it easily with the palm of her hand. He proceeded with a series of punches that Eden felt she could block with her eyes shut. Now that the playing field had evened out, she clearly held the advantage. Out of the corner of her eye, she noticed Titan edging away from the scene.

She considered going after him then Dominique gang tackled her from behind plowing her into Ringo. He smelled of expensive European cologne and decay. Eden nearly gacked right there. Using the motion to take Ringo down in a pile, she rolled to her knees and scooped up one of the stakes she dropped earlier.

Dominique snarled gnashing the elongated canines together. Eden watched the metamorphosis from beautiful vamp to raging creature in seconds. The jaw grew making room for a mouthful of wicked teeth. Cheekbones and brow bones stretched into a monstrous concoction. Eden shook her head in disgust. And people thought these things were sexy?

Lady Vamp went for another kick apparently not happy to land on her ass just once this evening. Twirling the stake into her waistband, Eden shifted and caught hold of her calf with both hands. Pivoting to the side, she forced Dominique to lose her balance and go down hard on her stomach. Growls of pure rage came from the grass while Eden stepped through into a kneel with her leg locked tightly around Dominique's.

No time for style points, she could hear Ringo approaching. Whipping the stake out of her waistband Eden drove it hard into the center of Dominique's back. Lady Vamp turned to dust instantly.

Ringo dove at her kicking and scratching trying to tear her apart. He tangled his hands in her long hair and Eden bit the inside of her jaw at the sharp stinging in her scalp. She managed to get her hands on his shoulders to brace with and kicked him over the top of her. Ringo did a somersault to his feet while she rolled quickly onto hers.

"You look like hell, bitch." Spit flew out of his jagged teeth.

"Not as bad as you're going to look in about three seconds."

Throwing furious punches, Ringo hurled his body at her. Eden stepped back, blocking.

"One."

She dropped the stake next to her foot and planted her weight soundly. Ringo struck out and Eden caught him by the forearm and shoulder, twisted and brought him down to the ground. "Two."

Holding him with a knee and one hand, she picked up the stake. "You know Ringo; you're one stupid ass Vampire. I told you guys to stay away, but still, you've got to come around."

Ringo struggled to free himself in vain. He knew Titan was long gone by now. "You may kill me, but you won't be able to stop what's coming. This was just a test."

"A test?" Eden rocked back slightly, considering, but enforced pressure on Ringo's twisted arm. "Really? Well then," Eden sighed, "I guess you failed." She plunged the stake into Ringo.

He evaporated into blowing ash.

"Three."

CHAPTER TWO

Eventually, she would thank Elliot for insisting she take advanced martial art classes. Eventually. But at the moment, still ticked off at Elliot Warwick and his uncanny omniscience, Eden scowled. Damn it, he'd saved her life and she was none too pleased with owing him.

She owed him too much already. Way too much to ever be able to pay him back and Eden found that way too uncomfortable. She liked the idea of making her own way through life. She knew what she was now, a confident, clever young woman who survived tragedy during a very formative time in her life. Did she endure because of her crusty outer shell? Eden survived because of the philanthropy of Elliot.

She'd started Karate at five years old for fun. Eden craved the discipline and control as she advanced. She discovered quickly she had a natural aptitude for karate.

Elliot thought a young woman couldn't be too careful these days. He enrolled her in Kenpo Karate and Hapkido when she fell under his care.

She used it. The philosophies of the Korean originated Hapkido and the Chinese Kenpo helped her to learn and grow. Working out the anger and aggression, both disciplines brought her out of the utter darkness. She felt draped in the death of her parents. Death surrounded her as if she walked into a plague of locust. She saw things, terrifying instances that a sixteen year old shouldn't see.

Life until then was something out of a bubblegum fantasy. School, boys, friends and a set of parents that were any teenagers dream.

Shortly before Eden lost her parents in a fiery car accident, she discovered she really wasn't like other teenage girls. She knew the Undead were real and she only began to fathom how dangerous they were. An only child of parents without any living relatives, Eden was destined for child protective custody. With no family, the state really had no choice but to put her into the system. Eden knew she had a choice.

She could run.

Strangely enough, ten years later, she still wasn't sure if she found Elliot or if he found her. Or if she was still running. Sometimes she wondered if that's why she kept her distance, closed off emotions and had only a few close friends. Avoiding difficult questions, awkward scenes seemed to give Eden a case of the nerves recently.

It didn't matter much anymore how it came about. Elliot found her, lost and alone. He and all of his money produced court documents stating he was her legal guardian until she turned twenty. She never understood why or how a twenty-nine year old British guy even knew her parents. Let alone how this same guy ended up the guardian of a troubled sixteen-year-old girl.

Don't dwell on it. All it did was stir sticky thoughts into her brain that were best left undisturbed.

Forcing those memories out of her brain, she picked dead grass out of her hair. The more she thought about her past and Elliot's involvement in her life, the more confused she became. The past was just that. She couldn't change anything and God knew, she certainly couldn't change Elliot.

The cemetery held an eerie quiet now. Eden didn't like the vibes. Gathering up her phone and gear, she slung the bag over her shoulder and headed out. Tomorrow, she would consider Ringo's threat. Right now, she needed a shower and some sleep.

Undercover police officers along with a battalion of uniforms crashed the Rave at ten after two on Wednesday night while Eden was busy with other things. Smoke, cigarette and tobaccos that were more exotic rolled out of the doors in blue gray clouds as the cops rolled inside. Music thundered out of the abandoned shipping warehouse with a bass designed to create a breeze through clothing. Patrons scattered like fleas the instant they saw uniforms.

The warehouse, located ten minutes off the strip in an area of Henderson scheduled for refurbishing, made a great place for a weeknight party. The party organizers liked it cause the rent was cheap and they made serious cash. Dealers liked it because of the easy access. Kids loved it because the music, alcohol, crank, whatever you wanted, was available. And Vampires loved it cause it was a smorgasbord.

Cops didn't know anything about Vampires. Or if they did, they refused comment on such an entity. Patrolling Vegas was tough enough without a supernatural threat. So, they observed the *don't ask, don't tell* theory and hung with it. Tonight, the tip came from a perp plea-bargaining down to a lesser charge. Supposedly, Mickey Wade, Meth dealer, would attend the Rave with a special product. Mickey always gave free samples of his new stuff and those that survived the trial got in on the ground floor.

Nobody noticed the pair leave quietly through the back door. If they did, they kept quiet. The undercover cops found Mickey and arrested him while the uniforms sited the bartender for serving underage drinkers. In the raid, they managed to round up seven teenagers and found a couple of kids passed out in the middle of the dance floor.

Buried under waves of suds, the two young men laid in a fetal position by the speaker tower. On closer inspection, the teenage boys weren't out cold, they were cold dead. The official cause of death would entail an overdose from Ecstasy and Meth. The coroner would list a few incidental wounds, cuts, bruises and some odd punctures near the jugular. The Crime Scene Investigator snapped a series of photos paying particular attention to the neck wounds.

Las Vegas police officers saw everything. Robberies, drugs, prostitution, the ever-present threat of terrorism gave the folks in blue plenty to contend with; Maya knew that from experience and continued snapping pictures. Sure, they got their share of crazies. Hotel jumpers bailing when their luck hit the skids, the cops in Vegas were never bored. There was always the periodic weirdness. Goth parties that got too out of hand for the neighbors. Space aliens seeping over from Area 51 but those were rare and often sillier than the press would believe.

Because the local law enforcement had enough to contend with, they chose, very wisely, to overlook the shadowy areas where most humans refused to acknowledge.

Weres, Vampires, dark mages, the rare demonid, and hybrids belonged in another category, hell they belonged in another dimension. But since Vegas was one brilliant neon fantasy crawling with people from all over the world it became the perfect breeding ground for the others.

Eden shouldered her worn canvas bag and continued down the walkway to the parking garage. She worked the three to eleven shift at the Desert Wind Casino and Hotel four days a week as a

Security guard. Funny thing, Security was what she did on her off time as well. Her lips tilted in a quirky off center smile, you could call it *security*.

The overhead lights buzzed with neon gas and she heard the heavy whir of the air conditioner as she walked to her Nissan Pathfinder. A golf cart buzzed past and the driver waved as he continued on his rounds. Eden waved back and hit the remote on her keychain to shut off the car alarm.

Darkness, people feared it or fell hypnotized by the lure of what lurked beyond the shadows. Youth with its shallow belief of immortality beckoned the darkness. They romanticized the others ignoring the danger. So, the young became easy prey for the Vampires. They were more than willing to provide a deadly kiss in exchange of wicked excitement. While the young were eager to experience the danger and promise of heightened ecstasy, the old ignored the warnings that something wasn't quite right with the nightlife in glamorous Las Vegas.

Six months ago, vague, disturbing rumors along the underground brought Eden to Las Vegas. That, and a job offer from the ever present, frequently mysterious, Elliot.

Eden climbed into her silver SUV and started the vehicle with an easy motion. If she were a suspicious or paranoid personality, she might dwell on her meeting with the eccentric man. Instead, she considered his timely arrival as a lucky twist of fate. Elliot Warwick, odd English rich guy turned guardian, probably saved her life.

Pushing a CD by Linkin Park into her player, she backed out of her parking slot. She sniffed the air curiously picking up the strong scent of rum. She'd slipped out of her casino uniform before leaving the building because a guy managed to dump his entire drink down the front of her chest but the inebriated patron's *Desert Volcano* lingered.

Rolling down the windows, she drove out of the parking garage and headed down the strip. Maybe she'd air out by the time she got to the Luxor. She had a reservation at the "Noodle Factory" and Lo Mein sounded real tasty right now. Maya would just have to get over her nice rum smell.

Her friend had some sort of allergy to the smell of alcohol but since she called Eden, and since Eden smelled like a distillery Maya would just have to suffer.

Eden sighed figuring Maya would try to make them a spa appointment when she saw her. A resigned sigh floated from her lips. Eden tried doing the girly pampering thing but she usually came out of the exclusive spas more stressed than when she went inside. Maybe she could pull her hair back in a long ponytail and sit on her hands during dinner. No split ends or chipped broken nails made Eden really happy.

Fridays were usually chaos except during the summer, and then it became extreme chaos, which was all right by her. It gave her time to think about the Rave Maya told her about.

As she drove through fairly light traffic, Eden

tried not to concentrate on the wildly different lifestyles between her and Maya Wright. The young criminalist balanced a scientific mind with independent spa loving, shopping demon woman.

Eden negotiated a left turn into the Luxor's self-parking area and reminded herself she was nothing like Maya. Which was a good thing considering what Eden did at night. Where Maya was open, Eden kept a close lid on things. Maya believed in science and fact while Eden was pretty damn sure she dealt with science fiction.

Eden Camden slayed demons.

And other various forms of evil that made the mistake of preying on Las Vegas. Just like Titan and his group of losers from the other night.

A tinted glass pyramid with a beaming peak greeted her as Eden pulled into the valet parking. Deep brown eyes scanned the Egyptian hieroglyphs decorating the entrance of the Luxor Hotel. If they only knew, she smirked to herself as she caught the tail end of a conversation between tourists.

Ancient Egyptians possessed powerful high magics as well as the origins of the hybrids. Eden didn't like hybrids much, condescending beings with a god complex. Of course, in ancient Egypt they were gods. In Vegas, they were a colossal pain in the ass.

Since Eden avoided Elliot like the plague for the past couple of days, it felt like walking barefoot on broken glass. She hadn't had the chance to ask him why he knew anything about magic.   Just another in the long line of bizarre topics she ought to discuss with him. Ah well, she felt the confrontation brewing.   She'd stay out of his way for another couple of days and see.

She hurried past the pings and lights of the casino and dodged people coming out of the elevators to duck into the Noodle shop.

Eden found Maya already seated in a booth near a Chinese bridge in the middle of the restaurant. She slid into the booth across from her and grinned.

Maya returned the smile. "I can't believe you can eat this late and not gain an ounce. I swear I want to know what gym you go to."

The Gym of the Undead. Eyeing the menu, Eden picked out a couple of favorites. "You didn't order already did you?"

Maya ticked off on her fingers. "I got you the House Lo Mein and Lemon Grass Chicken, a bowl of Egg Flower soup and Iced tea. I got myself some Cashew Chicken which you'll probably help me eat anyway."

"Well hot damn!   After three years, you're finally trained."

Maya twirled sugar into her iced tea. "You're just a laugh a minute. You know?"

Eden shrugged and sipped at the sweetened herbal brew. "What can I say? I'm particular."

"Yuh-huh.   Wish you were that particular about your hair."   Maya tapped a short clipped

French manicured nail on the edge of the table. "You've got all this gorgeous long hair and you treat it like a hay bale."

"Wouldn't be that you're jealous?" Eden practically purred as her bowl of soup arrived.

"Maybe. A little." Maya helped herself to a half bowl of soup. Her blonde tipped hair was short, curly and wildly chaotic and it went perfect with her chocolate skin tones. Eden didn't know if it was intentional or the woman had a lot of cow licks to deal with. Whatever it was, she was well aware her own hair usually had the consistency of straw. "I don't suppose I could talk you into a day at the spa?"

"I'm seriously doubting that."

Maya held up the envelope lying beside her on the booth. "I'm thinking it might be worth it for a look at some of the photos from the Rave."

Waiting till the waitress dropped off enough food to feed half an army, Eden accepted the envelope. "Had a little unauthorized action at the party?"

"I think you're the best judge of that." Maya dug into her plate of Cashew chicken with delicate persistence.

With a large spoon, Eden scooped up several hefty proportions of her dinner. "I thought things had finally quieted down. Silly me. Had myself a little party the other night. Loads of fun." The Lemon Grass chicken was delicately flavored and fabulous as usual.

"Don't elaborate, okay. Some stuff I just don't want to know about." Maya grinned. "Anyway, I would've chalked it up to incidental contact at the Rave. Normally." Maya waited to see if Eden reacted.

She reacted just not the way Maya wanted. Eden slurped up a noodle and thumbed the end of the envelope open. "If I open these, I'm not going to gross out the customers am I?"

"No, these are a little different." Maya inclined her head for Eden to open the envelope. "They're great if you're in to bubbles."

Bubbles? That caught Eden off guard long enough to halt the bite of mushroom. She pulled out the pictures leaving them on the seat of the booth. Out of sight was an exceptional idea when it came to crime scene photos.

Maya Wright worked nights at the Crime Scene Unit with Las Vegas. She was a level three criminalist with a degree in Biochemistry. When she met Maya three years ago lurking around a crime scene, Maya thought for sure Eden was some weird stalker. The two women became staunch allies and tight friends even though they had little in common.

Eden gave a cursory glance over the first photos. Two young men in their late teens or early twenties lying in foam, Eden flipped the photos. "Drugs?"

"Yeah, the tox screen came back positive for Ecstasy. And that's going to be the official cause of death."

"But, it isn't."

Maya provided two extra photos that nobody really wanted to see except Eden. Forking a bite of noodles, Eden examined the puncture wounds in the necks of the young men.

Jeez, when did she become so blah about looking at crime scene photos. A necessary evil she figured since it made her job more efficient. Eden loved efficiency. At home, she kept a monstrous database of evil doers. That was neither here nor there. Her eyes fixed on the punctures near the side of each man's neck.

Her cell phone rang and Eden dropped the fork on her plate of noodles. She dug around her waistband where the phone sang the opening bars to "Star Wars" and checked the Caller ID.

"You'd think I was fifteen." Eden groaned as she clicked the ring off. "Yes, Elliot."

Her savior, big brother, friend with the irksome idea that she needed mothering at twenty-six began this evening's round of questioning. The more he talked the more pronounced the British.

"Eden, you should've been home forty minutes ago."

"I should've."

"But you're not."

"No, I'm not." Eden manipulated the fork with her left hand and dug into the chicken. Rolling her eyes at Maya, she listened to Elliot's lecture on safety.

"You know it isn't a good idea to roam around

by yourself at night."

"I'm not by myself." Eden winked at Maya who smothered a snort.

A pause. Eden could almost hear the sigh. "I see." She imagined him massaging his temple as he did when stressed. "Well then, I will talk to you tomorrow."

"Night, Elliot."

Her attention clicked back to the photos. As much as she appreciated Elliot, he was a worrywart. She'd never met a man with his capacity to worry. Eden's breath hung in her throat like a dry piece of pasta for a mere moment. The first time she'd seen entry wounds like this she was on her first date. Time taught you a great many things, Eden learned in this world. The creatures that crept easily in the darkness and fed on humanity were a lot like everyone else.

Crap, this wasn't good. At sixteen, she tried explaining to her parents what she'd discovered. They thought she was on drugs. Sadly, they'd been on the way home from a drug rehab clinic when they'd died. Instead of a normal life and family, she found in her a power so rich and thick it flowed in her veins like molten lava.

Eden bit the corner of her jaw remembering the first time she'd come across *The Transformation*. A hideous form of cocoon surrounded the newly deceased for exactly forty-eight hours. The cocoon provided shelter to the victim while every cell in their body altered irreversibly and when they woke, behold, newbie Vampire. Nope, not good at all not when she'd seen her share of vamps on the Strip and none increasing their numbers through *The Transformation*. "When did these guys die?"

Maya raised a quizzical brow. "What official time?" Eden nodded her head, her full lips pressed in a tight line. "The M.E. put time of death somewhere around one-thirty Wednesday night."

Eden checked her watch. "Okay that gives us about ninety minutes. Can you get us in?"

Surprise dripped off Maya and Eden wondered if her friend was ready for this sort of endeavor. "Get us in where?"

"The morgue."

"Eeeewhh." Maya bit the tip of her straw. "What for?"

"Why does this bother you? You take pictures of dead people all day." Eden stuffed the photos back into the envelope. She glanced at her broken, chewed fingernails and dismissed them for their lack of manicured perfection. "If you're not good with this, that's fine. But if I don't get in there in the next hour, Vegas is going to see a murder spree."

Her friend gulped loud enough for Eden to hear. "Oh God, tell me you're kidding here." Maya shuddered. "Morgue's creep me out, Eden. Don't like 'em, don't go in them."

Eden sniffed disdainfully. "Give me a break, will you? You're destroying my macho scientist illusion." She polished off her iced tea. "Finish up, we need to head downtown."

CHAPTER THREE

The Clark County Morgue wasn't the slickest nightspot in town. Eden followed Maya's lead. Florescent lights beamed white across the polished tile floor and neutral walls. She couldn't quite place the smell, somewhere between scented candles and industrial strength cleaning solution.

Maya knew the clerk on nights and signed them in saying Eden was a well-known writer who needed a little research material. "She's amazingly talented." The clerk merely smiled and told them to have a nice time.

Eden hoisted the ever-present duffle bag that kind of reminded her about Batman's utility belt. Giving Maya a nudge, she grinned. "I thought you didn't have any imagination."

"I have an accomplished imagination, thank you very much. And right now, I'm imagining myself at home instead of trolling around the morgue looking for fledging Vampires." Maya suppressed a shudder as the continued briskly down the hall. "Let's just get this done. I mean how sure about this are you anyway?"

"To be honest, I hope I'm wrong." Eden ignored the twinge of apprehension traveling down her shoulder blades like ice water. "I've only seen this once and it wasn't pretty."

Maya gulped. "Swell."

"Be brave, Maya." Eden shouldered the door and let Maya lead the way into the dim security lit room.

"I don't suppose we could turn the lights on." Maya fumbled for a switch, seriously creeped out by the morgue.

"Any idea which friggie these guys are in?"

Maya wiped a trickle of sweat from her upper lip. Eden fought back a grin. "You are an evil woman at times, you know that?"

With a shrug, Eden headed for a logbook. "These guys should be in the latest entry." It took only a moment to thumb through the book and find the names she sought. "Almost bunk mates. Come on, Maya; let's see what we've got."

Locating the bodies, Eden slid the first compartment open and drew back as the tagged body rolled along the track into view. Death in its natural state created a hollow shell in the place of the eclectic energy that was life.

The two men she examined weren't dead and they certainly weren't alive. The skin appeared nearly translucent at this stage of the Transformation. Blue veins nearly purple as cells reconstructed at the base level. The Transformation tore down human DNA after the victim died. Reconfiguring the cell structure, bones, stomach, heart, and lungs took time and resulted in an epic configuration that was no longer human but something more animalistic. The translucence skin acted more like a sealing agent until the fledgling broke free. It hid what occurred underneath, the hideous exchange between life and the undead.

"You really ought to analyze this stuff sometime." Eden double-checked the toe tag with the logbook. "Vampire DNA could win you some scientific award."

"Ack! You're out of your mind, Eden. Outside of the fact that no one would believe the evidence." Maya turned away from the body. "That is an abomination. One of the grossest things I've ever seen."

Eden dropped the duffle bag on the floor and unzipped the bag. "You slay me, Maya. How can someone who takes pictures of crime scenes think anything is gross?"

Maya huffed watching as Eden continued digging around the bag and coming up with a syringe and a vial of some pale greenish liquid.

The needle went slowly into the rubber tip of the vial and Eden filled the syringe. "Creatox Nine stops the Transformation and returns the fledgling back to human. Developed in the Soviet Republic so Elliot tells me."

"For God's sake, Eden. Haven't you ever wondered why a geek encyclopedia has so much weird information for you?" Eden's motion halted as the syringe needle drooped in her hand. "Is it because he's so into you? Or maybe why you seem to have a thing for him?"

Eden nearly dropped the syringe. Almost but not quite, and she fixed Maya with a glare that would stop a demon in his tracks. "Come again?"

Maya looked down dragging her toe across a line in the linoleum. "Think about it for a second, either Elliot's the most dignified stalker I've ever seen or he's got the hots for you."

"Now which one of us is out of their mind?" Eden found a particularly large vein next to the clavicle and drove the syringe. "He's like a brother or something. And I'm way too uncivilized for a guy like that." Eden finished the injection and drew the syringe out then she backed up a bit to refill for the next guy.

The Creatox hit the vein causing a chain reaction in the fledgling. The man's body jerked convulsively and Maya let out a terrified squeak.

Eden grinned, "Looks like we got here just in time. Cut it a little closer than I'd like, but a little excitement's always good."

Creatox stopped the Transformation creating a nuclear explosion on the cellular level. You could almost see the lightning from the serum as it halted the change into the undead.

Maya gripped a countertop until her knuckles turned white as the Transformation ceased and the body stopped shuddering. Eden patted the guy on the chest and covered slid him back into the refrigerated compartment.

"One down." She glanced at Maya and held up

the syringe. "You want to do this one?" Maya shook her head so hard Eden waited for it to swivel a three-sixty. "Come on," Beckoning with the syringe hand, Eden did her best at coercion. "It's easy. Besides, you never know, you might have to do this sometime."

"Not just no, but *hell* no."

"Ah, you're no fun."

Ignoring Eden's easy chuckle, Maya folded her arms across her chest trying to appear indignant. "You're just mean sometimes."

"Yeah, sometimes." Taking the comment, Eden twirled it a moment then filed it away. If she hadn't noticed Maya's twinkle of humor lurking around her shiny eyes, she might've found the remark insulting. Since this type of banter was typical for them, Eden dismissed the remark. She'd tried to get Maya to stake a vamp on several occasions but the CSI just didn't have it in her. You'd think she'd be used any gore by now but Maya had a surprisingly sensitive stomach.

"Oh jeez!" Maya's breath came in sharp pants. "Eden, he's moving."

Pivoting sharply, Eden saw the young fledgling's eyes snap open and a hideous growl followed from low in its throat. "Damn it!" The beast tried latching onto her arm but Eden sidestepped him.

This thing wasn't finished cooking and yet it seemed cognizant of danger. How was that possible? During the Transformation, the undead were practically comatose. This dude was prepared to defend even though he moved with the speed of a drunk zombie.

"Damn, damn, damn." He snapped at her revealing new canines. Eden shoved the creature back and held him down by his forehead. No sense letting those cute little toofies near her for a bite. "Okay Maya, I need a little help here." With him flailing about, it would be hard getting the syringe into the correct vein. "If I've got to hold him down and inject him, I might miss. If I miss, we've got trouble."

The directions on the serum were pretty explicit. Don't inject into an already Transformed vamp or the undead could develop an immunity to the drug. This guy wasn't Transformed yet blue veins still popped out all over the place and he wasn't exactly a study in mobility. The other directive of Creatox, only inject near the clavicle. Apparently, when the testing occurred on this drug, an injection near any other artery sped up the Transformation. Instead of a fledgling vamp just hatching, you ended up with mean and nasty Master Vamp.

Eden leaned into the creature, pushing her elbow into its shoulder while twisting the syringe around in the other hand. "Maya?" Honey dripped from the words interspersed with growls. "If this thing bites me, I'm gonna stick a stake in your—"

"Okay! Okay!" Maya skittered to a stop behind her. "What do you want me to do?"

"Hold his arm down."   Eden shifted as the creature groped seeking a hold on his tormentor.

"I have to touch it?"

"I can't believe you're a scientist." Eden hissed placing the syringe between her lips. She reared back and slammed the creature in the vicinity of the heart with the heel of her other hand. The heart was the first organ to change under the Transformation. Until the undead fledged, the heart was even more vulnerable.

The flailing and growling stopped instantly. A groan escaped the lips and Eden took the syringe out of her lips. With the other hand, she moved his arm into position and injected the Creatox near the shoulder. She waited as the drug took effect, then slid the body back into its chamber.

Dusting her hands off, she dropped the syringe into a plastic baggy and zipped up the duffle bag. "Interesting evening, huh? Let's go, I'm beat."

Flames and thick gray smoke filled the night sky. She turned onto her street called Alexander where her apartment complex was located and knew in an instant "Hump Day" just elevated to "This Totally Sucks Day." Eden checked the clock on her dash, three-forty a.m. and a tiny little voice inside told her the evening would take a turn for the worse. Not like she hadn't already had a glorious night, this would just be frosting. Eden pulled her vehicle to a stop near the smoldering remains of her apartment complex and climbed out of the SUV.

The fire department contained the blaze while Eden watched dumbfounded. The smoke and flames burned her sensitive nose and Eden backed away into a passing fire fighter.

"Sorry about that."

The man swiped sweat from his forehead. "Not a problem."

"Any idea how this happened?"

"Looks like arson. A witness thinks they saw someone throw an incendiary object through the second floor window." The fire fighter shrugged. "It's hard to tell really. Some disgruntled boyfriend throws a Molotov cocktail through the window."

Eden frowned. Her apartment faced the street on the second floor. "Yeah, a boyfriend."

"Do you live here?"

A sigh escaped before she caught it. The noise sounded a bit whiny in her ears. "I used to."

The fire fighter coughed. "I'm sorry. Do you have a place to go?"

Running her fingers through her hair, Eden scratched the back of her head. If she were the slightest paranoid, she'd wonder about this. Really, seriously, wonder if Elliot had something do with it and only because he'd been such a nag recently about her moving into the hotel.

Since she knew Elliot wasn't a whack job, Eden tossed that notion aside as easily as she discarded all of her possessions in the apartment. She had no pets, no photos of family or friends, just some good rock CDs and a DVD collection that kicked. All of it she could replace in a matter of days.

"I've got a place." The fire fighter nodded and went back to work. Eden turned to go back to the SUV when something foul filled the air.

Pausing with her finger on the remote key, Eden tilted her head casually. She used to think something was wrong with people that they couldn't smell the stench of the undead. At about eighteen, she realized her sense of smell was different from most humans.

Excited or agitated, Vampires gave off a scent that Eden picked up. Dark, musty, a mix of earth and decay, she certainly didn't enjoy the smell. However, it had assisted her on a number of occasions.

Old garbage tweaked her nostrils and Eden narrowed her eyes as she focused on the side street away from the fire. Clicking the remote, she opened the door and reached for the duffle bag. Tucking a stake into the back of her slacks, Eden locked the car door. Why did she have the feeling the vamp here wasn't a coincidence?

She came around the corner and strolled up the street approaching the vamp from behind. Clearly visible in the streetlight, Eden growled in disgust.

Reaching up, she dragged Titan from his perch on a trash bin. "I swear to God, Titan if you torched my building, I'm going to tie you to a flag pole and let you swing in the sunlight." He landed on his but and the temptation to drag his redheaded ass down the street nearly overwhelmed Eden.

Titan got to his feet gently, brushing off his backside. He smiled as a small child with their hand caught in the goldfish bowl. "Eden, babe. What're you doing out here?" His canines reflected in the dim light as he cocked his head at her. "I thought you'd be tucked in bed by now."

"I'll bet you did." She wasn't smiling, not even a little and if Titan had a brain in his tiny skull, he wouldn't push. "The question is what are you doing here?"

"Hangin'."

"You want to be hanging from a tree?" Eden moved faster than Titan expected and had the stake leveled at his heart. "Now let's try it again. Why did you torch the building?"

Titan ran his finger around his collar, trying to inch away from the tip of death. "You were supposed to be in there."

"Really?"

Titan nodded slowly.

"I didn't realize you had a death wish." The vamp shifted and Eden deliberately scratched him with the stake. "I've got no problem hooking you up, Titan, cause right now, I'm pretty peeved about the whole thing." She shoved him back against the trash bin. "Where's Dominique?"

"Out and about, I suppose."

"You don't keep tabs on your girlfriend."

Titan brought the smile back. "She's a free spirit."

Eden sniffed. "Or she didn't want to get her

hands dirty." She adjusted her stance and made Titan painfully aware that she could look him eye to eye without any effort. She could take him down just as easily. "All right, Titan. You seem to be in an amiable mood tonight. I had no idea you were a fire bug, but hey, we've all got our quirky habits." Pleased to see a trickle of fear in his eyes, Eden backed up slightly. "I'll see if I can be as pleasant about this considering you torched my DVD collection."

"Jeez Eden, I didn't know. You should've been in there to rescue them or something." He chuckled, pleased with his remarkable sense of humor. She watched him as he glanced casually about for an exit.

There wasn't one unless Eden gave it up and she was pretty irritated that her "Terminator" disks were probably shiny puddles now. "I told you, you're a funny guy. I'm not laughing until you tell me what this bit was all about."

"I can't."

"*Ex*-cuse me?" Animosity glittered in her eyes. Something about Titan irritated her and entertained like a mosquito bite you really shouldn't scratch. She'd let him exist only because he didn't seem bent on killing humans and he generally stayed out of her way. "Can't or won't?"

Titan stroked his goatee. He opened his mouth then closed it pressing his lips together. "Can't. Really can't." His hand moved achingly slow toward the pocket of his long coat.

"Did I mention my "Die Hard" DVDs?" Eden twirled the stake between her fingers. The fire at the complex was out and the fire fighters were clearing the mess. Most of the onlookers returned to their homes as dawn would creep over the horizon in an hour or so.

"Oh I'll buy you some new DVDs, Eden." His hand was nearly to the pocket. "For someone who isn't dead, you seem pretty damn ungrateful."

Eden's hand snapped out and encircled around Titan's wrist. She leaned closer ignoring the dead floral scent of his breath. "Try any more of that magic crap on me and I'll snap this off." Vampires did possess regenerative capabilities, but Eden doubted they'd grow limbs back. "Cut the crap, Titan and talk or I'm barbequing you in about an hour."

The big vamp shuddered in distaste and shook Eden off. "All right, all right. Back up and I'll tell you what I can then I'm out of Vegas."

"Guess again, Titan. You're going to talk and then your ugly self will do exactly as I say." She moved back putting her hands on her hips and tilted her head at him. The look in her eyes dared him to run; too bad Titan was a giant, spiked haired chicken.

He held his hands up in a gesture mocking friendship. "You and I have had our quarrels, right babe? But we still manage to get by." Titan lowered his hands careful to keep them away from his pockets. "It was a warning, Eden. To you. I had no choice, you know?"

"So you're not behind it? Wow, and I was scared, Titan, that you'd finally turned into a killer." Eden drew in a breath and shifted her weight. She'd heard of vamps lending themselves to the mercenary business. She never considered they'd have balls enough to come after a slayer.

Interesting dilemma she plucked at it for a moment. Slayer's didn't usually receive death threats from the locals and vamps stayed away. "Spill it, Titan. What was the deal?"

"A warning, that's all I was told. Issue the slayer a warning. Let her know things are going to change in Vegas." Titan's eyes darted toward the horizon. "I don't know who's behind it. I just got a boat load of cash and a connection at the blood bank."

"Well hot damn!" Eden hissed, "Looks like you hit the jackpot." She twisted around and nearly planted the stake in his shoulder. "What happens now that you didn't get your target?"

Titan shrugged his big frame and managed a lopsided grin. "That's the thing, babe. I don't think I was supposed to succeed."

*****

She hated this. Walking past the glitz and glamour of the Desert Mirage lobby, Eden kept her head down and moved straight for the private elevator behind one of the high limit Baccarat tables. She hated having to ask Elliot for anything. Somehow, it made her feel like that frightened teenager again. If she were suspicious, she might think that Elliot had something to do with this. Hell, who was she kidding? Eden knew for a fact she was the most suspicious person she knew. Besides, who wouldn't become suspicious with Elliot acting so weird? He'd pestered her for weeks now saying she ought to move into the hotel for safety reasons.

Eden punched the button for the penthouse before sliding her keycard into the slot that would allow her access to the penthouse floor that Elliot inhabited. She didn't actually believe Elliot torched her apartment just to get her to move into the Desert Mirage. Tossing her bag into the elevator, Eden ran a finger along the burnished gold railing and lowered her head slightly. Although, he had the uncanny ability to maneuver things to come out exactly the way he wanted.

Eden liked her independence. A lot. And it grated on her like running your teeth over a drill bit every time she had to ask Elliot for help. As the elevator rose smoothly in the air, she did something she rarely allowed herself to do, dig around in her screwed up feelings for Elliot Warwick. It reminded her of kicking through piles of trash and suddenly uncovering smoldering embers. You never knew what to expect with fire. It had the nasty habit of unpredictability and Eden liked to know what was going on. What made things even more difficult was she always felt like she had something to prove with Elliot.

In ten years, he'd been a strong, solid presence

in her life. Always British, Elliot reacted with a formality that made it hard for Eden to reach out to him. His praise for her was positively sterling. Over the years, she moved from needing a guardian to becoming an employee. And would it have been so hard for him to tell her that she was strong, smart, and capable woman? It would've been a great start. But if she ever heard that out of Elliot's mouth, she'd probably turn to stone. Frozen in shock, yeah that would be the freakin' day, when Elliot said anything close to he was proud of her or she turned out to be a hell of a woman. That's all she wanted, really wanted was for him to put his stamp of approval on her.

She needed that, deep down in a place that was so iced over now, she didn't think it'd ever thaw. It was a deep, black hole inside her where she put things she didn't want to deal with. She'd discovered that place right after her parents died and used it to hide those feelings she couldn't deal with. Eden didn't cry anymore. She'd stopped crying the moment Elliot Warwick found her and now as tucked her silent longing for his approval away, she discovered it was one thing she could cry over.

She ought to leave. Head out and crash over at Maya's house and then she wouldn't need to deal with Elliot. The elevator door opened and Eden braced her hands on the entrance. What was the big deal? She'd known Elliot for ten years. He'd been her guardian and their relationship evolved, as she got older into an impersonal sort of employer/employee thing over the past couple of years.

Eden clamped down on a sigh. She didn't sigh, she wasn't prone to dramatic outbursts or fits of tears, but she was so damned confused these days, she just hated to be near him. She got this edgy, itchy feeling around him as if he brought on Poison Oak or some nasty rash. With a growl, Eden scooped up her bag and started down the short hallway. It was as if he knew how to overload her system and did it just for shits and grins.

The heavy, old wood, engraved, castle style door waited ominously for Eden to approach. She raised her hand and rang the bell. With any luck, no body would answer. Eden yawned broadly and glanced at her watch. Damn, it was after two in the morning, no wonder her body felt like she had eighty-pound weights wrapped around her limbs. Even if Elliot or his butler were awake she doubted they'd —

The door opened. "Miss Camden? Are you all right?" Elliot's butler looked pretty good for a guy who definitely had been asleep until just moments ago. Roland pulled the door further open and ushered her inside. Eden decided this was the best luck she could've hoped for. With Elliot asleep, she could get a room and not have to encounter him. Roland tilted his head slightly and sniffed. "Miss Camden, are you hurt? You smell like smoke."

Her lip curled and she tried to smile. She

pulled her tee shirt sleeve up and sniffed it. "Yep, smoke." Raising her eyes to Roland's, she could see the concern in his light blue eyes. "My apartment was torched tonight."

"*What?*"

Eden made a slashing motion with her hand before bringing her forefinger to her nose. "Ssshhh! Don't wake Elliot up, it's bad enough as it is without him knowing."

Roland's eyes shifted and Eden groaned inwardly.

"Elliot is awake."

Rotating on her heel, Eden turned to face him. "Crap," she muttered under her breath as Elliot came into the living area wrapping the belt of his robe tighter. She cleared her throat and forced her body to straighten no matter how tired she was. "I'm sorry about waking you guys up, but someone decided to burn down my apartment complex tonight and —"

"Are you hurt?" Elliot pushed forward away from where he leaned against the doorway and it reminded Eden of a jaguar prowling.

Eden shook her head. "It was cinders by the time I got there."

Elliot froze with his hands nearly on her arms. He seemed to reconsider – something – and for the life of her, the only thing Eden could come up with was he didn't want to touch her. Instead, he looked at Roland, "I've got this, Roland. Thank you."

"I could prepare Miss Camden a room if you'd

like, sir."

"No, that's fine." Elliot raised a hand effectively shooing the other man away.

"I'll see you in the morning then, sir." Roland turned and smiled sympathetically at Eden. "It's nice to see you again, Miss Camden. Despite the circumstances." Roland went left down a hallway that led into the kitchen.

Originally, Eden thought Elliot was gay when the butler showed up. Who kept around a guy that looked like Sean Connery when he played Bond? And as a butler? Just didn't add up in Eden's little book of statistics. Roland set her straight though the first time she'd delivered an innuendo directed more towards Elliot.

Something about the two of them as lovers didn't add up, really, but Eden pressed the issue and Roland only laughed. Then he assured her in his most clipped British accent that he wasn't gay nor was Elliot despite the fact the man hardly had any contact with the female of the species.

Elliot turned eyes the color of summer grass on her. They glimmered slightly in the dim light of the living room. Eden wasn't sure it was concern. She just didn't get it. A man that looked like this with all his money was single. He had his little idiosyncrasies, but what guy didn't? She scratched the top of her head and tried not to look at him. "Can I get a room, Elliot?"

"Certainly."

"Well, give me the key and I'll get out of your

hair. How's that?" Eden fingered the strap on her bag while Elliot smoothed his wavy golden brown hair.

He pointed down the hallway where he'd come from. "There's a room for you here. Always has been."

"I can't stay here."

He lifted to an already arched brow. "Why not? It's not as if you'd be staying with strangers."

"Here? You're kidding, right?" Eden turned completely around to face Elliot and dropped her bag. "You've got to be kidding."

"It's bigger than that rat trap you called an apartment. And you'll be safe here."

Eden folded her arms over her chest and noticed the distracted look in Elliot's eyes. She suddenly wondered what it'd be like to have tits like the showgirls. As quickly as that thought settled over her, Eden brushed it aside. "You're kidding, right?"

"I rarely kid at two forty in the morning."

"I hunt demons in my spare time, Elliot. What part of safety do you think I'm missing there?"

Rubbing the back of his neck, Elliot moved toward the hallway. "Your room's on the right. It's yours if you want it. I'm going back to bed."

Maybe it was his nonchalance, or the irritating way he had of making her seem like she was sixteen again. But Eden couldn't help herself as she came up behind him and snickered the laugh of someone who's either drank too much or just a part insomniac. "Isn't this going to cramp your style? Having a woman staying at your place and being the million dollar bachelor and all?"

Elliot paused at the door to what Eden assumed belonged to his bedroom. He looked at her a moment with a wicked glimmer to his eyes. "The women I socialize with wouldn't worry about a female who'd rather look like a boy than a woman." Elliot twisted the handle on his bedroom door and walked inside. "Is there some reason you prefer to dress like a boy?" He shook his head. The door closed quietly behind him leaving Eden on the outside as usual.

CHAPTER FOUR

"Sorry all my party dresses burned in the freakin' fire!" Eden yelled so loud it made her lungs hurt. She took hold of the door handle to what she figured was one of half a dozen guest rooms in Elliot's penthouse and wrenched it open. Just like that she turned into the defiant teenager again to his stern guardian.

Gilded gold and shades of moss greeted her as Eden moved slowly into the guest room. It looked like it belonged in a box of Lucky Charms. The room held more priceless artwork than Eden had ever seen. Van Gogh, Matisse, Eden gently laid her beat up bag on the thick carpet and wondered if she ought to lay a towel under it. She wasn't used to this kind of money or luxury.

Bending over, she untied the laces of her scarred work boots and pulled them off slowly. She laid each shoe next to the door. She pulled off her thick crew socks and noticed the hole in the toe. Another pair of socks down the tubes. Eden rolled them into a ball and launched a three-pointer into the gorgeous trash near the Louis the something writing desk. The socks landed in the trash with a satisfying thump and Eden almost wished she'd shoved them into Elliot's mouth.

Yanking off the long sleeved, thermal tee shirt, Eden tossed it over the back of a chair. Her fingers went to the loops of the belt of her canvas jeans and she wiggled out of them. She left them in a pile on the floor and padded barefoot into the bath wearing boy-cut panties and a black bra.

So she dressed like a boy. Big deal. What the hell was she supposed to wear out fighting demons anyway? Black Prada? Stiletto heels? Maybe some nice pearl earrings to complete the look. Eden reached inside the shower and turned it on full blast. *Shit.*

A hot shower was just the thing to wipe Elliot right on out of her mind. Eden blew a long strand of hair out of her eyes as she glanced at herself in the mirror. Okay so her hair could use a cut and maybe she ought to wear make-up or lipgloss periodically. Like a Vampire or werebeast paid any attention to her hair products or nail polish. The only thing those creatures cared about were how sharp and pointy the stake was that she carried.

Steam fogged the edges of the mirror and Eden wondered if she had a spare shirt in her bag. She didn't generally carry spare clothing. But sometimes she'd find an odd pair of socks or a shirt. Since she doubted Elliot would give up one of his silky pajama tops for her to sleep in, she was hoping for an old soft tee shirt.

Plodding back into the bedroom, to look for a clean shirt Eden pulled up short. Her heart hit her ribcage so fast it made Eden coughed. "Elliot? What the hell?"

Green eyes went as big and round as UFOs gazing at her in the dim bedroom light. Eden didn't know what to cover up. Her legs, her bare midriff or her cleavage. He starred at her with his mouth half open until he coughed slightly and it seemed to jar his body into movement. "I owe you an apology."

"It couldn't wait?"

He shook his head, "No. No, it couldn't." She watched as he skimmed his palms down the front of his burgundy silk robe that probably cost her more than a month's salary. "I had no right to speak to you like that."

"That's nice," she nodded. Elliot's eyes moved away from her body and Eden experienced a sudden loss of heat. Goosebumps broke out over her skin and she folded her arms over her stomach. "In case you didn't notice," she pointed at her lack of clothing, "I'm a bit underdressed here."

Elliot blinked. His eyes sharpened to laser pinpoints and that did a number on her eternal heat settings. Suddenly, it was very hot in here. "When did you get that tattoo?" His eyes narrowed in on the skin just inside her left hipbone.

"What?" Obviously, he hadn't noticed she was half-naked and to make matters worse, his clinical examination of her body reminded her of a doctor. Eden inhaled slowly to keep the steam from rolling out her ears. Shit, it wasn't like she was making moves on the guy but most men reacted a bit more pleased at seeing a chick half naked. Maybe she didn't dress too feminine but for crap's sake, she was all girl when you took the clothes off.

Grinding her teeth together, she placed her hands on her hips and took a combative stance. "Get out. I've got the shower going already and you're standing between me and some sleep."

"I don't care about the shower." Elliot advanced slowly, his eyes still on her tatt. *"When did you get that tattoo?"*

"I don't know. Six years ago I think." What the hell was the big deal? At first, she'd tried to tell herself she'd got the tattoo as a lark. But with the dude drawing on her, she realized it was more a symbol of who she'd become. The tattoo was a unique statement of her skill and ability as a Demon hunter. "What's the big deal?" It wasn't that big of deal.

Just an ornate dagger, with an wicked hilt pointing downward. Some of the guys she'd fucked thought it was a hint at what was below. Eden let them think what they'd like. The dagger had blue lightning encircling it. When she'd first looked at the finished tattoo, she'd thought the lightning was around the dagger then she realized she couldn't really tell where the barbed current left off and the dagger began.

The tattoo seemed to mesmerize Elliot. His fingers curled slightly as his arms reached out. "I have to touch it." He stepped forward.

Instinctively, Eden backed up. Somehow, their positions reversed and she stumbled over her stupid boots lost her balance and whirled to right her body. Instead of falling backward and smacking into the wall like a normal person might, Eden always did things different. She corrected her fall and managed to stumble into Elliot's chest.

Her fingers dug in, attempting to steady herself. The fabric of his robe was cool and slick, but the muscle she felt beneath it, seriously shocked her. It was hard, sculpted, and totally unyielding. She wasn't expecting muscle of any density at all. It wasn't that Elliot was out of shape. He stood about five inches taller than her, putting him around six feet and he was lean. She'd always seen him in suits or jackets with casual shirts underneath so she never really considered the guy might have a body.

Her knees buckled as her hands went up his chest and ended up gripping the lapels of the robe. Elliot's hands went under her upper arms and steadied her. His fingertips went down her arms slightly and her skin lit up like a bonfire.

"Let me go," she panted wondering why on earth she couldn't seem to catch her breath. The only reasonable explanation was exhaustion. Eden decided to go with that and hold on to her sanity.

"I need to touch your tattoo."

Eden shut her eyes for a moment and tried not to inhale. He smelled of cloves, citrus and wild rain. She nodded trying to convince herself she wasn't insane. Licking her lips, she managed to open her eyes and find Elliot's sparking emerald gaze. "The only way," it came out on a croak so she started again, "The only way you're touching the tattoo is if you're on top of me." She inhaled, gaining some equilibrium, "And since I'm pretty damn sure, I'm stronger than you, you should just back off now and get out."

"Is that what you want, me on top of you?"

She shook her head, "You keep putting words in my mouth. I said I was stronger."

His fingers bit into the muscle of her arms. Elliot tilted his head so that his lips were so close to hers she could feel his breath on her face. Her axis tipped again as she looked at his mouth. It was cut in harsh thin lines, but something about it suddenly made Eden wonder about things that never, ever occurred to her. Things like what did it taste like? What would that mouth feel like on the skin where the mark in question was?

He drew her right back out of her delirium with a soft smile. "Is that what you think, Eden?" His hands moved with such speed they sucked the air out of her lungs and she found her arms flattened against his chest and hips yanked hard against his. "Have you been fighting demons for so long that you believe all men are weaker than you?"

"That isn't what I said."

Elliot moved his lips next to her ear, "That's what you're implying though, isn't it?" She shivered as his words drifted along her skin. "You would be very much mistaken by that, Eden. Very much mistaken."

"I didn't say that."

His hands went up her bare back and Eden felt him singe her skin as the roughness of his palms flattened underneath the edge of her bra. "Tell me exactly what you're saying then because we seem to have an issue communicating recently."

Air hissed through her teeth as she tried hanging on to her concentration. "That isn't my fault. You barely acknowledge me when I talk to you let alone actually listen to me. Why would I think that you gave a rat's ass about me, Elliot? I'm your employee nothing more, nothing less." She wiggled one arm out of his crushing grip. "As your employee, I suggest you let go of me before I knock you on your ass."

"Is there something I've done to make you so belligerent?" He tangled his fingers around her free hand and the jolt that tore through Eden made her gasp in surprise. Allowing that much current to spark between two people was just wrong and shouldn't happen. "Why are you so hard on yourself? I thought I taught you better."

Eden couldn't take it anymore. She couldn't think, could barely see, and was sure breathing was no longer an option. "Let me go." She shoved and in the next second, she found herself pinned on the bed with Elliot kneeling over the top of her. Pinning her arms above her head, he used the weight of one arm to hold them while he leaned sideways against Eden.

She watched his eyes go over her body and down to her tattoo. He raised his free hand to hover just over her hipbone and then suddenly, he rolled off the bed. Eden breath came in ragged pants as she struggled to sit. "Come to me when you're ready." He moved to the bedroom door and opened it. "Goodnight, Eden."

*****

Elliot walked the short way across the hall to his room appalled at his behavior. In the ten years he'd known Eden, Elliot never used force. He shut his bedroom door and turned to face his bed. On the nightstand, Roland had obviously sensed he needed a drink because the man left him a snifter of brandy. Grateful, Elliot picked up the glass and swallowed allowing the heat from the alcohol to burn its way down his throat.

He'd gone to her to apologize. Instead, he'd made matters worse between them. Harsher and colder than they'd ever been and he simply didn't understand it any longer. They used to have such a friendly – Elliot shook his head and sat the glass down. No, he couldn't classify their relationship as friendly. Tolerant was a much better word.

A knock came on his bedroom door. He didn't really expect to see Eden. As he opened it he told himself, he wasn't disappointed to see Roland. "Can I get you anything else, sir?"

"No Roland, the brandy was fine. Thank you."

Roland cleared his throat, "Did you tell her?"

Elliot arched a brow. Clearly, he butler picked

up too much information on a daily basis. "What should I've told her?"

Roland's lips twitched, his eyes rolled dramatically, "About who you *really* are."

Elliot smiled slowly, "Who I *really* am?" He wondered what Eden would do if she knew. Would she turn that wild bobcat temper on him or simply seal her emotions up and bottle them away? More likely, the latter because he sensed she'd feel betrayed somehow by his omission.

"You know what I mean."

Pressing his lips into a thin line, Elliot nodded. "She wouldn't accept it. Eden's very hard headed when she wants to be and right now, she isn't ready to believe anything more about me than I'm a rich, boring guardian."

"You won't tell her?"

Shaking his head, Elliot pursed his lips. "I can't do that now."

"Why is now any different than before?"

"She has the mark, Roland."

It took the other man a moment, but Elliot saw realization dawn in his eyes. "Oh dear."

"She thinks it's a tattoo." Elliot rubbed the back of his neck in a weary motion. The tattoo covered a birthmark he'd known about years before he ever met Eden Camden. The birthmark of a Demon hunter appeared on every child destined to fight a world of darkness. But it wasn't the birthmark that concerned him now, it was the tattoo.

Eden claimed that she'd got the tattoo six years

ago. He guaranteed she wouldn't remember how or where the tattoo had been placed on her flesh no matter how hard she tried.

He could practically feel the magic emanating from the symbol of the downward dagger encircled by barbed lightning. That's why he'd wanted to touch it, to make sure it was real. And if he ever needed to trigger the symbol to protect Eden, he would eventually need to touch it. The dagger represented the force and will of the hunter; while the barbed lightning represented the magic and wisdom of the guardian.

Roland had been with Elliot long enough to know when to leave his employer to his own thoughts and Elliot considered that an amazing asset. "Thanks for the brandy, Roland. I'll see you in the morning."

"It will work out, sir."

"Hmm, I'm not so sure of that this time." Elliot closed the door and undid the belt of his robe. Laying it over the back of his reading chair, Elliot walked over to the mirror hanging on the wall. He regarded his reflection for a moment, scratching his jaw in consideration. Slowly, his long fingers went to the hem of the silk pajama shirt. He raised the shirt up over the washboard muscles of his abdomen to stare at the tattoo under his left breastbone.

It was a duplicate of Eden's. The same color, a black dagger surrounded by blue lightning. It appeared on his chest exactly six years ago when

Eden apparently got hers. Elliot stared a moment longer at the tattoo before letting his shirt drop. The girl had absolutely no idea of the implications of this. He wasn't sure he liked the implications much himself. He'd wanted to protect her from this and the possible consequences.

Shrugging of his slippers, Elliot went to his bedside and flicked on the small lamp. If she'd ever paid the briefest attention to the lessons he'd tried to teach her about the hunter/guardian legacy, she might've put it together. But she'd never been interested in history lessons. And any talk of magic seemed to bore her to tears. So, Elliot simply quit trying and hoped that the mark never appeared.

He yanked back his bedclothes and climbed into his large bed alone as usual. Bloody hell, she wasn't ready for this and he damn well knew he wasn't either. Six years ago, he'd known he'd spend this lifetime alone. His world revolved around protecting and guiding Eden into her destiny. She was enough to handle without having to deal with a lover too. He didn't have the time or patience to try to juggle women. He barely managed a civil relationship these days with Eden.

At one point in time, he thought they'd become friends. He assumed it was a typical outgrowth of his guardianship. They never actually progressed to that state though and it grated on him like nails on a black board. He wanted more from her than just casual indifference or an employer/employee relationship. Right now, she probably thought he was some sex starved pervert.

Now, because of that tattoo, an ancient prophecy was reborn. The prophecy claimed that when a hunter and guardian bore the same mark their souls were bound to each other through all time. She would need the protection the ancient symbol afforded her. But would she accept what else came with it? Elliot fluffed his pillow and switched off the lamp.

******

Breathing wasn't an option. Now that Eden knew the exact temperature it took to turn human skin until a hot, sticky puddle, breathing just didn't matter anymore. Her body reacted on a chemical level that was all.

It was the catalyst to this chemical reaction that she couldn't wrap her smoldering brain around. Elliot Warwick managed to reduce her into a steamy pool of lava in a matter of minutes with just the lightest touch of hand. Never mind that her pussy was slick and wet with hot honey. She wasn't even going to dwell on that. In fact, she refused to dwell on that.

She couldn't dwell on that. Hell, what was the world coming to? Elliot made her – Eden sifted her thoughts, trying to sort them like a file system. Only problem was, these thoughts just wouldn't sort. She'd wanted his hands on her and inside her and then she wanted his tongue, his mouth. Eden shook her head, and then peeled the damp tendrils away from her sweaty forehead. Her hands shook. This just wasn't right.

Eden tried to sit up. Interesting the melting point of her body seemed to fuse her into the bedspread. Eden peeled the heavy fabric away from her body. She inhaled slowly, half expecting her lungs to evaporate under the cool air in the room. Well, this was an unexpected turn of events. She pushed herself to her feet feeling a whole lot older now. Obviously, she wasn't needing a hot shower anymore. She wandered into the bathroom and headed for the shower. Good thing too, because it looked like all the hot water was gone.

*****

Eden nibbled around the edge of her toast before dipping the remainder of the bread into the yoke of her egg. Chewing on the soggy piece of toast, she turned her head slightly back to where Roland poured himself a cup of tea. "Is Elliot feeling okay?"

"Hmm?" Roland glanced out the kitchen window onto the flower garden in the backyard.

"You know, is he okay? Feeling up to par?" Eden turned back to her breakfast and picked up a piece of bacon. She twirled the bacon in the air, searching for a delicate way to put it. "Is he on any medication for um, mood swings maybe?"

Roland's teacup clattered on the granite counter top. "Miss Camden, are you asking me if I think Mr. Warwick is taking some sort of medication that might alter his state of mind?"

Eden considered a moment. When British guys

spoke they always sounded more official. More knowledgeable too, Eden thought it was cool. "Yeah, I think that's what I asked."

Roland snickered and picked up his tea. "You think he's on medication? Really?"

"Well, that would explain his weird moods."

"*His* weird moods?" The way Roland said that made it sound more like he referred to her. Suddenly, she had the distinct feeling the butler was trying to give her a hint.

"Okay, well so he isn't on Prozac." She picked up her cup of coffee and finished it. "He doesn't have any odd fetishes does he?"

"*Fetishes*?" Eden's head whipped around as Roland bit back a howl of laughter. "Like tattoos, perhaps?"

"You know about that!" She pointed a finger at him. "Come on, spill. What's the deal with Elliot and tattoos?"

"What makes you think it's tattoos, Miss Camden?" Roland poured himself another cup of tea. "Have you ever thought it might be you?"

"*Me*?" Eden gathered up her plate and walked over to the sink. She rinsed her plate off and put it in the dishwasher. "You've got to be kidding. I've barely been around him for the last couple of years. How could it be me?"

"Oh I have no idea, Miss Camden! Just an old butler speaking out of turn no doubt."

"You really think it's because of me?" Eden rubbed her forehead. "Why?"

"Why would a man be disturbed by a woman?" Roland picked up his teacup and started out of the door. "I really couldn't say."

"Hang on a sec, Roland." Eden put a hand on his shoulder so that the other man would face her. "Help me out here, okay?"

"I don't see how I can."

"Well," Eden began, patting him gently on the shoulder, "if you know something that could help me out, what's the harm?"

"I would help you, Miss Camden, if I could. But, I don't know how it's possible. It's really something that you need to sort out with Mr. Warwick."

Eden winked. She got the hint. Loyalty was something she understood and appreciated. "Thanks, Roland." She started to the counter for another cup of coffee and then turned as an afterthought, "Is he around?"

"Not that I'm aware of, Miss. I believe he left early this morning."

She nodded and poured another cup. "Thanks again, Roland."

He pushed the door open leading into the dining room, "My pleasure, Miss."

*****

Elliot knew where to find them. The freeway overpass under construction out on Pecos Road was a perfect, out of the way place for Vampires to take refuge. Sunlight didn't hit it due to the angle of the construction. Vampires in the form of bats considered it a unique rest spot. Elliot planned to make this their final rest.

As dawn broke over Las Vegas, rays of sunlight glinted on mirrored edges of hotel casinos as they rose into the sky. Elliot had stood on the balcony of his penthouse just before the sun rose, staring out over the city lights.

Closing his eyes, he allowed the form to take shape in his mind. The bone, the tightly honed sinew created a picture for him. It was one he knew well. Eyes blinked, refocused as he spoke the phrase, *"Shanar verinatas."* Arms folded into wings, height shrank into a compact form with enough force per inch, and he could take down a man with his talons.

He flapped his large, powerful wings in a slow steady motion heading southwest toward Pecos. Catching an updraft, he sailed for several miles without expending any excess energy. The morning air was still cold, but Elliot didn't notice. His gaze and attention was only on the overpass now.

The magic it required to change forms was a huge drain of energy, especially for a lesser magician. Elliot was no ordinary magician and the energy for complex spells, he channeled easily. As a Warlock, Elliot mastered altering forms years ago and it could change to nearly any animal he chose now at will. He preferred the Red Tail hawk though. In Las Vegas, it was relatively common bird of prey and easily accepted. He enjoyed the owl, but there weren't many within the city limits and Elliot required a great deal of anonymity.

Magic was an immense gift. A power so unique and complex it took years to master and even those that thought they had, couldn't change form. He'd been born to it. Studied it, reveled in it and then when Eden came along, he'd simply gloried in the possibility of it all.

In the form of a bird of prey, Elliot used the skill to hunt.

He landed gently in a tree three hundred yards from the overpass. With a ruffle of feathers, Elliot's landing didn't rustle the limbs at the top of the Eucalyptus. His pupils dilated as he searched out his prey.

He found them, seconds later. At least eight, perhaps more, huddled together in a familial group. Elliot knew there was nothing loving or familial about this group of bats. He launched himself into the air with a piercing cry and swooped in for the kill.

Talons pierced through skin and fur as Elliot slammed into four bats sound asleep under the overpass. The force of the blow crushed two before they could wake. Elliot swatted at the other two with a wing and shoved them against the cement. The bats didn't squeak but they rewarded him with a resounding snap and thud. He used the talons to rip and tear his way through the group as they awoke to utter chaos. In their groggy state, they were no match for a hawk. In any state, these Vampires were no match for a Warlock.

With half a dozen bats lying decimated in the dirt below, Elliot located the one he was after. A bat with a shock of red hair, the one Eden had mentioned by the name of Titan. He sensed this creature was behind the fire at Eden's apartment last night. The Vampire seemed to have some strange sort of attachment toward Eden.

Reaching his talons out, Elliot plucked Titan from his upside down position on the shaded overpass and rushed downward to the earth at a lightning speed. Elliot was careful to land. He had no desire to crush the bat. Flapping slowly, to break the landing, Elliot settled his prey in the shade. Raising one long talon, Elliot delicately tapped the unconscious Vampire.

"Open your eyes, fool!"

The bat woke slowly. Elliot saw the panic crawl into the creature's eyes as a scream of alarm came from its mouth. The bat struggled and Elliot closed his grip a bit tighter causing the bat to hiss. *"Are you the one called Titan?"* Elliot angled his head and opened his sharp beak slightly. *"Answer me, Vampire or I will simply squeeze the life out of your pathetic body."*

"I could change, right here, now and then who would kill who?" Elliot sensed the note of desperation in Titan's thoughts even through all the bravado.

Elliot leaned closer allowing the pupils of his light eyes to dilate slightly. *"Try it."* Elliot rotated his talons, tapping them lightly on the dirt. *"Please, try it."*

Titan reconsidered. His fleshy wings quivered in the dirt. *"What do you want?"*

"I want you to listen to me very carefully." Titan nodded with a tiny squeak of compliance. *"Tell your master it's time for him to change his plans. If he comes to Las Vegas, I will destroy him."*

A look somewhere between surprise and open obstinance appeared on the Vampire's bat countenance. *"I don't know what the hell you're talking about."*

"If your master comes to Las Vegas, he and all of his underlings will perish." Elliot stepped off the Vampire and folded his wings. *"In case you doubt me, ask Carlos if he remembers Elliot Warwick."*

CHAPTER FIVE

"Much as I love you, Eden." Maya sorted through several pairs of thongs, "There is no way, no way you felt the sudden urge to go shopping just for grins."

Eden found a stack of lacey panties in every shade of the rainbow. Thumbing through them, she found her size and grabbed a handful. "All my stuff was torched, I need clothes."

"Uh-huh."

"What *uh-huh*?"

Maya tossed several bras that matched the panties Eden selected onto the sales counter. "You're full of shit, girl."

Eden paid for her purchases and stuffed the bag into another larger one full of shoes. Her credit card could already feel the strain this little shopping trip put it under. But, she needed clothes. "Okay, I need some more girlie clothes." Heading for the exit, she counted on Maya pointing the way to sexy, stylish outfits she hoped would make Elliot's eyes pop out of his head.

"Girlie clothes? Okay Eden, what the fuck is going on?" Maya shoved a finger at her in the most accusatory manner that it made Eden feel just a bit guilty. "You don't wear girlie clothes, Eden. You never have. You wear the skater clothes that my little brother buys."

Examining her purchases, Eden lifted a lacey black thong out of the plastic bag. "How long does it take you to get used to these things?" Eden twirled the garment experimentally before dropping it back in the bag. "It seems kinda itchy."

"Oh lord, save me from amateurs!" Maya grabbed her wrist and dragged her toward another store. "With any luck the guy will be so hard once he sees you in it, you'll only have it on ten minutes or less."

"Guy? There's no guy." Eden pretended interest in an aquamarine tank.

Maya yanked the tank out of her hand. "No guy? Oh really?"

"Really."

Eden passed on the tank and found another in black. Maya shoved three other shirts and two pairs of jeans at her. "Try these on and let me see." She nudged Eden in the direction of a dressing room. "Until you tell me, you're under lock and key."

"Lock and key? What are you talking about?" Eden shut the door behind her. She kicked off her shoes and unbuttoned her relaxed fit jeans. She picked up the pair of jeans Maya selected for her and held them up to her hips, examining them in the mirror.

The color was "Midnight Ice" and the jeans slid over her hips resting just below the hilt of the dagger on the tattoo. Eden zipped the jeans and turned to examine her butt. She twisted around to get a good look. Oh yeah, these jeans would so kill him. Eden pulled her straggly hair back and looked down at her tattoo. Yep, this would kill him. Eden yanked open the door to the dressing room. She really wanted to enjoy this. A lot.

"So?" Eden propped her hand on a hip and thrust it out for effect.

Maya coughed, "Whoa girl, where did that come from?"

"What?"

Maya angled her index finger at Eden's tattoo. "I didn't know you were into body art."

Eden shrugged. "Me either. I went to a party one night, got hammered woke up the next morning and there it was."

"No shit?" Maya laughed. "You wanna tell me how someone managed to draw on you with a needle without your knowing about it?"

"Beats the crap out of me," Eden shrugged.

Maya chewed on the end of her thumbnail and Eden could see the gears working in her head. "That's freaky, you know. I thought your reflexes were like superhuman."

"Not when I'm drunk, evidently."

"Yeah, sure. I've seen you drunk before Eden." Maya examined the jeans and how the fit. "No body could take you down let alone color all over you hip like that without you knowing."

With a tuft of hair between her fingers, Eden

waved it at Maya in hopes of changing the subject. No way in hell would she explain how she went to bed one night and woke up with the tatt covering her birthmark the next morning. She'd spent two hours trying to scrub the thing off and finally accepted the new edition to her appearance as another quirk in her never-ending saga. "I think I want to color my hair. Darker maybe."

Maya tugged at her hair. "Well, it would be an improvement. Add some depth to that mop you've got going on now."

"Well...if you're nice...maybe I'll let you pick out a cut for me."

Damn, she pushed it too far. Now, Maya was suspicious. She could see the glimmer in her pale brown eyes. "What the fuck is going on?"

"Nothing. Why?"

Eden moved to go back into the dressing room. "Well, the jeans rock, girl." She was closing the door when Maya inserted very casually, "So get them all in every color and you'll have Elliot on his knees in a couple of days."

Eden's hand froze on the door, "*Excuse me*?" For a split second, Eden considered busting that smart-ass look right of Maya's face.

"You heard me."

"I did and now I'm wondering what you're smoking."

Maya sighed dramatically, "Like I said, spare me."

Eden shook her head and walked back into the

dressing room to strip out of the dark jeans. "You're nuts."

"You're going to need shoes with those clothes. Those clunky things you wear now aren't going to make the Brit want to climb off his pedestal."

"You're out of your mind!"

"Yeah, sure. How long have I known you, Eden?"

"Over three years, why?" Eden didn't like the train this conversation chugged on. "You want to see if they've got another shirt like this one?" She stuck it through the door at Maya.

"I ought to be grateful you're actually buying women's clothing. But I am nosy, you know?"

Yanking off the jeans, Eden piled all of her new clothing together. She pulled on her old canvas jeans and noticed an immediate difference between the two pair of pants. Those dark blue jeans were tight like a second skin that hugged ever curve on her body and made her ass to die for. It did something for her that Eden never expected. Not only did she look hot, but it made her feel hot. She let the pleasure roll over her like biting into a piece of Godiva chocolate. It blew through her mind on an exquisite burst of sensation, and something she never thought she'd ever have.

She wasn't vane. She didn't have the time or inclination to delve into the whole Jessica Simpson prettiness. Sure, the singer was startlingly gorgeous but she spent gallons of money and time to create such a fabulous effect. Besides, what Vampire would flee at the mere sight of Jessica?

Attractive wasn't anything she'd ever use to describe herself with, but now she wanted it. She wanted Elliot to look at her and see something more than a Demon Hunter or a smart-ass teenager. She wanted him to look and damn it all, she wanted him to want.

And she needed Maya's help to achieve that desired result because Maya was an absolute master in the realm of making men drool. But if she wanted Maya to help her, she'd have to tell her friend the truth because Maya wouldn't let go until she did.

Eden leaned her forehead against the mirror in the dressing room and wondered if she ought to pound some sense into her teeny weenie brain. The idea of her and Elliot was like Wolverine dating Darin from *Bewitched* and she was Wolverine in this lovely scenario. Vinegar and oil, lemon juice and sugar that's how much they had in common so it made no sense to Eden why she should all of a sudden want Elliot's tongue all over her body. Then, she wanted to taste him.

She'd been so fucking hot last night. Elliot could've slipped his cock into her pussy and she would've cum all over him instantly. The muscles of her pussy contracted and gripped imagining what his cock was like.

Get a grip.

Eden sighed. The only grip she wanted right now was her pussy gripped around his cock.

Inhaling slowly, Eden forced the ache that

threatened to become something uncontrollable, up into her stomach where she could manage it. She wiped the sweat off her forehead wondering where all the heat came from even though she could hear the air conditioning blowing. Her skin seemed white and pasty and Eden knew Maya would insist on make up now.

She opened the door to the dressing room to find Maya waiting patiently. Yep, if she survived today it would log into her mental journal as a miracle. Because she knew for a fact that her sad little piece of plastic was already trembling under the weight of her charges.

Three hours and fifty-two minutes later, Eden collapsed under the weight of her new and exotic *girlness*. It took a double espresso, caramel latte to rouse her from her semi-conscious state. That and a good chocolate biscotti.

"Your hair looks positively amazing!" Maya dipped her biscotti into her coffee then reached out and touched Eden's hair. "Oh man, that color is just – wow!"

"It's okay?"

Maya shook her head. "No, it's not okay, girl. It's freakin' stunning."

"I never thought about coloring it before." Eden blew on her coffee to cool it before sipping.

"Well, I tried to tell you."

"I know." Eden used her incisors on the edge of a biscotti. It made her all the more "boy-like" in

Elliot's eyes.   That her long, blah brown out of control hair was put into a ponytail or worse. Well, it didn't matter now, she was more girl then she'd ever been and Elliot better thank his lucky stars cause she'd just spent two months salary on all this stuff.

"So what's the game plan?" The jolt of caffeine still wasn't enough to make Eden more coherent. She stared at Maya with a glazed look that made Maya cringe. "How are you going to get in the Brit's pants?"

The coffee hit the back of her throat with the consistency of oil clogging all paths of oxygen. Eden choked, "Why do you suddenly think I'm after Elliot?"

"Probably because he is hotter than hell and so unavailable he'd make any woman who saw him want." Maya shrugged and picked at another piece of biscotti. "I'm just so proud my little girl has finally noticed boys!"

"Bite me."

"She knows we eat at seven." Elliot toyed with his wine glass trying to push his irritation down from his fingers and into the crystal.

"Yes, sir. I believe so." Roland cleared the plates as efficiently as usual.

"Then why isn't she here?"

Roland shifted the plates to balance on his forearm.   "Perhaps, she didn't feel welcome to dinner."

Elliot stood up, shoving his chair back. Wood slid along the marble tile. It made a muffled squeak. "How could she not feel welcome?"

"I'm not sure, sir. Did you actually ask her to dinner?"

"Well of course not." Pushing the chair under the table, Elliot picked up his glass of wine and started for his study. "Why should I?"

Roland merely smiled and mumbled under his breath, "And that's why she didn't come to dinner."

Elliot chose to ignore the remark and continued down the hall to his study. In all truth, he wasn't sure how he would've reacted to Eden. He realized now that he was pleased she'd avoided him all day. Pleasure shot through his body last night like a torch tossed on gasoline when he'd pushed Eden down on the bed. It certainly put a wrench in things. He didn't expect sensation. Or what came with it.

He'd wanted her.

Elliot sighed and pushed the door open. He didn't bother with lights. Raising the glass to his lips, Elliot swallowed some of the Merlot. He'd known her sense she was sixteen, known of her sense she was ten. They'd never had a child/parent relationship. Eden was an adult when she was eight years old and she'd always been independent.

He was the Guardian. His only role in Eden's life was to guide, teach, and protect. The creed of the Guardianship was a long and arduous one. Elliot never intended to choose that for his life but magic drew him in. Once he saw Eden Camden, he knew he would do anything to keep her safe.

Over the years, he'd bandaged countless wounds, tended to a bruised ego, and butt heads with Eden thousands of times. He'd taught her everything she willingly accepted and force fed her the lessons that would eventually keep her alive. Sweat, some blood and more than few tears fell to the ground from both of them, but they managed.

He'd touched her before.

Elliot dragged his fingers through his wavy hair. The frustration made him want to rip it out at the roots. Why the hell was last night any different than before? A couple of years ago, he'd tended a bruise on her hipbone and he'd felt nothing. Perhaps, less than nothing, until last night.

He never expected to react like that in Eden's presence. Elliot reached out for his wine glass and finished the Merlot. For God's sake, she dressed like a damn teenaged boy most of the time and that wasn't the least bit alluring. Until last night when a blade of current cut into his spine.

All that skin, Elliot inhaled recalling her vague scent. Dark, hot, and mysterious as spices from the Orient, he understood what it was to need. The pads of his fingers itched and Elliot rubbed his fingers together. He pressed his body up against the side of Eden's and the surprise at seeing that damn tattoo threw all his normal, orderly thoughts into a tailspin.

A tap on the door brought his mind back into a

reasonable facsimile of normal. "Elliot?" The door opened without waiting for his reply. "What are you doing sitting in the dark?" Eden flicked on the overhead light and strolled into the room. "You're not pouting cause I missed dinner, are you?"

"It's customary to call. Roland held dinner."

"Sorry," Eden muttered as she came around the chair where he sat to plop onto the loveseat beside him. "I'm sure it was still good."

"Palatable." Elliot refused to look at her. "Barely." Maybe he was pouting, but at the moment, his mood was surly.

"Oh come on, I've ate Roland's cooking before. He could put white sauce on a shoe and it would be fantastic." He heard a rustle of fabric as Eden crossed her legs.

Odd, he couldn't recall Eden ever making fabric rustle. Elliot adjusted his body in the chair, using his hands to shove back slightly on the arms of the chair. "Did you need something, Eden?" He turned his head to look at Eden.

"Well, I was going to apologize to Roland but it looks like he's gone to bed already so I thought I'd apologize to you."

"It wasn't my meal you ruined."

Eden sat forward leaning her forearms on her knees. "Are you trying to start something?"

He heard the edge in her voice but ignored it. All of his attention focused on the shadow of Eden's cleavage within his grasp. His tongue swelled and Elliot forced air through his nostrils. It was hot, thick like gelatin, clogging up his throat and his lungs.

"No," his voice was raw, wet sandpaper. Good Lord, what had she done to herself? Elliot's eyes sharpened to pinpoints in the light. He allowed himself a moment of pure pleasure as his eyes did a thorough examination of his slayer.

"What are you looking at?" Eden twitched, leaning back a bit. "Do I have a bug on me or something?"

"No," he thought he shook his head, but wasn't sure if he moved at all, "No." Lava began to seep into his veins heating his blood. "You look…"

Eden stood up and put her hands on her hips. "I look amazing, right?" She rotated her weight, angling one of her hips at him.

She wore a tank in turquoise cropped just under her breasts. Colored stones dangled from her ears sparkling in between locks of wildly layered blue-black hair. Elliot's eyes narrowed at the subtle sparkle of eyeshadow and then the gloss over her lips. "What have you done?"

Eden frowned, "You don't like it?"

He shook his head, totally baffled. He couldn't remember ever seeing her in sandals, let alone, heels. Elliot rubbed the back of his neck. The muscles didn't relax, only tensed under his touch. His eyes slid up her jeans, tight smooth denim went up Eden's long muscled legs and over her hips.

"Elliot?" She clucked her tongue at him. "You know, you might say you don't like it, but I think you do."

"Why should you care if I like what you're wearing?" Control shuddered around him and he could sense the tingle, the sparks of loose magic snap and pop around him. His eyes went to her the bare skin of her stomach. The low-rise jeans gave just a teasing view of the tattoo.

She was trying to kill him.

Eden blew out a long breath. "You know, I don't get you. I wanted to try something new. Maybe I was tired of looking like a boy too."

"I didn't mean –"

She held up a hand, "It doesn't matter." Eden shrugged, "I needed new clothes so I got some." Her hands went to an earring and unhooked it from her earlobe. "But right now, I need to blow off some steam."

Elliot could think of several ways to blow off some steam and all of them had Eden in bed with him. Her legs locked around his waist while the muscles of her hips clenched and released. He wanted to slide his cock inside Eden. Deep, hard and revel in the sweet wetness as her pussy held onto him. Elliot never imagined this, never expected such fierce need. He closed his eyes for just a second to gather a hold of the magic blasting around him.

She couldn't see it. He still had enough strength to hold onto it and keep from making an utter fool out of himself. Gold, silver, green sparks like fireworks tripped and danced around him. Half of him wanted Eden out the door, the other half wanted to see just what kind of explosion they might create with each other.

"I'll see you tomorrow at work."

He moved, faster than she expected. He saw the glimmer of surprise reflect in her dark eyes. One second, he was sitting down and the next moment he trapped her against the doorframe. "You want to blow off steam?"

Eden swallowed then licked her lips. "Yeah." She turned her head to the side. Elliot saw her look at his arms on either side of her face. "That's what I said."

He tried not to lean into her, tried not to want to touch. "Down at the gym?"

She shook her head and strands of that impossibly black hair fell across the bare skin of his forearms as if it were silk. "Ah, hunting."

"Yes."

Elliot rocked back on his heels and smiled, "I'd change my clothes if I were you." He reached out and trailed his fingers over the hem of her tank before he could help himself. "You wouldn't want to ruin them." Eden shuddered at his touch and it made him pause a moment.

Her fingers reached out and curled around his muscled forearm. They gripped, testing his strength before running slowly up and down the hair over his arms. "I will." Eden pushed at his arms in an effort to move past him and found her body pressed against his.

Eden's hands fell from his arms in a weak slide. Elliot angled his head slightly, so he could look at her eyes as well as consider her mouth. That gloss slicked over her lips. He wondered what flavor it was. "You should get on then."

"Uh huh," Eden sniffed, angling her head toward his throat. "Is that Armani?"

"Hmm?" Distracted, his fingers tangled into the ends of her hair. It was soft as the most exquisite silk and he couldn't think of anything he wanted more than to have it spread out over his chest. He blinked as her question registered. "Armani? Yes, I think so."

She inhaled deeply and her breasts brushed over his chest. Elliot tensed. His body turned to liquid metal, superheated and instantly malleable. He tilted her head closer and his breath mingled with hers pulling him further under her spell.

Eden raised her mouth, parted it willingly. Her lips reminded him of petals, soft, ripe, and enticing. "Elliot?"

It wasn't much more than a whisper. He could hear the confusion laced around his name as she searched his face with her dark eyes. She didn't know where they were now, or the dangerous ground they trended, and he didn't like the look on her face. Elliot lifted his head slowly, trying to fight the pull. He wanted to devour her with his mouth, but he needed her with him.

Elliot twisted his right wrist up to get a look at his watch. "You'd better get a move on then, you don't want all the good Vampires taken."

It squashed the mood just as he intended. He stepped back a good two feet allowing Eden access out the study door.

"Yeah, yeah," Eden hastily brushed back her hair with a hand that shook. She moved stiffly, almost as if he'd struck her. She reached back and searched for the door handle, missing it twice, before closing it behind her.

Relief flooded him with the icy fury of a winter blizzard. Eden wasn't ready. He certainly wasn't ready. Certainly not for what his body had done to him. His cock was so hard he knew it would take hours to relieve the agony. The alternative was something he didn't consider. A paltry substitute wasn't anything he even considered now. He hadn't fucked a woman in such a long time he'd actually started to think he was immune to desire. Now, he knew different.

Blood burned so hot through his veins heating his skin. Elliot wiped a fine sheen of sweat from his upper lip. He needed to focus and control the magic raging inside. Magic acted on instinct and intense emotional or physical reactions of the wielder. The last thing anyone needed now was magic bouncing around the building like small atom bombs.

Walking over to the study window, Elliot opened it wide. Most hotels in Las Vegas sealed windows unless they were in a suite. In Elliot's apartment, all the windows opened. Tonight at least he would have the satisfaction of watching his slayer in action.

CHAPTER SIX

Elliot walked over to his sofa table and picked up a five-inch crystal globe. He rotated it around his palm for a moment before stepping out into the moonlight. The globe caught the rays of silver from the moon and began to glow. He gathered the energy of the night, shaped it as he uttered the words to his *Spell of Sight*. "Oracle of sight, I summon thee. Visions in the crystal reveal to me. Show me what I wish to see, show me what my slayer does not wish me to see."

It fell over her like some sort of tropical fog. Hot, thick, and oppressive, Eden didn't realize it was the heat generated off her own body until she got back to her room and stripped off her new clothing. A fine sheen of sweat covered her skin and Eden knew for sure she was about to self-combust. She managed to lay her jeans and top over a chair before running into her bathroom.

Eden turned the cold water on in the sink on high and stuffed a hand towel under the flow. She needed an ice bath, but hopefully this would work to lower her temperature. Wringing the towel out, Eden ran the wet, cool towel over her face and down her neck. The chill of the fabric was a shock to her overheated skin and Eden flinched.

"Damn it all to hell!" Eden tossed the towel over the tub and twisted the water off. This was just one big fat pain in her ass. She wanted to fuck Elliot's brains out. She considered Elliot's cock for a moment. She wanted it. Wanted to know if was long and thick and if when he slid it inside her tight, wet pussy, if she would come instantly. Eden gripped the side of the sink as a shudder ran over her entire body.

The bare skin of his arms was all he touched. Hair-roughened over tightly muscled sinew made her even more hot. She wished she'd gotten a look at his chest. Her fingers clenched and she forced herself to relax. This was not happening. If she believed in magic, she'd think someone put a hex on them or something.

For God's sake, it was Elliot! She was hot for Elliot. She wanted to bang her head against the wall. British, stuffy, boring, irritating Elliot made her so damn wet she could barely walk without squeaking.

Striding back into her room, she picked up her ratty pair of canvas slacks and slipped them on. On an impulse buy, she picked up a pair of basketball shoes to wear in her slaying choirs. She figured they'd cushion her feet better than the old work boots anyway. She bent over, tied the laces, and snatched up a tee.

She needed to kick some Vampire butt. That

would blow this bizarre fascination with Elliot Warwick right out of her head. It made concentrating painful and breathing became difficult around him these days. Eden thumped the heel of her hand into her head, she knew what Maya would say: "Go fuck him."

Because it took her two hours and twenty-eight minutes to scratch up some paltry Vampires, Eden wasn't in the mood to play when she located them. She found them hanging out near the entrance of a high end strip club. The chicks that danced here were pre-med, pre-law, pre-big-giant-future-ahead of them. The made serious cash and a lot of them got off on the whole sex goddess fantasy. Eden never was a sex goddess so she couldn't get into dancing for a bunch of horny guys with cash.

There were only two of them. Damn, she really wanted a good workout. Four or more was worth some cardio. These two dweebs sucking donor juice out of an old wine bottle were barely worth a cough and a spit.

"Hey guys, gotta light?" Eden pretended to dig around in her pockets for a lighter.

He had greasy matted hair and wild, bloodshot eyes. He wiped the excess blood from his lips with the back of his hand. "If that's your costume, bitch, you've gotta long way to go to get some rich fuck's rocks off."

Eden licked her lips and widened her eyes. "Wow, all I wanted was a light, and I get a greasy assed puke giving me attitude."

The other Vamp backed up just a bit. Eden could tell all he wanted was to stay alone with his bottle of blood. Well, too damn bad cause Grease ball pissed her off and she was really in the mood to snap things in two.

She hadn't brought her bag. Tonight, she wanted it rough. Hand to hand, pulling hair and rippin' hearts out bloodfest. The muscles in her neck and shoulders tensed tight as drawn violin strings. Eden took in a breath of the smoke clinging to the air around the strip club. She hated cigarette smoke; it burned her lungs.

Grease ball passed his drink off to his friend and pushed away from the wall leading to an alley. She watched him grab hold of the top of his head and crack his neck. It popped with a hideous snap. Eden cringed slightly, if the guy'd been alive, he would've just snapped his ugly head off. The closer Eden got the more it stank. Body odor, piss and the dead rot of a Vampire who by the looks of things had been a drug addict in his former life filled her nostrils all at once and nearly made Eden gack. She turned her head away, hoping to suck in clean air but got her lungs full of thick smoke as the doors to the club opened up.

Later, she wonder if she'd done it on purpose. But she let Grease ball have an opening and the Vampire took it. He had her by the throat in a second, his long, dirty nails digging into her cotton tee, snapping and snarling like some rabid dog. His breath was rotten sewage that'd baked in the sun all day and Eden's stomach rolled as if she'd swallowed some of that same sewage.

Working the heel of her right hand up to his breastbone, she shoved hard. "Okay," and she broke his grip, "you are so going to back up here cause goddamn, you fuckin' stink!" She got him to arms length and used her foot to his hip to kick him back some more.

He tripped over his own two feet, landed on his ass. "You bitch, I'm gonna suck the life out of you."

Yeah, yeah. Like she hadn't heard that shit a hundred times before. She wished her shirt had longer sleeves as she tried to wipe the stench of Grease ball out of her nose. "Shit man, you smell like you fuckin' died two years ago."

The Vampire sailed at her his jaws cracking open even wider as he screamed at her, "I did, bitch!"

Eden smiled and shifted easily to a ready stance. Rocking her weight onto her rear foot, she waited until the Vamp reached the apex of his launch. In was a move she'd practiced and used so many times that now, the tightening of her thigh muscles and the lift and then extend didn't bother her in the least. Her brand new, high-octane court shoe met Grease ball's Adam's apple with a solid smack. His head snapped back like an umbrella opened in a hurricane.

Grease ball hit the ground with a thud. She scanned the outside of the club with the speed of a missile homing in on its target. While Grease ball coughed and choked, Eden decided to use his blood bottle on him to finish the deed. Eden started for the wimpy dude and then bottles then decided the piece of metal sticking out of the alley trash would work wonders instead. She'd let the other one stew in his own little puddle of fear while she found something nice and pointy.

"You shouldn't have done that," a strong young arm wrapped around her throat and a man's voice breathed quietly in her ear, "Don't you know what tonight is?"

"Sorry, no." Eden checked her watch and sniffed. "Is this something special?" She could smell the decay and with this one, the odd, misplaced scent of roses.

"Very special."

Eden sniffed loudly, and brought her hands up to a defensive position. "You wanna get your hands off me, now or would you like to have your arms broken off?"

A rustle of movement behind her had every hair on her neck standing up. Eden drew in a slow breath. More than one now, she could sense them, pick up the mystical vibe radiating off all extraordinary creatures. Vampires emitted a blood red haze that she could see, feel and very nearly taste. Metallic, coppery, if she had to define it, she'd say blood.

Well, the good thing was, she'd wanted a challenge tonight. Some drop down, rip your nails off fight that could get her mind off fucking Elliot. Looks like she'd get her wish, the only problem was she was unarmed.

Bad for her.

Good for the creep force.

"And what makes tonight so special?" Keep it casual, Eden's eyes searched the perimeter. In the dumpster, she couldn't see anything useful sticking out. Her eyes went further down the alley, something had to be around that she could use.

"Vampires night out."

"Sweet." Eden moved in a liquid motion. Slipping all her weight into the Vamp, she used her shoulder and hips to rotate while she clutched his arm. She had a good grip when she rolled her weight forward. Rose smelling Vamp sailed over her shoulder and into the dumpster. She somersaulted forward and then came up in a crouch to face six Vampires that appeared in various stages of intoxication.

Shit! Fuckin' drunk Vampires. Now, this wasn't what she wanted at all. Drunk Vampires were a bunch of crazy ass fools that would bite through cement in all their fury. Amazing how quiet an alley was at night. She could hear crickets chirping as her fingers reached for and closed over a sharp piece of glass from a broken jar.

One of the more predominate myths surrounding Vampires was the whole wooden stake through the heart thing. She liked wooden stakes because of their feel and she made her own so they balance perfectly in her palm. But she found out early that the wooden stake was more for her benefit than the Vamp. That little rule only applied to a Master Vampire and she could count the Master's she'd met over the past ten years on one hand. The little ones though, under a hundred a fifty years of age, Eden brought down with anything that pierced the heart. If you could flip a bottle cap hard enough, it would work. Maybe she'd practice that sometime, but right now, she intended to filet a couple.

With deadly accuracy, Eden hurled the sliver of glass into the closest Vamp's chest. Shock went through the group like a boulder plunging into still water. The Vamp coughed and broke in ash. Eden took hold of two more pieces of glass and smiled, "Who's next?"

She moved before any of them could react by firing blades of glass into the hearts of two more Vampires. Ashes to ashes, and creeps to dust. Satisfied, she dusted her hands and stood up folding her arms across her chest. "Well?" Eden laughed, "What no takers?"

One of the Vampires trembled with rage. He charged forth only to find himself yanked back by his pals. "You'll regret this, Slayer. Those were *his* little brothers."

Eden glanced back at their pal digging his way out of the trash. She jerked a thumb at him. "Oh well sorry about that. A broken fence post came out with him. Eden pounced on top of the trash and ripped it out. She plunged it into Rose Vamp's back and watched as he promptly turned into a nice mulch. She grinned, "Tell him I'm sorry. Would you?" She looked back at the three remaining only to find they'd gone.

Run away, vanished, whatever, the three left beat feet that was probably a smart thing. Eden snickered. Damn, just when it was starting to get interesting.

The light of the moon reflected blue shadows off his impossible long, curly black hair. The wind lifted it created a halo of darkness around him while he drifted silently over the cemetery grounds located off an incline that looked out over the city. He'd wanted to see this Sin City for a long while now. Something about this city sparked his interest for a long time yet he hadn't found a reason to leave his home until now.

Carlos Venturi surveyed the gems of light flickering and waving along the Las Vegas Strip. It was brilliant. Color. Sound. And ah yes, the humans. The anticipation grew to a fine hum through his body. Tourists from all over the world – ah, the variety!

He came to Las Vegas at the request of Seraphina and her Renegades. Apparently, they'd developed a bit of pest problem. A problem so dire that it needed a Master to intercede. Carlos found it interesting that Seraphina petitioned her case personally to him. Something about a Slayer and her Warlock, Carlos smoothed a long strand of hair from his face as he considered that particular combination. He couldn't remember the last time a Warlock actually joined with his charge and it was up to Carlos now, to make certain that didn't happen.

He moved through the cemetery like a black wraith. Carlos wore black as a habit. It accented the polished olive complexion of his Spanish heritage. Tonight, he favored a long, black coat over dark jeans and a black silk shirt.

His deep brown eyes found Seraphina and her Renegades waiting near an intricately carved marble statue. Mist seemed to cling to him as he moved closer creating an eerie fog and concealing his feet. Seraphina and her group of six Vampires dropped to a low bow when they saw him.

"Master, you honor us with your presence."

Carlos made a sweeping motion with his long-fingered hand. "Rise."

"We've secured the grounds for you here, Master. If you find them lacking, we've prepared three other sites." He noticed as Seraphina spoke, she kept her eyes downward. Her six other were afraid to look him in the eyes. As much as he adored the attention, after all he'd once been the heir to the Spanish throne, some eight hundred years ago, their bowing and scraping wouldn't get them anywhere.

"My Elite have already surveyed the sites and found this one to be suitable."

"As you wish, Master."

He stepped forward, the fog clinging to him like an unseen guardian. "Seraphina," he stopped in front of her and lifted her chin so that her eyes met his, "I require only common respect. You and your Renegades may treat me as just another of your clan."

He tilted her chin slightly. She had a warm willing mouth that he claimed. His tongue pushed past her full lips to tangle with hers momentarily. He'd known Seraphina a long time, knew of the passion inside and the complete and utter darkness that lurked there as well. Its taste was deadly and sinful and he knew it'd bring a lesser man to his knees.

Carlos broke the kiss. He knew better. "The party has been planned."

She nodded, using her index finger to wipe the smudge of lipgloss from her chin. "For the weekend, just as you asked."

His eyes went over her group. "Meager numbers, Seraphina. What's happened?"

Venom flared in her eyes. "It's that damn Warlock, he's been picking my people off while they *sleep!*"

"Not very sporting of him, is it?" Carlos' smile was entirely too friendly. "When you came to me, you didn't tell me the names of this Warlock and his Slayer."

Seraphina appeared confused. "I thought you knew."

"Knew what?" Even the moon had only just

reason to its peak of the night, Carlos was anxious to explore. "You leave me to guess?" He jerked Seraphina forward. "You know my appetites, Seraphina. I don't know if you'd be up to satisfying my current hunger."

A male Vampire snickered behind Seraphina's left shoulder. When Carlos fastened his dark eyes on him, the young one had the intelligence to appear frightened.

Seraphina cleared her throat, "Elliot Warwick. The Slayer is called Eden."

His lips twisted as he thought. No, he couldn't say he remembered encountering a Warlock by that name before. Of course, it didn't matter much to him, he'd yet to come across a Warlock he couldn't defeat.

Footsteps pounded over the fresh earth and Carlos sensed the male running before he actually became visible through the trees. Several of the other Vampires tensed but at Carlos' raised hand the tension eased out of them. "He's one of mine."

The young male skidded to a stop and knelt before Carlos. "My lord."

"Where are Reynaldo and Dumas?"

"We came out of a club and we noticed a fight in an alley. You know how willful your brothers are my lord, they wished to investigate."

Carlos folded his arms, "Indeed. Get up, Anthal."

The other man rose slowly, almost as if he preferred being on the ground. "Myself and two others barely escaped. They're off feeding."

"And my brothers?"

Anthal shook his head slowly, "I don't know how it happened, my lord, I swear to you."

Carlos studied the large black man with long dreadlocks, a carry over from his days as a pirate. He'd know for centuries how wild and impulsive his brothers were and he'd known just as well how it would eventually be their demise. "Tell me everything."

"There was a Vampire. Down and out from the looks of him. He insulted this girl." Anthal folded his huge arms over his massive chest. "We were coming out of the club when she snapped his neck with one kick. She sauntered into the alley looking for something to finish the poor creature off with and Reynaldo ran after her."

"You had no idea what she was?" Carlos found that hard to believe. Anthal was nearly as old as he was, he would've seen a half dozen Slayers by now. "You disappoint me Anthal. I thought you were more knowledgeable than that."

The other man sighed. "We'd been in the club for a while."

Carlos scratched in between his eyebrows with his index finger. "What kind of club was this?"

A sheepish grin appeared on his dark face. He shrugged, "Well, we are in Las Vegas." Carlos fixed him with a black stare. "Oh, it was a strip club. Lots of willing women, if you know what I mean."

Unfortunately, Carlos knew all too well what

he meant. Pretty women and men with a sexual hunger and an unnatural thirst, if you threw alcohol in that mixture it became an ugly picture. "And so, you were all drunk."

"Maybe."

"*Maybe?*" Carlos clenched his fists. It was a wonder he didn't throw Anthal across the cemetery. "There is an issue of honor here, Anthal and I will deal with that when the time comes. But for now, you and I know that my little brothers were both stupid, pains in my ass. They were bound to get killed sooner or later."

A snicker of laughter from behind Seraphina got his attention. Carlos noticed a large male with flame colored hair and a goatee suddenly coughing. Carlos dismissed Anthal with the wave of his hand, "I'll deal with you later." He moved his body away from the male and turned to face the redhead. Extending a long finger, he motioned for him, "You there, come over here."

The Vampire stood about six foot five and was at least, five inches taller than Carlos. Instead of showing intimidation, Carlos merely smiled. "What's your name, young one?"

"Titan."

Carlos tilted his head. This was the one the warlock released, he remembered Seraphina mentioning it. "You survived a Warlock?"

Titan shook his head. "I didn't survive anything, Master. He released me out of choice." Carlos was stunned when the youngster grinned. "I guess he liked me."

Carlos pursed his full lips in thoughtfulness. "Interesting. Aren't you the one Seraphina sent to torch this Slayer?"

"I'm not too good with fire."

"Evidently." Carlos stepped up and used his thumbnail along Titan's cheek. It cut a blood red line through his skin. "And you sleep in a place children with pellet guns could pluck your existence from you in the blink of an eye." Carlos smiled a slow, sinister, and somewhat seductive smile. "Listen to me, young one. As clever as you believe yourself to be, you are no match for this Slayer nor her Warlock. I suggest you trend carefully from now on."

*****

As dawn rose, it cast a hazy glow over the city that refused to sleep. The alley, strewn with trash, emanated a strange combination of odors. He walked confidently to the spot where he'd seen Eden battle the Vampires through the crystal. The odor got stronger with each step and Elliot's nose twitched at the smell. He entered the alley and raised his right hand, *"Twan ne' dwar."* It was a simple spell that revealed the remnants of the undead. The ground shimmered with a faint blue glow. Elliot watched as it revealed two dark shadows on the street. Elliot walked over to the shadows and bent down to scoop up a handful of dirt.

The dirt melted to dark, nearly black ash as he

examined it. Elliot tilted his palm and let the ash blow away in the morning breeze. It was as he suspected. The Vampires had already called the Venturi clan. A small smile played about his mouth. It appeared that Eden's encounter last night was with two of Venturi's brothers. She'd defeated them easily. Elliot turned, brushing his hands off. Maybe he had nothing to worry about after all.

CHAPTER SEVEN

"So what did I do wrong? Exactly?" Eden stretched out on the chaise lounge and readjusted her towel. Sun blazed down creating shiny diamonds on the pool's aqua ripples.

"Okay, tell me again. Everything from the beginning." Maya stirred her drink with a straw.

Eden focused still not in full swing. Switching shifts wasn't Eden's cup of tea. She barely managed to drag her weary butt out of bed and get to work at seven this morning. Smoothing her hair back, she leaned into the chaise and adjusted her sunglasses on her nose. This was worth it. There was even some serious eye candy at the pool today. The fact they were ogling her and Maya made this afternoon more fun.

"How many times do I have to tell you this? Shit, it was humiliating enough the first time out. Now, I get to relive this eighty times for your enjoyment." Eden adjusted the skinny waistband of her new bikini. "That's just cruel and unusual punishment." Eden sighed. Who was she kidding? She still hadn't gotten over last night and nothing had fucking happened!

"Look, just tell me again. I think I missed

something here."

"I got home late," She turned her head and dropped the sunglasses down on the bridge of her nose so that Maya could get full effect, "because of you. Elliot was in a pissy attitude."

"Why?"

"He said because I was rude for not calling to let them know I wasn't going to be there for dinner."

Maya nodded as if all this made sense.

Eden turned her head back and laid it on her towel. "So I go find him, hanging out in his study as usual and try to apologize. But no, he doesn't want an apology. Then he makes some snotty remark about how I was dressed."

Maya pushed herself out of the reclining position. "Snotty? Elliot?"

"Yeah, Elliot."

"Mmmm…"

Eden reached over and picked up her iced tea. "What does that mean?"

"It means, tell me how he was acting."

"I just told you that." Eden slurped the tea to the bottom of the glass. "He was acting snotty with a weird look on his face like he couldn't decide if he wanted to eat me or beat me."

Maya laughed, "Well there you go."

"Okay, obviously I don't have the kind incite you do here even though I think you've met Elliot what? A half dozen times over the past three years." Eden waved her empty glass at the waitress walking by.

"You send he wanted to eat you, right? He probably wanted to do that. But was just afraid or didn't think the timing was right."

Eden rubbed her temples. The back of her head was throbbing and she could feel it creep into her skull and land behind her eyes. "English please?"

"He wants to fuck your brains out."

Eden's hand slipped on the glass of tea as the waitress handed her another drink. If it wasn't for her reflexes it would've landed in her lap. "No way."

"Why? You think I'm wrong?" Maya huffed, "Oh please."

"You really think he wants to have sex with me?"

Maya shook her head. "I said he wanted to fuck you. Guys don't get all bent and twisty unless a woman seriously gets under their skin. Tell me if you haven't been getting under Elliot's skin recently."

"Afternoon, ladies."

Elliot's voice sent shivers of pleasure over her skin. With the afternoon breeze, she hadn't been too hot even sitting out in the sun, until now. Two words and Eden's body turned to kindling. This just wasn't right. She'd never reacted like that to a man in her life.

She tried to look bored when she lifted her gaze, but damn that failed as soon as she saw him. He had taken off his tie and undone the top two buttons of a pale peach dress shirt that went really well with the sand colored jacket and slacks he wore. Guys weren't supposed to look good in those colors.

"Hey Elliot," Eden smiled or tried to be casual but it was really hard when she kept thinking about how good he looked in his clothes, he was probably phenomenal out of them.

"Hi Elliot, how's it going?"

Elliot smiled at Maya and Eden experienced a stab of jealously that wasn't altogether pleasant. "What are you slumming or just touring the kingdom?"

"You're usually not even alive at this time of day. What's the occasion?'

"Needed some sun."

He raised an eyebrow. "Since when?"

This time Maya had the gall to laugh. "Oh Elliot, you're a stitch! Where else could she show off such a fabulous bikini?"

Eden was about to "stitch" her up until she saw Elliot's eyes drift over her stomach. Sand, her throat turned to sand as she watched his gaze drift up over the curve of her breasts. She shifted her shoulders with a great amount of satisfaction. Especially when his eyes dilated slightly, and Eden wondered what cosmic force prevented her from jumping his bones at that moment.

"I need to speak to you."

Eden lifted her hands up. "Speak away."

"Privately."

Maya took the hint. "You in the mood for a

margarita yet?"

Eden nodded, "Sure." As Maya got to her feet, she grinned, "Thanks."

She expected Elliot to sit in Maya's chaise lounge across from her. He moved and sat beside her near her knees. She shifted her hips to put more space between them but when one of his palms skimmed over her thigh, she froze. "What are you doing?" Eden cocked her head slightly, that did not sound her own voice all breathless and sexy.

Elliot pulled off his sunglasses and tucked them into his breast pocket. His eyes were more like stones, rich and intensely colored. "Take off your sunglasses, Eden. I want you to listen to me."

She raised her chin. "I'm listening."

"When you're listening, you look at me."

Her skin was hot as if the touch of his hand branded her. "Why don't you sit over there?" She pointed to the other chaise. "It's not like I'm near-sighted or something."

"You're acting like a child." He reached out and plucked the sunglasses off her nose before she could react. Her eyes widened, she couldn't remember him ever exhibiting reflexes that rivaled her own.

"First, I look like a boy. Now, I'm a child." Eden pushed up in the lounger and gave him a good view of her half-exposed breasts. She saw his eyes flicker. Satisfaction was such an interesting thing. Right now, any little bit she received was so pleasurable it made her forget how badly she wanted his hands on her body. "You're not scoring brownie points here."

"One of the Vampires you killed last night –"

"How do you know I killed any last night?"

He ignored her question. "One of the Vampires you killed last night was related to a Master."

"Big deal."

"I think Seraphina and her group of Renegades called for him."

Eden sniffed, a hint of irritation lashing over her skin. "I told you, you should've let me kill that bitch last year." She reached out and took his sunglasses. "But you wouldn't and I think it's because you've got something going on with that chick."

Elliot blinked. "Going on?"

"A little somethin' somethin' on the side."

His spine straightened like she'd just shoved a fork up his ass. "Are you insinuating what I think you are? Oh for God's sake!" He started to stand up and she laid a hand on his leg. "You must be joking!"

The fabric of his slacks was a tight, soft weave. Her fingers tightened feeling the curves in the muscles of his thigh. "When did you start working out?"

He jumped as if she'd hit him with a taser gun. "What? Eden, for God's sake, try to stay on target here."

She swallowed hard. Her brain was a massive tangle of wild thoughts and exotic colors swirled together around Elliot. "I can't, Elliot. Don't you see?" She dropped her sunglasses on the table and took hold of one of his hands. She looked down as their fingers twined and a fiery current sped through her arm. "You can feel that can't you, Elliot?"

His nod was so brief she wouldn't swear she saw it. He shut his eyes. "Eden, please." She brought his hand to her neck and drew it down the side of her breast. It sent a hot tingling down into the pit of her stomach before streaming into her pussy. "I'm trying to protect you."

"From what Elliot? Myself? You?"

He drew in a deep breath and shuddered. Suddenly, satisfaction didn't mean so much to her anymore. All she wanted was for him to touch her and then kiss her like he meant it. "I'm trying to keep you from getting killed." He pulled his hand away and took hold of her shoulders. "Are you ready to deal with a Master?"

"I've done it before." How he managed to throw ice water all over her sweaty body, she didn't know. But her heart beat an odd rhythm in her chest and she knew the cool off would last only for a short while.

"Not like this one, you haven't."

She released his hand. "Okay, no biggie. I'll study up on him take a few more training sessions." She fluffed out her hair and resettled in the lounger. "As long as they don't come with magic, I should be good to go." She turned slightly to look at him and then it occurred to her she'd never asked him about the other night.   "Where'd Titan learn a spell anyway?"

"Simple ones can be bought and sold."

"And how did you know that I was under attack?   How did you know how to release it anyway?"   She reached out and hooked his chin feeling the scrape of his growth of beard on her sensitive fingers. She pulled his face up slightly and relocated his gaze. "And why the hell do you seem to be so fuckin' obsessed with my tattoo?"

He took her wrist in a gentle touch and moved her hand into his lap. Elliot held it between both of his hands. "You have a lot of questions. How many do you want answers to?"

She glanced down at her hand then back to his eyes. "All of them."

"Do you remember when you got the tattoo?" At her nod, he angled his head and his eyes narrowed. "Did you specifically request the tattoo?"

"Sure, they don't just draw on you."

"No?"   Elliot stroked his fingers across the top of her hand. "Were you drunk?"

"Have you been talking to Maya?"

"Eden, even the most gifted tattoo artist couldn't just imagine this design."

"So what?"   She tried to pull her hand away, but he wouldn't let go. He watched her with those disturbing eyes of his and made her wonder how much he really knew. If she admitted that tattoo just showed up one morning, what did that say about her skills? Someone was able to sneak up on her and draw with a needle didn't make any fuckin' sense.

So Eden did what she did best when things got a bit itchy. She changed the subject. "What about that spell? How did you know what to do?"

"There's a store out on Flamingo that specializes in this sort of thing." His eyes left the tattoo and he favored her with a rare smile. "I'm not a complete ignoramus you know?"

Eden wanted to devour him in that moment. That smile, lit up his face and his eyes glistened with magical mischief. She let her hand fall from his chin. "And they just let Vampires buy this shit? Are they out of their minds?" Before she realized it, she'd stroked her fingers over his chin. Eden tried to pull her hand away once more. This time, he raised her hand to his lips and she crumbled. "What are you doing?" He drew the back of her hand over his mouth. Eden was stunned at how soft his lips were. Oh man, like silk, and when he turned her palm up, Eden had to bite back a sigh.

"The store doesn't know who they're selling to."

"Maybe they should." She tried to look away, tried not to let the fire blaze into her belly. "What are you doing?"

"You can't police everything." His eyes reflected so many colors, they reminded her of a piece of stone chipped open to reveal a surprising center.

"Elliot, please."   She clenched her thighs together as the wet heat traveled into her pussy. If he was trying to make her squirm, well, it was working. "Stop this. I can't think when you do this."

"What am I doing to you, Eden?" The fingers that had just held her hand now stroked over her thigh. He watched her with a small smile playing about those soft lips. "Did you put on sunscreen? You don't want to burn."

"Why do you keep going out of your way to irritate me?" She passed him a tube of sunscreen. "Here."

"I didn't know I was irritating you. I didn't think I had any effect on you whatsoever." He flipped open the tube and squirted some sunscreen into his palm. "But now, I beginning to wonder if that's not the case, because you do seem to be reacting to my touch."

Smoothing it across her thigh, Eden realized that the whole sunscreen thing was a really bad idea. He rubbed his hand over her thigh and down her knee before he ran up her inner thigh and Eden bit the inside of her lip. "Would you stop this please?"

"You wanted the sunscreen."

"Yeah, well I also want you to rub it all over me while we're both naked and since I don't see that happening, you can just stop now before I do something really dumb." Eden tried shoving his hand away. He only moved his other hand to rest on the seam of her bikini bottoms.

"You've never done anything dumb, Eden." His hand slid around her leg and pinned her by leaning forward slightly. "I'm sorry if I've ever done anything to make you feel inadequate in any way." He reached out and brushed a strand of hair that blew across her face. "You're a beautiful woman. Smart, strong and damn near invincible."

He bent closer to her and she could smell faintly, peppermint on his breath. He was so close. All she had to do was raise her chin a fraction and her lips would be on his. Her mouth parted and she could practically taste him already.

"Oh damn, they put salt on yours again and I told them – oh shit!" Maya drew up short as Eden watched Elliot spring to his feet. "I'm sorry guys, I didn't – well, I just didn't –"

"It's okay, Maya." Eden swung her legs off the lounger and reached for the margarita. If she ever needed a good shot of tequila, it was right now.

Elliot put his sunglasses back on his face. "Will you be home this evening?"

And there was Mr. Ice again! How could she keep letting that slip her mind? He could turn off emotions faster than anyone she'd ever known and it was enough to make a girl dizzy. Dizzy with need and desire and just plain caught in a brain freeze, she nodded slowly. "Yeah."

"I'll see you then." He smiled at Maya. "Nice seeing you again, Maya." He walked back toward the casino entrance and Eden sucked down half the margarita without a pause.

"Holy Moses, girl! I'm so sorry, I had no idea. Well, I had an idea, but shit!" Maya reached for her own drink. She pointed a finger at Elliot's retreating figure. "You know, he really has a nice ass." She grinned at Eden, "Never noticed that before."

Swallowing half the margarita, the crushing icy blow of brain freeze was enough to scorch some of the steam cascading over her skin. "Christ, I'm not going to survive this."

Maya fanned herself and chuckled, a sound that irritated Eden only because she knew what the laughter was about. "Slow down there, sweetheart. You don't wanna be smashed by dinner."

Eden finished the drink and sat it on the poolside table. "Yeah, I think I do."

"Mix alcohol with that fire you've got going on between you two and kaboom! The hotel goes into orbit."

"You're just a laugh a minute, you know?" Eden signaled the waitress.

"Hey, I'm just telling you what I saw. And no one's pushing you into this, Eden. I mean, you've known the guy ten years and you're just now noticing that maybe, just maybe there's something there." Maya shrugged. "I think the two of you have spent so much time ignoring the obvious that now, it's smackin' you both in the face, and you haven't got a clue."

"So what am I supposed to do?" Eden didn't know what to do anymore. In fact, it seemed like a real good idea to just put the whole idea of her with Elliot away in the back of her mind. "I move closer, he pulls back. I show him my clothes, *my new girl clothes* and he looks at me like I'm a hooker."

"I doubt that."

Eden frowned. "You weren't there." She thought he'd show a glimmer of interest at the bare skin and all that but nope, nothing. Nada. Just that bland, bored British stare he seemed to perfect over the years.

Maya spritzed a bit of mineral water on her face and then turned to look at Eden. "Okay, I hesitate to ask this. Mostly because I'm scared you'll kick my ass."

"I'm not going to kick your ass."

Maya licked her lips. "Uh-huh, just wait. I have a theory."

The waitress brought her another margarita, which Eden greedily scooped up. "All of a sudden, I'm not sure I want to hear this."

"Yeah, probably not but I'm going to say it anyway cause I think it needs to be out there."

"Wow, you're confident aren't you?"

A smirk played around Maya's lips as she watched Eden drink her margarita. "Well, if you don't like what I tell you, there's always my news on the Goth front."

That got Eden's attention. But damn if she didn't want to know what Maya thought about her and Elliot. Personally, she didn't think there was a chance in hell. How could two people not notice each other for ten years? That was just silly.

"I think sometimes people just don't see what's right under their noses. Maybe because they don't want to or maybe because they're afraid."

"You think I'm afraid?"

Maya shook her head. "I didn't say that. I said some people might be."

Eden lifted her hair off the back of her neck and then let it settle on her shoulders. This was nutty. She searched her mind for any signs of an attraction. If she was honest, she could come up with a few times that she thought Elliot Warwick looked devastating. But it was always when he was on his way to a benefit where she figured he'd be with some sexy blonde. "You don't think it could be some sort of magic spell, do you? Something designed to screw with my head?"

"I'm betting it was there all along. Whatever magic you're experiencing is all your own making."

"I don't know that's what I'd call it. But damn, I go to bed at night thinking about him touching me." Eden discovered she'd finished her second margarita and decided to call it quits. "I wake up in the morning all tense and edgy. I even went out last night looking for some Vamps to take the edge off."

"You've got it bad, girl."

"I don't know. The whole thing just feels weird. Like he's hiding something or maybe he's just not interested in me that way and doing the whole polite British thing is his way of telling me to back off." This time Eden sighed aloud. It didn't make her feel any better. She was supposed to out here relaxing but as soon as Elliot showed up, her whole body coiled.

"I'm no expert on British guys, from what I've heard they can be a bit repressed."

"Swell." Eden tried to stare at a couple of body builders coming down to the pool. It didn't work. "Why don't I feel any better?"

"I never said you would."

"Well fuck, Maya. That's some pep talk you give."

Maya grinned. "Now I guess is a good time to tell you about the Goth rumors."

Eden pressed her lips together. The business of slaying always managed to get in the way of her ever having what people considered a normal life. She'd never noticed it until this second. Not many men would find the idea of her slaying normal and some might even think she was crazy. Who believed in demons and Vampires and the assorted other creatures populating her world? It kept you from getting close to people. Except Elliot who knew everything about her.

He was the closest thing to family she'd ever had. Eden blinked. Maybe, just maybe that's why she'd never seen it. She'd refused to see it because it'd mean changing how things were. And sometimes, when you changed things, you screwed them up.

And she couldn't stand to lose Elliot.

Eden cleared her throat. "Tell me what you've

heard about the Goths."

Maya looked at her funny. Eden could tell she wasn't going to press. But it was in her eyes. "I kinda overheard some of the detectives talking. Seems there's a few rumors floating around downtown and on the Strip about a big party coming up this weekend out past Blue Diamond."

"Standard Vamp party zone."

"The cop's are staying away." Maya stirred her drink. "Not even a traffic violation out there this weekend."

"Gotta a date this weekend?"

"Why?"

Eden smiled. The predator buried in her existence coming to the surface. "I'm in the mood for a party."

Dinner was a strained affair at best. Roland served a pasta dish that Elliot knew was a favorite of hers. He didn't care much for it but as a gesture, he was more than willing to eat noodles and garlic. If it meant a chance that Eden might open up to him. He drank a half bottle of Merlot and he couldn't remember the last time he'd drank anything more intoxicating than tea.

"Did you get a tan at the pool today?"

"Not much," she stuffed a mushroom in her mouth. "Must've been all the sunscreen you smeared on."

He nodded. What else was there to say? Feigning interest in the food, Elliot waited.

"I figured I could use a little sun. Don't want to look like one of those Goths."

"That wouldn't happen." Elliot lifted his glass.

Eden's eyes narrowed a bit. "Thirsty, Elliot?"

Elliot twirled the wine in his glass. "Perhaps." The dining room table seemed too long and much too formal all of sudden. He sat at the head of the table as was his habit but it surprised him that Eden sat as far away from him as possible. The tension in the air wasn't so much thick as it was uncomfortable. It disturbed him on so many levels he couldn't begin to assimilate it.

Her fork slipped out of her hand and clattered on the plate. She scooped it up and flashed him an irritated glare. "Look, I've got to tell you. This kind of dinner doesn't do much for my digestive tract. I feel like I'm at finishing school or some crap like that."

"You didn't have to sit down there. I'm not going to assault you." It was a poor choice of words, he knew that, but he was sick and tired of walking on eggshells with her. "Don't you find it strange that we can't even pretend to be friends?"

"I didn't know we weren't friends. Something changed since this afternoon?"

Elliot forked a vegetable and bit into it. Too much garlic. You could repel the entire Vampire population of Las Vegas with it. There was so much to tell her. Things she needed to know about magic and prophecies. How they affected them and how the outcome could change them irreparably. He couldn't begin to calculate the fallout from that one.

"No nothing's changed," he smiled slowly, forcing it up to his eyes. Now wasn't the right time for this. She'd existed her entire life without knowing he was a Warlock. Might as well wait a few more days, what could it hurt?

"So tell me more about this magic."

Elliot frowned, his brows drawing together. "What magic?"

"The stuff the Vampires are using. I need to be immune to that shit." She twirled what looked to Elliot like a half cup of pasta up onto her fork before stuffing it in her mouth.

"You think more of them will use magic against you?" She nodded and gave muffled grunt that Elliot assumed was an affirmative response. Elliot considered a general protection spell but it wouldn't take the creatures long to counter that.

"They might," Eden washed down the pasta with a swallow of tea. "Titan seemed to get a kick out of incapacitating me."

"I'm sure he did," Elliot watched her over the top of his wine glass. How was it he never noticed how lovely she was? How vibrate and alive her eyes became when she talked about the hunt and over a good dish of pasta. It made him curious about all the other things he'd missed when it came to Eden. "I'm not sure I understand your relationship with that one."

Elliot could've easily killed the creature the other not but chose not to due to the strange affection Eden had for the flame haired Vampire.

"No relationship. He does stupid shit and I remember not to kill him because he usually has accurate information."

"I see."

Eden picked up her plate and walked over to the serving table for another helping. "What do you *see*, Elliot?" Deliberately, she sat her plate next to him and pulled out the chair. "Because I'm thinking you are pretty blind when it comes to stuff."

"And what sort of *stuff* would that be, Eden?"

"You know, social stuff. And what about that magic business? You never did say how you knew to call me."

He regarded the wine for a long moment. Sometimes, it took a moment or two to catch up with Eden's train of thought. It was a fascinating display to watch her mind shift gears. When Eden was uncomfortable, she deliberately jumped topics in the span of a heartbeat. He'd gotten used to it over the years but it was often hard to keep up.

He raised his head and smiled deliberately. "Do I get to pick the questions I answer?"

Eden sniffed the air and raised her chin. "I only asked one question."

"But I'm curious, what social skills do you think I'm lacking?" He angled his head slightly. "After all, I'm British, Eden. We excel in social skills."

"You seem to be lacking when it comes to women."

He raised a brow and tried not to smirk. "Really? I don't recall ever having any complaints."

She inhaled on a sharp breath. "You know, that whole British thing gets annoying when you flaunt it."

Elliot's eyes widened. "I'm sorry that offends you. But I bloody well can't change the fact that I'm British."

"I didn't mean it like that."

"No, of course not, you never bloody mean to offend people!"

Eden shoved back, "Hey, all I said was you're not real good with women."

Elliot got to his feet. He was around the side of the table before Eden could react. "Get up."

"I'm eating."

"Get up before I pull you out of that damn chair." He reached down and curled his fingers around her wrist before she had a chance to react. Her eyes gleamed with a mixture of shock and the hard edge of anger. He ignored it totally, pulling her up against his chest.

"Going for the caveman routine, Elliot?"

Releasing her wrist, he slid one hand around her slender waist. Kilowatts of power vibrated through them causing Elliot to rethink his impulsive move. But she was so lovely, so vibrant and full of power, he couldn't resist. Ever so slowly, he raised his hand to cup the side of her face. When she leaned her cheek into him, he found time to inhale. "How could I not have seen this? Not in ten years."

Elliot shook his head, disbelief clouding his mind. "What was I thinking?"

"I don't know." Her words weren't much more than a breath of soft air filtering over him.

He used the pad of his thumb to stroke over her sensual lower lip. She sighed and Elliot bent his head slightly as her lips parted beneath his touch. It baffled him. Utterly baffled him that he could've known this woman for so long and this was the first time he'd really looked at her. Wanted her. With a quiet desperation that seemed so out of place yet something he needed to exist.

Roland cleared his throat, "I'm sorry, sir. You have a call."

Elliot closed his eyes and nearly groaned aloud. "I'll be there in a moment." He heard Roland's steps retreat down the hall. Turning his gaze on Eden, he noticed the cloudy haze in her eyes. "I'm sorry."

CHAPTER EIGHT

"You know I wouldn't call you if it weren't important."

The voice on the other end of the line was rough with an edge like steel. Elliot recognized Garridon Blackthorne's distinctive timbre instantly. "What can I do for you?"

"I have the information you wanted."

Interesting, Elliot thought. "And in exchange?"

"Stop using that magical chemical Creatox on the fledglings."

Elliot sat down on the leather armchair behind his large desk in the study. "Well that would depend on the information you have."

There was a hesitation from the elder Vampire. "Do you want to know the identity of the Master in Las Vegas."

Garridon Blackthorne had no reason to lie to him. Of all the Vampires in residence on the Strip, the Blackthorne brothers were by far the most honorable. It wasn't wise to trust them as a whole but like anything, there was good to be had among the lot. Elliot scratched the side of his head. If Garridon knew who the Master was, it would be much easier to plan a defense for Eden. "All right."

"Is that a yes, Warlock?"

"Oh indeed, Vampire." Elliot didn't miss the sarcasm there. "Provide me with the name and you and your kind are safe from Creatox." Elliot didn't consider that much of a loss anyway. From what Eden said about the drug, the process was rather messy and eventually, someone would notice the remnants. "Who is it?"

"Carlos Venturi."

Elliot schooled his emotions before responding. He drummed his fingers across his desktop for a moment. "Your information is accurate."

He could practically see the smile forming on Garridon's lips. "Very."

"Would you care to impart the source of your information?"

"Depends." There was an eerie chuckle on the other end of the line. "Are you planning to kill him?"

"Well that would depend on a great number of things."

"Hmm, all right. This particular Vampire passed on the name of the Master at great peril to himself. He also does seem to have some odd sort of affection toward your Slayer."

A flare of thought burst into his mind. "That red-headed fool!"

A chuckle came across the phone. "Yes, that would be him."

"And why the hell shouldn't I kill him?"

"Mostly because he is on your side in a

roundabout sort of way."

Elliot chewed the inside of his jaw. "If you're lying—"

"What would I gain from that?" Garridon practically growled at him. "Do you believe I have a death wish?"

That almost made Elliot smile. "Vampires have never been known to be foolhardy."

"I had no idea you had a sense of humor."

"Neither did I." Elliot hung up the phone.

Eden's past was about to rear its ugly head and if Elliot didn't do something, this time, Carlos Venturi would succeed. He'd known about Eden when she was six years old. He'd been selected as her Guardian and was sworn to protect her with his life if need be. Over the years, he'd watched. He'd traveled to her home on several occasions placing protective wards around the property and even the child as she slept.

At sixteen, Eden was an angry, confused young woman. Hurt and dismayed by the accidental death of her parents, Eden could've ended up in state custody if he hadn't intervened. He'd brought her into his home under the guard of a Warlock.

That kept the assassin at bay.

Now the only thing that could protect her completely was fulfilling the Prophecy. And he was loathe to even try to fulfill it. Pinching the bridge of his nose, Elliot lifted the ancient tome holding the legend of the Slayer/Guardian prophecy and the spell work involved. It was an ancient volume of

spells he'd acquired years ago.   Like all of his
spellbooks, Elliot locked the pages with protective
wards and another spell to keep prying eyes away.
He   wasn't   necessarily   concerned   with   any
household members, more those that wandered into
his home with a more sinister nature.

He picked up his reading glasses and settled
them on his face before staring at the old writings.
Even though it was a complex spell filled with
careful enunciations and Elvin phrases, Elliot had
memorized the spell the second the tattoo appeared
on his chest six years ago.

He'd known the day would come.   Eden
Camden's parents didn't die in an accident. They'd
been   deliberately   targeted   by   the   Vampire
population upon the birth of Eden.   Elliot and the
rest of the Guardian population knew her parent's
death was a result of a Vampire assault.   A Slayer
was a death sentence when she reached maturity.
Eden became a death sentence to creatures of the
night well before her sixteenth birthday.

He acknowledged the Prophecy years ago even
though he'd never expected to see that damn tattoo
on Eden. It just made things all the more precarious.
His own feelings for Eden, still new and powerful
yet so undefined made him wonder what would
happen if the spell became active. Elliot closed the
spell book and removed his glasses. He needed
some quite time to think. To remove all thoughts
from his head except the task of protecting Eden
from the Master.

Elliot unbuttoned his shirt and pulled it free of his dress slacks. He undid the buttons at the cuffs then tossed the shirt on his chair. He stepped out of his shoes and tugged off his socks before walking to the oversized arcadia door that led out onto the balcony. The balcony ran across to his suite and Elliot could've easily changed there.

His fingers went to the belt of his slacks and as he undid the clasp, he imagined it was Eden instead. It burned hot as syrup dripping over his bare flesh as he stripped down even though the night air was relatively calm. Elliot closed his eyes to focus the power roaring through ever cell in his body and spinning around him like some crazed cyclone. He couldn't let his need for her interfere when it came to the magic. The magic needed controlled influence over it. Otherwise, you simply released chaos into the world.

Tonight, he wanted the owl. Over the planes of existence, Elliot called to the wise bird to join with him and allow him to take its form. Bone reassembled into cartilage as his body twisted into a new form. Irises changed and pupils turned to round disks. The transformation wasn't painful, it only disoriented much like a roller coaster ride. Elliot learned a long time ago not to fight the sensation but to flow with the spell and allow the energies to do their work.

In moments, the man became bird. A Great Horned Owl, nocturnal by nature and just a bit over two feet tall stood in the place where Elliot had been. He stretched his wings expanding the grey feathers over a light brown cast until they were nearly five feet in length. It felt good.

A predator by nature. Great Horned Owls could hunt cats and even known to strike out at humans while defending their nests. Elliot always thought it was an interesting aspect that the owl was monogamous when all he could think about was Eden Camden. He tucked the wings against his side and looked out into the night.

She didn't bother to knock. Her hand twisted the doorknob and pushed the door open to the study. "Elliot, we need to talk." A gust of hot wind smacked her in the face and nearly pushed her into the wall. She squinted into the semi-darkness of the room. "Elliot?" She released the doorknob. "Where the hell did you go?"

Hoot.

Eden practically leaped out of her own skin when she saw the giant owl on the balcony. "Holy shit," she breathed, listening to her heart pound in her ears. "Where the hell did you come from?" Eden moved closer, taking slow, tentative steps. He was huge, with big golden eyes and such an inquisitive look on its face. Eden had never been so close to an owl before. She had no idea they were so beautiful and exotic. And this one, wow, you put Elliot's reading glasses on him and --

"You're very pretty, you know that?" Eden took a step closer, not wanting to frighten the bird.

"Aren't you a long way from your home? Hotels aren't exactly a place for birds."

The owl flapped his wings and flew up to the balcony fence. Eden stared for a moment. If you looked really close, the bird had interesting features and an intelligence about him that was almost frightening in its intensity. He gave her one last look, at least Eden assumed the bird was male and then dove off the balcony into the night sky.

Well, obviously, Elliot wasn't in here. Piss! How were they ever supposed to get to the bottom of this if he continued to avoid her? At least, she thought he avoided her. Scratching the top of her head, Eden tried to sort through all his mixed signals. Eden growled under her breath. God, she hoped it was mixed signals. She'd hate to think that all this came from a weird case of hormones gone bad.

Eden took a look around the room and walked up to the desk. Elliot's clothes were in a neat pile on the chair. Eden's eyes narrowed. Weird. She figured that the study connected to his room since the balcony ran the length between them. But she didn't think Elliot was much of an exhibitionist.

Repressed was a good word for him. The man sure wasn't in touch with his feelings. If he had feelings, and this wasn't a figment of her imagination which Eden was seriously beginning to doubt. She reached out and fingered the collar of his shirt. The material was incredibly soft with a bit of a ribbed texture to it. Before she realized it, she'd picked up the shirt and held it against her cheek. She stroked it over her cheek and down her neck inhaling the scent of Elliot's cologne.

Oh man, it was so good. Armani, she thought. Rich, sexy and made her wish he was here right now, so she could do all those things she'd been imagining. She called Elliot repressed. She probably wasn't much better. After all, she'd denied her feelings about him. Just like she buried the scattered emotions that blew around her after her parents died.

She inhaled the fabric once more. Elliot represented things in her life that were at the same time chaotic and balanced. He was the anchor. The one force in the world where she knew it would always be safe.

Eden drew the shirt away, with a hesitation that spoke volumes. She never thought she could want someone like this. Ever. It simmered inside her. Bubbling, oozing as if her entire body became magma at just the thought of him. If they didn't do something about this soon, she'd be making real good friends with the vibrator Maya bought her for her birthday last year as a joke.

She folded his shirt back up and laid it on top of his slacks. Well, might as well go check out a movie on HBO or something cause she wasn't getting anything here except way too hot. Eden turned and noticed the large book lying on Elliot's desk.

It was about the size of a phonebook.

Beautifully bound in leather with some gorgeous etch work on the cover and spine, Eden picked up the book to take a good look. She loved first editions and this one sure looked like an antique.

She flicked on the desk light, and examined the title. Either her eyes were going or this wasn't English. Maybe it was that old English stuff or something just as flowery. The lettering was a gold inlay with a heavy brocade style script. She could imagine how much a book like that cost.

Eden ran her finger along the edge of the cover. She loved books and was forever collecting a stack of *To Be Read* material. Maybe she'd just take a look at this one and see if it was something she could get into. She preferred reading to watching television anyway. Eden took hold of the corner of the leather cover and opened it up.

She skimmed her fingers over the title page and winced. Damn paper cuts, Eden sucked the tip of her index finger that throbbed as if she'd stuck it into a blackberry bush. She flipped the page over and saw something that looked like a poem. She tried to wrap her mind around the words but it was like learning a foreign language.

"*Aflanish maaveen* –" Eden found herself whispering the words aloud as she tried to sound them out. What the hell kind of –

A gust of wind shook the glass panes of the arcadia door. Eden's head turned at the sound. Icy wind blasted around the study and blew like a frozen dust devil. Eden took two steps forward toward the door to close off the gust and screamed as the wind grew arms and reached for her. She didn't even have a chance to inhale before the limbs caught her and threw her against the farthest wall.

She hit so hard her teeth rattled. "Shit!" Eden shook her head to clear the cobwebs and that took too much time. Eight, no ten, red orbs that seemed like tiny missiles slammed into her so hard it made her vision swim. The next thing she knew she was pinned to the wall with her feet about eighteen inches off the ground.

Eden tried to pull her shoulders off the wall. Nothing. The wind that swept into the room seemed to dissipate just as magically as it arrived. She kicked her feet and they didn't budge. "Shit! Fuck! Goddammit! Somebody get me down from here."

Magic.

The thought surfaced quickly. Stupid freakin' magic. And it was probably some creep ass Vampire that managed to cast the spell on her that left her pinned against the wall. Eden growled under her breath. She wiggled against the wall looking for any leeway.

"Damn it all to hell!" Where the fuck was everybody? If Elliot was in his room taking a shower or whatever, he ought to hear her. And Roland was everywhere all the time except right now.

Crap. Crap. Crap.

Stuck like a freakin' human dartboard against

the wall just hangin' out till someone wandered in. And she wondered what she was going to do this evening.   Obviously, her plans were made now. How fucking humiliating!

If she could've twiddled her thumbs, she would've.   Why the hell couldn't see get a decent bout of magic like some hot honey to do her bidding all night?   Instead, she always managed to stumble into shit like this.

As far as she was concerned, no magic was the only good magic.   You couldn't control the shit from what she'd seen, and to Eden, control was paramount.

Elliot folded his arms across his chest as he leaned against the door jam.   "How long has she been up there?"

"At least twenty minutes, maybe longer."

It was almost comical.   What was Eden doing in his study?   And, why was she snooping around his spellbooks?   He'd never expected Eden to come into his study tonight.   He didn't think he'd get an opportunity to ask her about it either.   He tilted his head slightly to look inside the study.   She looked madder than a wet cat.   "I appreciate your notifying me."

Roland nodded.   "Have a good evening, sir." Roland turned and left him to deal with his inquisitive Slayer.

He thought about his options.   He could release her from there.   Eden would think the spell wore off and growl her way down the hall to her room. That was by far the simplest answer. She looked rather like a victim of a bizarre exercise in bondage at the moment. That thought brought all sorts of erotic imaginings with it.

And then it came to him.

"A release you seek from your binds, but in this night you are all mine. Open your eyes, see and feel, for tonight, even dreams can be real." Elliot opened his hand and the entire room shimmered as if sprayed with mica. He waited a few seconds then entered the room. When Eden woke the next morning, she would think this was all simply a dream. Perhaps, not a simple dream but a dream nonetheless. Elliot wasn't sure if it was a good idea but it would answer a few questions.

"Hanging around?" He pushed the door open and walked into the study.

"Fuck you!"

"Indeed." He moved closer, rubbing his hand down the sleeve of his sweater.

"You wanna get me down from here, Sherlock? Or are you just going to leave me up here like a freakin' deer head?" Eden snarled trying to pull herself away from the wall.

"What makes you think I can get you down?" Elliot moved to stand next to her moving his desk chair out of the way. His eyes flitted over the disarray of the study. He really should've considered Eden might show some curiosity about his books. He'd hoped she would show some interest and now that she had, she was stuck to his wall like Velcro.

"You got me out of the last magical mess I was in. Do something, damn it!"

A small smile played over his lips. This was his opportunity. He shifted his body until he was facing her and planted his feet so that his face nearly aligned with her hips. "Is that what you want, Eden? Truly?"

"Yes!" Then she managed to bend her head so she could look down a bit. "Do you think I like looking like I'm the donkey. In the pin the tail on game?"

His hands went to her hips pretending to make an attempt at pulling her down. Instead, they spread over her jeans. "Mmmm, tail. What an interesting concept."

"Elliot, what are you going to do?"

"Nothing you don't want me to do."

"I want you to get me down."

He smiled slowly as his fingers went to the hook of her jeans. "How about I get you off?"

"Whaaa—t?"

He unzipped her jeans hearing each tooth of the zipper click. The torture was exquisite. Her skin was so soft and tempting. He let the tips of his fingertips smooth over her bare flesh. "You're so tempting, Eden. How is a man to resist you?"

He wouldn't touch the tattoo. He knew that. When that time came, Eden would know it was no dream.

"Yeah, I'm a regular sex goddess.   Quit screwing around, Elliot and let me go."

"Ah, screwing would be a delicious bit of business." He peeled back the material of her jeans and then slowly tugged them down her hips.

"Elliot, what are you doing?" He head bumped against the wall as he tugged the tight jeans off her hips.

"I must admit, I've always been a bit fascinated with the concept of bondage."   As enticing as the scrap of material covering his prize was, Elliot yanked the thong down to her knees to join her jeans. Her pussy hair had been shaved into the shape of a tiny diamond.   His entire body went rigid. Fire poured into his cock.

He bent down and slid her shoes off. They hit the floor with a clunk. If Eden wasn't under the dreamlike state of the spell, she would've noticed that he'd repositioned her feet with the movement. Then, her jeans fell to the floor as well.

Instead, she sighed.

"Do you want me to taste you, Eden?"

"Oh hell, yes!" He saw her fingers move, claw at the air as if trying to reach for him. "I've wanted this for so long.   Longer than I ever really imagined."

Elliot leaned his head forward. He puts his hands on the wall to brace himself. He opened his mouth and skimmed it over her pelvic bone. He used his tongue to glide slowly over her warm flesh, tasting her softness. Her skin smelled like gardenias with just a hint of spice. His palms spread over her pussy and he used both index fingers to spread her folds to allow him easy access.

With the tips of his fingers, he pinched her clit. Rolled his fingers over her until he felt her swell and Eden groaned in delight. "Do you like that, Eden?"

Her teeth gritted together and Eden managed to nod, "Gawd, yes!" He watched her body bow slightly and marveled at her strength while he slipped his fingers deeper inside drawing out her juices.

To say his cock was hard was such an understatement. He couldn't remember when his shaft was more like a steel rod than an appendage. Elliot used to his own frustration and bent it toward Eden. He drove his fingers deep inside of her pussy, twisting and rubbing like some sort of crazed vibrator.

She was so wet he could practically feel his cock slipping inside to fuck that tight wetness so hard that the only thing Eden ever thought of at night was him. Three fingers deep inside her and Elliot felt the walls of her pussy contract. "Elliot! Please!"

She got her legs around his shoulders then. "What?" He pumped his fingers in and out and twirled them slowly until she shouted his name. "What do you want me to do?"

"Oh gawd, Elliot! Please, fuck me."

He wanted it.

He wanted her so badly. More than anything

he'd ever wanted in his entire life, he wanted to fuck her until she screamed. Until he screamed.

"Eden…"

"Elliot, get me the hell down. I want you now."

It was like a wave from the Pacific crashing over him leaving him shaking and soggy. Elliot leaned forward and clutched at her hips. "I can't." His movements were staggered, hesitant as he pulled her jeans back up over her hips. "I'm sorry."

Elliot released the spell and lowered her into his arms. "I'm so sorry." He scooped her up and her head fell against his shoulder as his spell rendered her into sleep.

*****

"I've gotta tell you, girl, you have some superior dream skills!" Maya dipped a piece of calamari into some spicy marinara sauce.

"I'm going out of my mind here, Maya." Eden lifted her glass of ice tea and swirled it slowly. "Seriously, help me out. What am I supposed to do sort of going into his room naked?"

"Maybe you should."

Eden choked. She sucked down the remnants of her tea. "You're kidding?"

"It might work."

"Or he could just think I'm some nympho who's in love with him."

Maya stopped in mid bite. "What did you just say?"

Eden plucked up a piece of calamari. "Hmm?" Maya picked up her fork and stabbed her in the hand. "Ouch! What the hell?"

"You just said you were in love with Elliot."

"I did not."

A smirk appeared on Maya's mouth, "Yeah, babe. I'm afraid you did."

"I didn't say that."

"Face it, Eden. You are so far gone, it's not even funny anymore."

Eden's eyes narrowed slowly. She dropped the calamari onto the plate. "You're out of your mind."

"At the risk of you probably killing me, I've decided to state the facts here."

"Maya, I appreciate your ability in the whole crime lab thing. But you don't know shit when it comes to me and Elliot."

Maya huffed and signaled the waiter. "Bring us to Appletinis." The waiter scurried off. "I've never seen you go out of your way for anyone. Ever." Maya tilted her head slightly. "I know you want him."

"I've pretty much taken out a billboard on the Strip advertising that. The only one who doesn't get the message is Elliot." Eden accepted the martini gratefully. "Cause he ain't getting the message, that's for sure."

"You know, if I hadn't seen the two of you out by the pool, I'd really have to rethink this. Maybe suggest you move on."

"I was thinking that last night or this morning after that wet dream." Eden swallowed a taste of the Appletini. "I want him. Really bad, Maya. It's gotten to the point that I'm having a hard time thinking straight around him." She shrugged, "Maybe I'm just pathetic inventing a relationship when there isn't one."

"Hey he's British. Give the guy a break."

"So we going to that party?"

Maya's lips twisted slightly as if she was trying to keep track of the conversation. "I think I can manage it. There's a police detective I want to come along."

"Since when?"

"Since this detective seems to be interested in Vampires."

*****

"I have to say, sir, I'm surprised." Roland laid a plate of eggs and toast in front of Elliot in a proper manner.

"At what, Roland?" Elliot speared an egg. It was over easy. He didn't eat runny yolks. Turning his head, he lanced Roland with his eyes. "What's this?"

Roland sniffed. "Your eggs, sir."

"I don't eat eggs like this."

"You don't?" Elliot could see Roland's smirk flatten into a dull stare. "How silly of me, sir, to overlook your needs when I've known you for such a long time."

Elliot shoved his plate away. "Do you have a point, Roland? If not, I suggest you take this slop and feed it to the garbage disposal."

"I was only trying to point out that perhaps,

Miss Camden's needs ought to be recognized and you might enjoy fulfilling them."

Elliot bit back a sigh. "I don't know that we're ready for that."

"Eventually, there won't be a choice in the matter."

Looking at his cup of coffee, Elliot avoided Roland's eyes and the subject. "There are always choices."

"You need to tell her the truth."

"About what?"

Roland reached out and picked up Elliot's plate. "How you feel about her. That's why you haven't told her the rest." The plate clattered into the sink. "You have feelings for you, don't you sir?"

"I don't know what you're talking about, Roland." Elliot picked up his cup of coffee and tasted it. No sugar. The bitter surge of caffeine nearly made him choke. "Roland, I suppose that means you forgot I took sugar in my coffee."

"No I didn't forget, sir. I just wanted your attention for a moment."

Elliot let the coffee cup clatter onto its plate. He turned slowly in his chair to fix what he hoped was an irritated glare on Roland. "You have my undivided attention."

"All I'm trying to say, sir, is while you're trying to figure out what you should do regarding your feelings for Miss Camden, she may assume you aren't interested and find other forms of entertainment."

Elliot tilted his head, absorbing the words.
Could Roland have the key? Was he so busy trying
to allow her freedom that he could inadvertently
lose her instead? And if he lost her, how did he live
with himself?

Elliot stared at Roland. The light bulb was dim,
but as he sat there, it became brighter until it was
glaringly obvious. By trying to do right by her and
keep her from knowing about the Prophecy and all
the politics around that, he could very easily lose the
woman he'd fallen in love with.

"Your sugar, sir." Roland sat a sugar bowl in
front of him.

"Why do I have a feeling you know
something." Elliot spooned sugar into his coffee.

Roland picked up his plate and refilled his
coffee. "I don't know what you're talking about."

"I think you know exactly what I'm talking
about. You know everything that's going on in this
place, this hotel even, probably more than I do. So
tell me, what do you know?" Elliot stirred his coffee
slowly, carefully, wondering if Roland would like it
if he slammed him into the sugar bowl. "And I
wouldn't hesitate, because stuffing you into the
sugar bowl is quickly becoming an option."

"I may've overheard her speaking with her
friend, Maya, I believe."

Elliot tried not to grimace. Maya was a wild
thing. Far more than Eden was when it came to men
and a wild lifestyle. Elliot sensed Maya was behind
Eden's sexy makeover – not that he complained or

anything. It was just so completely unexpected. It made his stomach roll and his heart and lungs twist into some sort of bizarre braid. "What are they up to?"

"I'm not sure exactly, but it sounded like some big party this weekend. Lots of men, evidently."

"And you mention this to me, because…"

Roland smiled, "I want to torture you."

Elliot's lips twisted into a slow smile. "Hmm, I guess a raise wasn't anything you had in mind for the future either."

A frown pierced Roland's full lips. "I should've thought about that."

Now, Elliot's smile became a bit greedy. "Yes, you should've." He picked up his coffee cup and got to his feet. Moving slowly, he decided to go into the office. He had some paperwork to do before his morning rounds in the casino. "I assume this party is this weekend. Who is the lucky host?"

Roland shrugged, "Neither seemed to know or care."

Elliot nodded, "And the location?"

"Out past Blue Diamond road."

Elliot pushed open the swinging door that led out of the kitchen. "Interesting."

The sensation burning over his stomach lining wasn't easy to identify. It could've easily come from that hideous breakfast Roland served or it could've been the bitter taste of jealously. If he truly wanted honesty, he hadn't felt that sensation ever. And it was because Eden hadn't shown any serious interest in men since he'd known her. All at once, a surge of gratefulness filled him as if he'd stumbled into a spring rain shower. A delicious reprieve – in the past six years he'd stamped his own emotions into the dirt, he hadn't worried about Eden's.

Evidently, Roland was right. She'd grown bored waiting for him to make a move. Elliot sighed as he entered his study. If he made a move, the bloody Prophecy would bind them together for eternity. He didn't know if Eden wanted that. Could they possibly make the change from barely friends to lovers with such intimate knowledge of each other every breath you took belonged to the other?

CHAPTER NINE

Eden pressed the back of her hand up under her nose. "My God, this place reeks!" She followed Maya down a ravine where a huge tent had been set up and lit like the Fourth of July. She'd never seen a rave like this one. Most were held in vacant warehouses behind the casinos but this one was in BFE. She couldn't believe out in the middle of the desert was a party of this size.

"What are you talking about?"

"You can't smell *that*?"

Maya shook her head and delicately avoided a pothole as she maneuvered the terrain. "Obviously not."

It smelled like a cross between manure and rotting flesh with a weird heavy overlay of exotic florals. Enough to make the normal slayer-type gack with revoltion. "I can't believe you can't smell them."

"By them you mean Vampires?"

Eden nodded. "I figure the entire population of Vegas, Phoenix and LA are here now." Damn, she should've worn something else besides the sexy stuff. These boots with the three-inch heels were hell walking in the dirt. She'd break an ankle if she wasn't careful.

"Just get a high octane drink when we get in and it will kill your sense of smell."

"You think that'll help?"

Maya dug into her wallet as they stepped into line. "It'll help you get over the cost of this thing."

"Excuse me?"

"Yeah, chicks are twenty. Guys are forty."

Eden snorted and dug her fingers into her pocket. "Great, we get the pleasure to pay to have Vampires hit on us."

"Just think of all the potential targets for you."

"Funny." Eden bared her teeth. She might be sexually frustrated, but taking on three hundred Vampires at one shot wasn't her idea of fun. More like suicide. She wasn't stupid. Horny, yes. Irritated as hell, oh yeah, but stupid? No freakin' way.

"Oh lightin' up, Eden. We're here to have fun is all. Take a look at the weirdness or whatever." The line advanced at a pace that surprised both of them. Maya handed the bouncer her money. "Just fun, Eden. And who knows, it might do you some good to bump into someone besides Elliot – if you get my meaning."

Eden stuffed a twenty into the sweaty palm of the bouncer. "Yeah, yeah. Drink and dance is all we're doing." The thunder from the subwoofers nearly blew them back outside. Maya clutched at her arm. "Shit, we're going to go deaf."

Maya's fingers dug into the hem of her shirt

and yanked. "First a drink, then a dance, then if we can't hear, we'll get out of this place."

Pierced, tattooed, dyed Goths littered the tent like cattle about to go to slaughter. Another time or place, she'd try to warn them, but there were at least eighty of them just in her line of sight. Vampires galore, Eden couldn't hazard a guess as to exactly how may were at this rave. Celebrities, shit! Eden shook her head in disgust. Vampires were now the *in thing* in Vegas? The danger, the darkness – people just didn't have a clue.

She sidled up to the bar just as a bartender with muscles on muscles shook a huge bell and shouted about the music. "Free drinks for the girls, next ten minutes on our host!"

Trays loaded with shot glasses hit the floor. Chicks in all sizes and colors descended on them like a pack of hungry beasts. Eden managed to snag a couple for her and Maya. She passed one to Maya and raised the glass in a toast. "To an interesting evening."

She tilted the shot glass back and swallowed. It wasn't bad. Sweet, fruity, but nothing she wanted to drink all night. Leaning across the bar, Eden tapped the glass on the bar. "Got anything with more of a kick?"

"How much of a kick are you after?" He grinned at her and then Maya. "We've got a special going tonight. Drink that's been around for over a hundred and eighty years."

Eden looked over at Maya and winked.

"Sounds good."

The bartender sat two, small liqueur style glasses on the bar in front of them. They had tiny handles on the sides and looked quite expensive. From under the bar, he pulled out a bottle the same size as a gallon wine jug. It was black and the liquid that came out of it appeared nearly emerald in colored light bouncing around the walls. He placed a tiny spoon on top of each cup and plopped a sugar cube in the spoon.

"Well, this is kinda cool." Maya winked at Eden.

A drizzle over the top of the sugar cube, with some other alcohol and then the bartender pulled out a candle lighter and lit the sugar. "Wait till it burns down a bit." He leaned forward as if mesmerized by the flame. "Look at the color." He tipped the fiery sugar into the glasses and nudged them forward. "Down it in one shot, babes and you'll have free drinks all night."

Maya used two fingers to pick up the glass and examine the now blue fireball drink. She shrugged at Eden. "Hey, it's what we're here for."

Eden picked up her own glass and reconsidered for a moment. Maybe downing blue fireballs wasn't such a smart idea. But what the hell? A girl needed a bit of wildness sometimes, a bit of rebellion. She'd been tied to Elliot Warwick for so long she was surprised they weren't actually growing each other's appendages now.

She tipped the glass up to her lips and for a

second, she thought she noticed the bartender signal someone in the back of the tent. But that must've been her imagination. Even though she could see that far, the place was packed like sardines in a tuna can.

The weird drink rolled over her tongue like a backdraft. The fire hissed out and for a second, Eden knew what it was like to be a dragon. Smoke steamed out her nostrils as jet fuel slipped down her throat in a wild array of berry and spice.

"Holy crap!"

The bartender snapped two wristbands on them before they could blink. "There you are, ladies. Free drinks. And I know you'll want another one of these soon."

Maya shook her head, "Holy crap!"

"I said that already."

"Yeah, but I meant it." Maya shouted about the band that just took the stage in the center of the tent. "What the hell was that?"

Eden's brain turned into a basketball that resembled a disco, mirror ball. "Beats the shit out of me. But what a buzz."

"You wanna dance?" A guy in his mid-twenties with long blonde hair wrapped an arm around Eden's waist and the other around Maya's shoulders.

"Absolutely!" Maya volunteered before Eden could decline.

The basketball that was her brain became dribbled and passed down a court of wild color and insanely loud music. Eden wasn't sure at what point she became some erotic sex dancer. Maybe it was after the second or third fireball but she gyrated with the best of them.

The band changed tempos or maybe the band just changed period but the whole tent seemed to shift and tilt with weird vibes and streaks of blues and reds. Sweat trickled down the back of her neck as she managed to get a Coke from someone and noticed she'd lost track of Maya during the last bump and grind.

Narrowing her eyes, she did her best to focus. One minute the tent was bold and blinding with light, the next it flickered to one candle. She blinked. It looked like there was an orgy going on next to the stage. Well, that was a different take to a mosh pit.

And it was hotter than hell, in there. She wiped the glass of ice across her cheek and down her neck trying to cool her overheated body.

Damn, was she the only one sweating? Eden looked around. Maybe there were more dead people in here than she thought. Everyone else looked fresh and ready for another three hours of this aerobic sex adventure.

Eden glanced at her watch and nearly fell over. It was already a quarter to two. Shit, they'd been there over four hours. Where the hell had the time gone? Absently, she dug around in her pocket for her cell phone ready to call Maya and call it a night.

"Oh my darling, you can't think about leaving

now. Not when I've just found you." A man of average height and the longest, blackest hair she'd ever seen, took her by the hand. "Come my love, we have much to talk about."

Eden's tongue stuck in her mouth like a rolled up wad of cotton. He pulled her through the crowd that parted effortlessly as he walked by. "I'm not yer love." That sounded funny so Eden focused on enunciation. "You are cute, but I don't know you."

"Not yet."

Normally, cocky guys weren't her cup of tea. So she decided to blame her sudden shift on Elliot. After all, if he'd shown the least bit of cooperation, she wouldn't be at this party. She let him lead her into another part of the tent.

It was dark and mercifully cool. It was probably the party host's idea of a VIP lounge. The small area was covered with velvet pillows and lit with tiny red lights. At the moment, it was just Eden and her new boyfriend. "So what's you're name?"

"Carlos."

He passed her another fireball. She hadn't seen him move. Eden narrowed her eyes again and tried to focus as he raised the glass to her lips. "Mmm, sexy name." She swallowed the fireball enjoying the burn of jet fuel down her throat and eating through her stomach lining.

He laughed and somewhere it registered in Eden's head that that wasn't a sexy laugh. It was dark and very, very cold. "Sit down, Eden."

"How do you know my name?"

Then she was sitting or sprawling over mounds of funky pillows. "I know a lot about you." The man, Carlos, stroked a hand down the side of her face and down her neck. "You are far prettier than I expected."

"You were expecting me?" He nodded and she noticed his eyes were the same color as his hair. Against a fairly dark complexion, she figured sexy Carlos was probably European.

His fingers went to the back of her halter. "Oh yes, I through this party for you. I can't tell you how happy I am that you decided to attend."

She felt the material slide away from her breasts. Instead of cool air, the air that draped over her skin was hot and oppressive. "What are you doing?"

"Nothing you don't want, Eden." He trailed his fingers over her nipples. "You wanted your warlock to do this, didn't you?" Carlos bent his head and licked his lips. "That's the trouble with the British. So indecisive. Don't take what was right in front of them and then moaned about it when it was finally gone."

Eden brushed his hands away and shoved herself up on her elbows. "Look buddy, you have me mistaken for someone else." She sniffed and though it was subtle – really subtle, she could smell death on him. She reached for her top. "You must think I'm one of the Goth groupies."

Carlos' teeth clicked together. "No, I know

who you are." He leaned over the top of her and his breath smelled like cinnamon. "And I know what you want." He pressed her back and trailed his long tongue over the tip of one nipple. "I can give it to you."

Her breath came on a hiss. Whoever, whatever he was, he had one hell of a tongue. Strands of silky black hair trailed over her belly as he made his way down. "What do you have that I can't get anywhere?"

He slid his thigh between hers and Eden swore she heard a zipper. The guy was undoing his fly? Okay, she was lit, but she wasn't fucking some stranger she just stumbled into. Then his hand reached for hers and the next thing she new, she had a cock the size of a foot long in her hand.

"That's what I can do for you." He arched his back as he guided her hand up and down the length of his hard, heavy cock. "You intrigue me, Eden Camden. More than I ever thought possible."

Maya would die for a cock this size, just tip over and fall dead on the floor in a puddle of girl ooze. Eden wasn't sure what to do here. "Great, nice to know I'm an overachiever."

He pressed the weight of his hard body into her and pushed back her hair before licking the side of her neck. "Ah, I can taste the power. You would be delicious."

"No, I'm not. I'm pretty sour." Eden fought the haze clogging her mind and the heavy intensity that came from this man's blatant sexuality.

She blinked and he eased her jeans off. "Tell me, you want it." His hot cock stroked over her inner thigh. Another hiss of breath followed by the strange sensation that she was drowning and Eden was torn between struggling to get away and giving in. "Say it, Eden. That's all you need to do. Invite me to give you pleasure."

He buried his head between her legs and used his tongue to pry open her folds. Eden swallowed the sharp blade suddenly lodged in her throat. His long tongue prodded her clit and made her lurch forward. He licked in hard, fast, wet strokes until Eden dug her fingers into his hair to keep from screaming.

Carlos lifted his head, "You like it, don't you?" He shifted back on his knees to stroke his cock until it stood straight up like a branding iron. "You can have it all, you know?" He smiled slowly, drawing his hand over the engorged head. "I can show you pleasure beyond your wildest dreams."

Eden reached a hand out for her clothing. Something was really wrong here. The red light in the small hot room seemed to dim, replaced by a pale yellow. Eden squinted. Good God, she could make out the outlines of at least four other people – no wait, six other people in the room watching them. Somehow, that cleared the mist from her bounced about brain. "What the fuck, I'm not into a gang bang."

Carlos snickered, a very unpleasant sound. Then, he licked the tip of his index finger and traced the edge of her tattoo. His fingers leapt back and Eden swore she saw smoke coming from them. "Kristov, explain to her." There was no doubt the skin singed when he touched her tattoo.

Another man with dark chocolate brown hair with auburn highlights came out of the shadows and standing next to him was Titan. "Oh you have to be fuckin' kidding me! You are all Vampires." She snatched her jeans up to her waist. "You know, this was a seriously bad idea." She rolled to her knees, "I'm just going to get the fuck out of here, and you all can party on."

The one called Kristov slid behind her and bent his head to examine the tattoo. "He hasn't activated the spell yet." He pointed a finger at Carlos. "If he had, you'd be a torch by now."

"So there's an opportunity here." Carlos tucked his hard cock back into his fly. "You can activate and she'll belong to you which means, she'd be my personal concubine."

Eden buttoned her pants and yanked her shirt over her head. She started to stand, but Carlos caught hold of her calf. "Let go."

"Not yet, dear Eden." He rose to his knees. "Aren't you the least bit curious?"

"About what?"

"Magic and your part in it."

Twisting her shirt back in place, Eden bit her lip and struggled to keep up with the conversation. "You guys are all nuts."

The one called Kristov, smoothed back her hair.

"He hasn't told you yet, has he?"

"Told me what?"

"The tattoo you bear is a magical glyph. It is an ancient prophecy binding a slayer to her warlock through eternity." Kristov licked his lips and Eden witnessed pure greed shining in his eyes. "I'm not your chosen one, but I believe I could unlock the power." He leaned closer. "You and I would have immeasurable power."

Carlos laid a hand on her shoulder. Gentle, yet very firm, his touch wasn't nearly as seductive as it'd been a few minutes ago. "And then I'd kill you both." He grinned, white teeth flashing against the olive complexion. "You will bind her to me."

On a wave of clarity, Eden pushed herself up and shoved both men back. "Nobody's binding me to anyone. And you, you magic fucker," she pointed her finger at Kristov, "just keep you're fucking shit away from me. I don't do magic. Period."

"Is that a fact?" Kristov snickered and glanced at Carlos.

"Yeah, it's a fact."

Carlos lifted a slender brow. "Now, that makes me wonder. Is your guardian as honorable as he'd like you to believe, or does he have an agenda of his own?" He reached for her hand and Eden shifted away.

"What *are* you talking about?"

The room seemed to roll with laughter. Carlos held up a hand and silenced them. He moved from a sitting position to standing in a second. "You really have no idea?"

Eden heard giggling. It was an obnoxious sound like birds chirping outside your window at five in the morning. She turned her head and saw the outline of Titan against a back wall. Son of a bitch, this bender got better and better. She figured she had enough strength to snap the redheaded firecracker's neck before the others pounced on her.

Her eyes spun back in her head as Carlos gripped her upper arms. "Elliot Warwick is possibly the most powerful Warlock in the world."

Air blew out of her mouth and caught her front teeth turning into a cross between a snort and a laugh. "So is it the whole blood thing that makes you guys insane or am I missing something here?"

Kristov's lips twisted. "I'm not a Vampire, Eden. I'm not insane either."

"Yeah well, that makes it all better."

"Your perfect guardian is a magic user."

She folded her arms around her chest. How much alcohol did it take before you became delusional? "Elliot is a tight-assed, no nonsense British stick in the mud."

"That's redundant." Titan moved from the wall and took a position near the doorframe.

"Screw you."

He parted his lips revealing sharp fangs. "Love to."

"Silence." Carlos picked up a strand of Eden's hair and sniffed it. "Think back, Eden. Your stuffy

Elliot hasn't been acting out of character recently has he?"

Eden inhaled. The damn *tattoo* started all of this. She pointed to her hip. "What did you say this was?"

"It's a glyph. Once activated it is supposed to fulfill an old prophecy involving a slayer and her Warlock guardian."

"He's using you, Eden. To get to what he wants."

Her mind spun again, that disco ball whirling counter clockwise. "What's that?"

"Power."

The explosion of music, light, and voices raised in an effort to carry on a conversation nearly blew Elliot and Roland back out of the front entrance to the rave. "They're here. Somewhere."

"With how many beasts around them?"

Elliot ignored the shouted comment threading his way through the crowd. It was a maze of Gothics, Vampires and assorted other bizarre pieces of humanity. Most of them draped around each other in macabre displays of sex and Elliot knew instantly this party was nothing more than a Vampire feeding frenzy. "We need to find them. They have no idea what kind of danger they're in."

"You really think a Master is here."

His nod was abrupt. He had a very bad feeling about this. He couldn't sense Eden in this meat market and that wasn't good. In fact, it was very bad. He reached out for a young woman with the same style hair as Maya and spun her around.

The girl's eyes got his attention immediately. Dilated pupils with an odd glow around the rim of the iris made Elliot release his hold. The girl wasn't Maya. Bloody hell, this was worse than he'd imagined.

Elliot made his way to the bar. The temptation to *Fast Freeze* everyone in the room until he found Maya and Eden was great. Unfortunately, it would reveal certain things about himself that he wasn't ready for the general population to know. In some cases, it was best to conceal things.

The line at the bar was three deep, but he managed to shoulder his way up to the long piece of plywood serving as the bar. There were four bartenders serving up alcohol as fast as they could pour. Elliot took a closer look – three of them were low level demons. Always looking for a way to advance themselves, this trio probably assumed a night at a Vampire party was a step up.

"Be with you in a sec," one of the demons told him.

Elliot smiled in a patient practiced manner. Demons rarely had the ability to detect Warlocks. And these three wouldn't possess the power combined to figure out who he was.

Leaning over the side of the bar, Elliot scanned the offerings. Everything looked like alcohol and it certainly smelled like a distillery back here. But all wasn't what it seemed, Elliot used his right pinkie in a subtle gesture. "Find."

A simple spell that didn't display a great deal of magic. Designed to locate any inanimate item the Warlock sought. It came in terribly handy when you lost your car keys. Right now, he was looking for Absinthe.

Absinthe known as the Green Fairy was a high alcohol per volume drink created in the Victoria era. Unique tasting, the liqueur infused flavors derived from variety of herbs. The Green Fairy nickname came from its color and its humble beginnings as a miraculous cure all. Absinthe's coloring was the result of the chlorophyll present in the herbs. These herbs included anise, hyssop, veronica, fennel, lemon balm, angelica and last but not least wormwood. This last ingredient made it illegal in most countries with reasonable liquor laws. Wormwood produced the psychoactive constituent thujone, which created anything from mystic dreams to bizarre hallucinations.

Blend Absinthe with the blood of a Vampire and you essentially created a sex-starved zombie in a drugged fog willing to do the Vampire's bidding. From the looks of this crowd, they'd had enough of this drink to slit themselves wide and watch while the Vampire's fed off them.

A bottle wiggled from behind the counter and fell over in a domino effect. It spilled out onto the floor and even in the darkness, Elliot could see the lime green color of the Absinthe. Two of the demons scrambled to retrieve the bottle and Elliot turned away from the bar.

He found Roland searching the crowd and put a hand on his shoulder. "Find Maya and take her home. I'm going after Eden."

Roland's brows knitted together, "What's happened?"

"He's got them all in a thrall of Absinthe." Elliot pointed to a group gathered around a group of young women having way too good of a time. "Bloody hell!" He shoved three men off of Maya who laid across another one. This man had his hands on her tits. "Get off her you lazy fool!"

He yanked the man away by his collar and lifted Maya up. Digging into his pocket, Elliot produced a small vial. He popped the cap open and held it to Maya's greedy mouth. "Drink this, Maya. It won't clear away all the poison, but it's a start." He poured the blue liquid into her mouth and she swallowed while leaning hard against him.

Shifting her body into Roland's arms, he put the small bottle back into his pocket. "Take her home, remove all remnants of the Absinthe."

"Yes, sir."

Elliot parted his way through the crowd, his patience wearing. If he didn't locate her soon, he'd start exploding Vampires shortly. Two girls, they were little more than girls wrapped themselves around him and began groping and trying to lick their way across him. He shoved them back, too firmly, he knew, but time was of the essence here.

This Vampire, this Master made a bold statement with his wild party and blatant serving of a drink most considered poisonous. He'd invited half of the nightlife in Las Vegas to this little gathering and Elliot could only assume it was an effort to assert power. It hit him hard and fast like an out of control train crashing into a mountainside, this entire party was to get at Eden.

Panic, a viable, tangible entity slid over him like green ooze and threatened to suck the life out of him. He struggled against it. Moisture evaporated out of his mouth leaving his tongue dry and tasting like sand. It squeezed his ribcage and Elliot gasped for air.

He wouldn't lose her. Not like this. Not in some drugged haze where she found herself bound to a Vampire. "Eden!"

The sound reverberated off the walls and bounced into the beat of the music. Elliot bent over coughing as he shook the panic. No matter what she thought of him, no matter what the outcome here he wouldn't let that Vampire get his claws in her.

"Elliot?"

Elliot turned to see Eden wave at him. She was up against a wall with her arms spread while three men fondled her. He took two steps and caught two of them by the shoulder. He was built like an athletic, lean and muscled, and at six two had a strength that most didn't expect. He shoved them off her and the third that was nibbling along her neck, Elliot took hold of and smacked his head into the ground.

He reached out for her arm, "Let's go."

"Elliot," Eden wrapped her arms around his neck and pulled her up against him. "I've mished you."

"Bloody hell." She had one helluva grip on him. One hand tightened around the back of his neck while the other went straight for his crotch. "Eden, stop. We have to leave."

"Nah, we're having fun." She practically spit the words out on his cheek. "Great pardy, where's Maya?"

"With any luck, home by now."

"Awww, that's a shame." She pinched his cheek. "Wanna fuck?"

"Bloody hell, Eden! You're drugged! Can't you tell that?" The girl was amazingly strong. Viciously strong. "Stop this. How much have you had to drink?"

She shrugged. "I dunno. A few." She took hold of his wrist and pulled it toward the waistband of her jeans. "Come on, Elliot. Show a girl a good time."

The feel of her skin distracted him. Hot, soft and oh so smooth that he never noticed her head move. One of her hands shoved his down the front of her jeans and at the same second, her mouth latched onto his.

Elliot nearly dropped to his knees. Her mouth, the sweetness of it would drive a man to madness. Her lips were soft, full and he simply couldn't resist her any longer. Oh dear God, it was so sweet he couldn't imagine anything in this world more heavenly. Her tongue pushed past his teeth to engage him and it crushed him with the sadness and utter beauty of one simple kiss.

He tasted the poison. Combined with the thousands of exotic flavors that merged to make Eden, Elliot swam in a sea of passionate darkness. His lips burned against hers and his fingers slid lower under the fabric of her jeans. He shut his eyes and gave in.

The kiss was his absolute undoing. It reminded him of lightning, the raw power, the electricity pouring through his entire body. He shuddered and somehow managed to yank his mouth away. "We need to leave, do you understand?"

"Why?" She shifted angling her hips into him. Elliot's cock grew hot and hard in a matter of seconds.

"This place is full of Vampires. There's a start."

"Big deal. You're the big wizard. Zap 'em."

Her comment didn't register. He was too busy conducting a thorough examination. The aura surrounding her was dark, gray and oppressive. His hands slid over her as he released the magic and allowed it to flow freely through his veins. The Vampire had touched her, he could taste it on her lips as easily as he could taste the remnants of the Absinthe. His hands glowed, a pale gold in the dim light of the tent as he ran them over Eden, clearing the cloud.

"Nice," she murmured against his ear then trailed her teeth down to his lobe. "Feels warm with a little vibration. You could market this." Her leg curled around his calf. "Be the next thing in girl's toys."

He bit back a laugh. They closed in on them. The darkness, the vile foreboding that came with a clutch of Vampires filled the tent. They circled them, closing in like a pack of hyenas. He put his hands on Eden's shoulders and shoved her hard against the side of the makeshift wall. "Look at me!" Jerking her chin up, he got a good look at her eyes. "I said 'look at me.'"

Her lips curled in snarl, "I am looking at you." The hostility was Eden. The glazed aspect to her eyes was all drug induced.

"You let him touch you. I can see it on you, the dirt." Jealously reared its head and snarled in a maniacal rage. It dug and clawed its way into him, twisting and yanking his innards.

Her hands went to his chest and she tried to push him back. But the magic swirling around him only added to his physical strength. "You *wouldn't*. He *did*." She smirked, "I think I like him better now." She snickered and it was a highly unpleasant sound.

Elliot leaned in, bringing his face so close to hers he could practically inhale her. Her hair brushed against his cheek and a few strands caught in the stubble of his beard. "You don't know what you're saying."

"I don't?"

"You've been drinking Absinthe all night tainted with the Master's blood."

Eden wrinkled her nose, "Eeeeewww!"

"Exactly."

"We need to leave."   His hands on her shoulders gentled. He wanted to get her out of this place. They needed to be alone together, he needed to get his hands on her before he went completely lost his mind. "Can you feel it?"

She moved her head, her eyes brightened wildly. "Your hands, oh yes, I can feel it."

"They're circling us, Eden. Like a pack of wild dogs."

Eden looked around, moving her head from side to side.   "I don't see anyone watching us. They're too busy bumping each other."

"We need to go, now."   He brushed her hair from his face.   "I can't hold back this many Vampires without it turning into a bloodbath."

"Hold what back?"

He tried reason. The glow in her eyes still worried him. "Eden, what did he tell you?"

She snorted and Elliot wanted to shake her. She was putting them both in danger by this. She might not realize it but she ought to be responsible enough to notice. He trained her better than this. Elliot twisted his body and started to turn away. His eyes moved through the crowd and he counted at least fifteen Vampires making a slow steady path toward them.

"You lied to me, Elliot."

"I don't know what you're talking about." He reached for her wrist and she clamped onto his own wrist with the grip of an anaconda.

With the other hand, she flicked open the button on her jeans, then shoved his captive hand down the front of her pants. "He wanted this. You didn't."

Elliot sighed heavily. He'd made a mistake. He should've told her six years ago. Instead, he kept it to himself. His fingers found the lips of her pussy and urged them apart. "You have no idea what I want." It was more a growl than anything else as his lips tangled with Eden's.

Lava poured through his veins. Boiling past the point of reason, Elliot's fingers worked Eden's clit in fury of fire. He leaned against her, absorbing every nuance that was Eden.

She used her teeth on his chin. Her arm wrapped around his neck as her fingers tangled into his wavy dark blonde hair. Eden shuddered, engulfed in flame as his fingers swept into her wet pussy. She wanted him so bad, she'd fuck him in front eighty-seven Vampires and enjoy it. Her mind still spun with the dizzying effects of the disco ball, but she still hungered.

Even though he'd lied, she still wanted him. Needed him.

"Don't stop." The words came out on a pant.

"They will try to kill us." His fingers danced

around her clit and Eden's knees buckled.

Whoever *they* were, she didn't care. Elliot was touching her and the entire city of Las Vegas could explode right this second – it didn't matter. She'd waited what seemed like an eternity and she was damn well going to enjoy herself.

Man, that Absinthe stuff was some good shit. Inhibitions, brainwave activity just blew on out the door. What did you need that stuff for anyway? Her body was happy swaying to the beat of the music and letting Elliot work magic on her. Eden sighed as she licked the side of Elliot's neck. Her leg curled around his waist and she could nearly feel his cock inside her oh so wet pussy.

Did he say something about Vampires?

Eden's brain bounced against her skull. She couldn't remember. Rubbing her leg up and down against his ass, she hoped he got the hint. She lifted her head from the side of his neck and got a blurry look at the crowd.

Eyes.

She saw eyes. Red, tinged with blood rage glowed in the laser light of the rave. It permeated the thick fog in her head or maybe it was the silvery glitter dust Elliot sprinkled. She didn't know. But those eyes, scared her when little else did.

Fear sprinkled along the base of her spine and danced its way up into her lungs and throat. She gripped Elliot hard and fast, "We need to get out of here." The desperation in her hoarse voice stunned her but not more than when Elliot twisted his body around. His fingers still worked her clit into a hard, eager nub while his attention turned to the party of undead they'd attracted.

Blocking her, he faced the Vampires, right hand extended and shot what she could only describe as a wave of energy at them. *"Back!"* Elliot's voice reminded her of a growl and a concussion blast that roared over the crowd.

If she had any doubts about what Carlos and Kristov had told her earlier, well, they just crumbled like ash seeing this. "Shit." She looked at Elliot's face and saw the fine sheen of perspiration – Elliot didn't sweat – on his face. He was holding the growling group of Vamps and curious Goths back with the power flowing through him.

Eden's body jerked as his fingers dove deeper inside her. She couldn't think straight. Sensations burst across her body with the rage of a thunderstorm. It drew her entire essence into a realm where she'd never gone. She wanted this, all of this, but a niggling sense of fear triggered some logical remnant in her brain.

"We can't walk out of here, can we?"

Sweat dripped off the hair at his temples when he shook his head. "Not now. Someone is pushing against this barrier. With magic."

"Alternatives?" Eden twisted around and searched the group for Kristov.

"Your reflexes are too slow to fight. Like I said, if I do anything inside this space with this many people—"

"I get the picture." She brushed his damp hair back and leaned into him. Gawd, as much as she loved his fingers rubbing her clit, it sure as hell made it hard to concentrate. "So what's the plan?"

"I can blink us out of here." She watched the strain form on his face, drawing lines deeper into the curve of his mouth. His eyes turned to stone as the press of fifteen Vampires bared down on him. "But if I'm going to do that, it's going to have to be soon. I wasn't expecting to expend this kind of power tonight."

Power.

The word clattered around in her head like some crazy drum. There were all sorts of implications to power. The lies that surrounded it. The knowledge it gave and the desire that seemed to rock her world. Eden swallowed, she'd deal with the implications later.

Right now, she had no desire to become these fuckers midnight snack. With one, hand she pulled Elliot's fingers from her pants. "The guy with the light brown hair standing next to Carlos is a Warlock."

Elliot's body absorbed the words like a physical blow. "We could be in more trouble than I suspected." He inhaled and blew out a ragged breath. "To blink, I have to drop this barrier. When I do that, we're sitting ducks."

Eden bit the inside of her lip, considering the ramifications. "Ah, we're screwed then." She noticed Kristov raise his hands and fire some sort of missile at them trying to breakdown the magical barrier. People around them just thought it was part of the light show. Eden knew they wouldn't think it was so entertaining when blood started flowing. "You know, I really don't want to be eaten in the literal sense."

He nodded, "I know." He said it threw gritted teeth. Elliot didn't grit his teeth or strain. Now he worried her.

"What can I do?"

"I need another power source." He adjusted his footing. "When we blink, it will help hold the barrier. Then it won't matter if they have a Warlock with them."

Power. There was that naughty word again.

"Elliot, what do you need?" She breathed slowly, "And what's a blink?"

"A vanishing act."

"O…kay."

"Like Star Trek."

Eden's eyes narrowed. "You're going to beam us out of here."

"In a matter of speaking."

She had a feeling she knew what it was. But she wanted to hear it from him. She could judge his actions later. Good or bad, whatever it took they needed to get the hell out of there. Cause now, she could see the reds of their eyes and it was pretty disgusting and scarier than she ever imagined. She was about to have all her atoms scrambled in some weird spell and that was better than these bloodthirsty Vamps.

She understood now what normal humans saw. Blood red haze and mindless rage, not a pretty thing. How could anyone believe in a seduction from creatures that existed on death?

Eden swallowed hard. Her mouth was so dry, she really could use a Red Bull right about now. "Touch it, Elliot. Use whatever you need but get us the hell out of here."

The hand that showed her pussy magic flattened against her hipbone. Placing his palm flat against the tattoo, he whispered words that were so melodic, Eden let them lift and draw her into a trance.

"Shit!" Eden screamed as the outline of her tattoo became a line of lit gunpowder. It sparked, snapped and she jerked away but the currant charged into her body and sealed her against Elliot.

There was a blinding blast of light and icy wind blasted in her face as her body and Elliot's vanished from the rave tent. Her cheeks vibrated from the force of the wind. Eden hung on to any part of Elliot she could catch hold of. They moved so fast she couldn't even manage to peel her eyelids open to see where they were going.

An icy torpedo, that's what they were, sailing through the air at the speed of light. Wasn't magic just the coolest thing? Yep, she was drunk. On a bender from that Absinthe stuff. She'd never drink anything green in her life again. Her body shook, goose bumps rose on her arms and back like moguls

you could ski over.   She opened her mouth to
scream once more and swore she inhaled ice
crystals.

A freakin' roller coaster from hell had nothing
on this ride. When the bottom dropped out on them
and they plunged downward at the speed of sound,
Eden only hoped that when you splattered it was
quick and fast.

CHAPTER TEN

Fused together, Eden and Elliot fell in a heap onto his bed. Disoriented, Eden tried sitting up but only could push the tangle of hair out of her eyes. "Jeezus, what the hell happened?" Her hands shook as she reached out to touch Elliot to make sure he was still breathing. It was hard to tell since he landed on her, but if she listened, she could hear his breath come in short pants. "You okay?"

He nodded slowly. Raising his head, Elliot smoothed a hand down her arm to her hip. The fabric from her clothing melting away and heat enveloped Eden. No, enveloped wasn't the right word – enveloped sounded like a blanket or something. This was hot, sticky and so disturbing in its intensity, Eden wasn't sure what would happen next.

She was naked. She blinked. "Well, isn't this magic shit handy?"

She reached for Elliot's shirt and tugged it over his head. His arms were strong, well muscled with a sprinkling of hair while his chest was smooth. Smooth with amazingly defined pectorals and the most superior abdominals she'd ever seen.

Her fingers reached out to touch that hot skin

and paused. Her gasp sounded hollow and eerily odd in her own ears.

Elliot had the same tattoo she did.

His hands moved over her shoulders and cupped her breasts. She sucked in a deep breath as that syrupy heat invaded her lungs. The tingle running along her skin sparkled through her like a crystal goblet flashing in sunlight. The prism danced over her body. Her nipples turned to hard buds as his thumb stroked over them.

Processing any kind of logical information was impossible. Whatever processed logical thought in her brain currently pinballed back and forth in her skull. He had the tattoo. Just like hers only it was below one pec. So the Vampires were telling the truth? Or trying to tell the truth.

Elliot's lips went to one of her hard nipples and Eden moaned as a rush of fire went through her breast and burned its way to her pussy. Her hand tangled in his hair while she used her other to maintain some sort of balance.

The concept of Elliot lying was so utterly foreign to her the thought itself threatened to make her ill. There was no way he'd do that. He just wouldn't. Elliot was a straight arrow. Upper crust and all that British rot stuff, he wouldn't hurt her like that. Her stomach tilted on a bizarre axis and nearly rolled away from Elliot to puke off the side of the bed.

He touched the side of her face in a caress that twisted her heart and settled her stomach. "I've waited so long."

His lips brushed over hers in soft, teasing strokes. His eyes burned a golden hazel as they watched each other's reaction. He eased her back and she ran her hands up those glorious abs. His skin was soft and hard at the same time. A delicious contrast that made her want to taste and touch more of him.

His mouth latched onto hers. She'd remember this moment for a long, long time. Remember it and hold it close no matter what happened.

Eden tasted spice, smoke and the cherry brandy she knew he liked, when their tongues met in a wildly choreographed duel. No one led, nor followed here. They were both adventurers eager to discover and find pleasure.

Elliot pressed her back into the pillows and for the first time skin met skin. The air around them sizzled and popped. Eden inhaled and the heat stung her nostrils. He smelled of cedar and oak leaves with just a hint of moss. Earth and man were a heady combination. One that Eden couldn't resist.

His chest against her breasts was the most exquisite of brandings and she couldn't get close of enough. No matter how it burned, the hotter it got, she needed to be lit up. The kiss left them gasping for breath. Hands became eager to seek and explore, Eden ran her hands over his pecs and lower.

The second she touched his tattoo, Elliot jerked as if she put a live wire in his hand. He stared at her with those hot golden eyes and pressed his lips together. "Tell me to stop." He brushed her hair from the side of her face and smiled gently. "Tell me to stop now, Eden."

"I can't." She shook her head back and forth against the pillow. "Not now."

He used his palms to part her thighs and slid two fingers deep inside her honey-coated pussy. His mouth worked one nipple, laving and sucking. Eden was already on edge. Bristled, angsty whatever you wanted to call it – Elliot worked her into such a twisted state she knew there was only one way to unwind.

With his fingers pumping in and out of her, Eden's hips rose to allow him more access. His palm massaged against her clit. Eden bit back a groan, trying to focus. It didn't do any good. Her blood burned orange hot turned to liquid metal at his touch.

It built deep within, rolling to a vicious release that made her scream. "More, please! Elliot! I need it all. I need you!"

It was a plea. Eden couldn't remember pleading for anything. Not even when her parents died. She didn't beg or cry – she'd just accepted.

This was so different. And that made it so very dangerous. He had her body and soul. If power was all he wanted, she'd already gifted him with it. Even though Elliot Warwick had yet to entirely possess her.

He shed his slacks in one smooth motion. Finally, she got to see his body. Beautifully nude.

Firm skin, over granite muscle his body reminded her of one of those Greek statues at Caesar's Palace. Dark golden hair trailed from his navel to the most impressive cock she'd ever seen. Long, smooth and thick, Eden licked her lips at the idea of this sword plunging into her wet pussy.

His hands rough and eager as he positioned her thighs around his waist, Eden could swear she could see little stars dancing around them. But then her vision blurred as he slid the head of his cock along her clit.

"Do you like that?"

The engorged head slid along her clit like lava. So very hot and it made her clit so hard it began to tingle and Eden twitched uncontrollably. "It's driving me insane!"

Her pussy hungered and it raged through her like a lioness during a hunt. She wanted to swallow that cock and pump him dry until neither of them could move. Her hips twisted as her heels dug into the mattress trying to urge Elliot's hard cock deep into her pussy. Her short nails dug into his shoulders and she jerked him forward. "Enough teasing already."

She looked into his eyes saw the hunger that matched her own, saw the need that was so indescribable at this point, it could only be a tangible entity.

"I'm not teasing." His mouth whispered next to her ear before traveling down her jaw. He took her mouth in a desperate kiss, tongues fought while

Eden's body tensed praying for release.

There was nothing left of his control. Magic, laced with passion, raged in his blood and burst chaotically around the bedroom. What little sense he had remaining was in his cock. The only thought it had was to drive into Eden as hard and fast as it possible could.

His balls tightened and if possible, he got harder. Sweat trickled down his temples. He looked at Eden, wanted to see her face when he possessed her. He wanted to taste her pleasure and absorb it into his skin.

His fingers bit into her thighs as his cock probed the opening of her pussy. It'd been such a long, long time and she was hot and so incredibly wet that Elliot feared he'd come as soon as he slid into her. Slowly, ever so slowly, his cock entered her as he slid up her body and one hand tangled into her hair. "Look at me."

"I am."

Eden shuddered and dug her nails into him again. It was the most exquisite sensation. The sting of her nails and her hot, wet sheath enveloping his cock nearly drove him over the edge. He yanked her hair roughly as his face moved next to hers. "Open your eyes, Eden. I want to see what this is doing to you."

He knew precisely what it did to him. Fucking Eden had become an obsession that he never thought would happen. He'd thought of it every night, alone in his bed. He'd imagined what she'd feel like, taste like. And the reality, was not even close.

Her eyes were black with desire and unfocused. Doubt niggled along the base of his spine forming a pool of cold sweat. He was fucking a girl under the influence of Absinthe. Even though he'd cleared the poison from her, her mind was foggy. His hips moved without his control and his cock slipped into her pussy inch by inch.

He'd worry about self-recriminations later. He was a bloody selfish bastard and he knew it. He'd waited for so long and the need was just too great. Elliot kissed her gently persuading her mouth to meet him. With his cock deeply embedded in her, air shuddered through his partially opened mouth. "Bloody hell!" Eden's legs cradled him and he bit the inside of his jaw until the coppery taste of blood got his attention.

Her hips raised while her legs squeezed and Elliot felt like a stallion spurred into action. He pushed away and went to his knees withdrawing his cock. "Tell me what you like. Slow and easy or hard and fast."

"I don't care. I like it all. As long as it's you."

Elliot didn't think he heard that right. There was an odd roaring in his ears. His cock missed her heat and he gripped the base to aim it back to the source. Everything inside him threatened to burst into a million pieces. His cells brought to a boil by Eden's glorious body. His hands skimmed down her thighs before digging his fingers into that tight ass and repositioning her body for deeper access.

"Put your legs on my shoulders." He rocked back and forth and stirred a tsunami to life at the base of his balls.

"What?"

"Put your legs up on my shoulders. My cock will go deeper inside you then." Eden put her legs up over his shoulders and be began to pump into her harder. "I want you feel all of me. I want to feel all of you."

"Ohmigod!"

Elliot spread his legs apart. He needed more traction. The walls of her silky pussy clutched at him tightly. Squeezing her ass, he slammed hard and fast into her, again and again with long deep strokes of his cock. This couldn't end. He wouldn't let it. He wanted to fuck her until he lost all sense of everything. Time, space, all coherent thought seeped out of him as the first blazing hot spew of come traveled from his balls and into his greedy cock.

Eden's entire body jerked and shook as flame licked across her body. Her body was the bow and Elliot the arrow pumping hard and fast. Her legs squeezed so hard around his neck she thought she'd strangle him. But he was killing her, catching her up in this firestorm of passion. He yanked her up and Eden's legs slid down his muscled back. His strength amazed her. He pumped into her so deep it shook Eden to the core.

The undertow hooked hold of her and Eden gripped for anything solid to hold onto. Her arms were around his neck as he lowered half her body back to the mattress.

"I'm going to come, Eden. I can't hold back anymore."

The words torched the rest of her feeble mind. Her pussy tightened automatically around that thick cock and clenched. One leg was still somewhere around his back her other used his legs as she fought to get some sort of leverage. She managed to get hold of his forearms, digging into the hard muscled flesh. "Harder, Elliot." She gripped him as tightly as she could while thunder and lightning pounded over her, through her and inside her. "Harder."

"Eden, come for me." The stubble of his chin scratched her cheek. "I need to know you got some pleasure out of this."

The first spasm wracked her body in a mindless burst. Somehow, she managed to touch the side of his face. "Feel it, Elliot! For God's sake, feel what you're doing to me! Do you know how much I love that?" The walls of her pussy tightened and she watched him jerk in response. Seared alive, that's what she was when his cum spurted hotly into her pussy. "How much I love you?"

Elliot continued pumping and a wild groan tore from his lips. They shook uncontrollably and for Eden the world splintered breaking apart into a million crystallized pieces.

"If you're wrong about this, Kristov, I'll snap you in half." Carlos ran his index finger over the rim of the goblet. He enjoyed savoring a nice Bordeaux. Especially when it was filtered in human blood.

"If I'm wrong about this, you won't be able to catch me."

"Perhaps," Carlos chuckled. He liked it when his associates didn't fear him. Courage was such an interesting concept. On one hand, he found it an irritating obstacle but a Warlock with courage was useful.

"He didn't activate the spell."

Carlos' dark brow rose. "How do you know?"

Kristov smirked, "I'd sense a disturbance in the Force, Master." He reached for a grape and popped it in his mouth.

"I enjoy your humor, Kristov. But let me explain something to you." Carlos lifted the goblet and swirled it slowly. "I want you aware of the fact that if you can't turn her, I will kill both of you."

Kristov swallowed and Carlos was pleased he'd finally managed to make the Warlock nervous. You had to keep them in line – the magic users – otherwise, they got the idea they were in charge.

"I'll monitor the girl. And Titan can keep an eye on her at night." Kristov shrugged, "I have to sleep periodically."

"I'm not playing games, Kristov." Carlos sipped at his wine. "I want Eden Camden. I was assured you were the Warlock that could do this for me."

Kristov rubbed his chin in a thoughtful motion. "You didn't give me all the details up front."

"What details?"

A slight smile appeared on Kristov's face. "The details about who the Warlock protecting your demon slayer was."

Carlos shrugged, nonplussed by his omission. One Warlock was just the same as any in his line of thinking. Some were more powerful than others for certain, but most just troublesome insects. "I assumed you'd be up to the task." Carlos smiled thinly, "Was I wrong?"

He watched Kristov's eyes dilate and he could sense the fear in him. Kristov straightened abruptly. "I'll handle it."

Carlos waved him off, suddenly tired of the Warlock's mouth. "Go find your amusement elsewhere. I have a hard on I need to use." Kristov got to his feet, cast a quick glance around the room and made haste exiting.

Carlos made his selections early in the evening. A pretty Hispanic with tits the size of watermelons, a nubile Black woman with the longest legs he'd ever seen and a petite redheaded girl. Yes, they were a pretty trio.

He approached them, naked and bound lying seductively in a stack of satin pillows. He decided he wanted the tits. Stepping out of his jeans, he began stroking his cock. All three girls were blindfolded and as he approached, he noticed they spread their legs eagerly for him. His irritation at not getting to fuck the slayer wouldn't spoil his evening.

Rolling the girl over onto her knees, he slid his fingers into her pussy and then began to rub around her asshole. He released her bounds and untied the too others. The two other girls began fondling him. Carlos smacked his prey – er girl on the ass before driving his cock deep inside her hole. With a low groan, he took hold of the redhead around the waist and sucked her ample tit.

He ran his tongue over her nipple as his eye teeth lengthened into fangs. Sex always made him hungry and he planned to have a smorgasbord this night.

Humming *Love is in the Air*, Roland strolled into Elliot's bedroom with a loaded down breakfast tray. "Morning, Mr. Warwick, Ms. Camden. What a lovely day it is!" Roland put the tray on Elliot's bedside table and pulled the drapes. "I hope you're both hungry."

Eden managed to yank the sheet over her breasts and gave Roland a sleepy smile. "Got coffee?"

Roland lifted the lid on the tray. It was loaded with eggs, bacon, toast, and fruit. Coffee, orange juice and Eden noticed a small bowl of the jelly she liked. "Hmm, smells great."

Elliot snuggled at her side, reaching for one

of her breasts. "You smell great."

Slapping his hand away, she shrugged at Roland. "Elliot, wake up. Breakfast."

"The only thing I want to eat right now is –"

"I'll leave you two to enjoy your breakfast and each other." Roland smirked and headed out of the door.

"Good God, Eden! Why didn't you tell me we weren't alone?"

She scrambled over the top of him and reached for the tray. She let the sheet fall away from her body. "Hey, I tried to tell you." She stuffed a piece of buttered toast in her mouth. Man, she was starving. She picked up a fork and dug into the eggs. "This is fantastic."

"It's a side effect of the alcohol." Elliot turned his head, averting his eyes. "Would you like some clothing?"

Eden paused there was something in his tone of voice. She watched him get out of bed and slide into a pair of lounge pants. The man had one fine backside that's for sure. "You okay?"

Elliot cleared his throat and picked up a cup of coffee. He sat at the chair next to the window. "Yes, yes. Of course I'm fine."

Definitely, something weird here. Eden sat cross-legged on the bed with the sheet folded at her waist. "Not hungry?"

He kept looking out the window. Like he was scared to look at her or something. Eden swallowed and the egg hung in her throat. Her stomach seemed as hollow as a well. Using the juice to wash the egg down her throat, Eden tried to smile. "I guess I'll take a t-shirt or something. Then maybe you'll look at me."

That motivated him. "Certainly." He got up, put his coffee down and nearly sprinted to the dresser where he pulled out a white cotton tee. He handed it to her keeping his eyes down.

She took the shirt and before he could withdraw his hand, Eden gripped it. The current that danced between them nearly made her jump back. She held on just like she wanted to hold onto him. "Elliot, look at me. Please."

His eyes raised, lids shuttered. "I owe you an apology."

Eden pushed the tray aside. Then she reached out with her other hand and stroked it over the top of his hand. "Sit down, please."

He sat at the edge of the bed with a sigh. Eden noticed he kept his back to her. It was a defensive posture. She'd used it herself over the years. "Eden, I owe you an apology. I took advantage of you. I know I shouldn't have, but I couldn't help myself."

"You're sorry about what we did?" Wow, she hadn't expected it to hurt so much. She really hadn't expected that. Bad on her for not taking a closer look at the big picture. Eden let go of Elliot's hand and used both hers to reach for the cup of coffee. It was the only thing she could do to keep her entire body from going into shock. "Okay, okay..." She sipped at the coffee. "You wanna tell me why?"

Elliot closed his eyes. "I'm your guardian. I am supposed to protect you."

"Well you did that." She sat the coffee down on the tray with only a gentle rattle. Every breath she took hurt. She didn't want to do this. So maybe the timing of the fuck of the century had been rotten but she wasn't going to wish it'd never happened. Far from it, she'd fuck him right now – if she could get him to face her.

She'd never even thought this would happen. Never believed they'd ever spend a night like that wrapped in each other's arms and drunk on each other. Eden never thought she wanted that or him. But now, now...

She didn't want any other.

So the question was, how to handle this. Her relationship experienced sucked. She'd pretty much never had a real relationship. Not one that counted anyway. Eden slipped the shirt over her head and pulled it down into place. Leaning forward, she hooked Elliot's chin and gently turned his eyes to hers. "So what do we do? Forget about it?" The breath from his sigh warmed her fingers. "I can't do that, you know?"

Elliot moved, coming to kneel in front of her. "Neither can I. Eden, you have no idea what you've let yourself in for."

"What are you talking about?"

He touched her cheek and she leaned into his palm, helplessly. "Finish your breakfast and get dressed. Meet me in the study."

Eden watched as he got up and walked into the bathroom. She flipped her fork off the plate and stuffed another forkful of eggs into her mouth. "Gee, that went over well."

CHAPTER ELEVEN

Eden tapped on the door to the study and this time waited for Elliot to open the door. It was only a moment before he did and gestured for her, "Come in, Eden." He stepped back allowing her room to enter before closing the door firmly behind him.

The room was dark anyway, but with the blinds closed, it was positively cave-like. Eden let her eyes adjust as Elliot moved around her to his desk. He sat down. "Sit."

"Is there a reason it's so dark in here."

"It's cooler."

"Yeah, that makes sense." Eden felt her way to the chair across from his desk and sat down.

He flicked on the desk lamp. "You're used to the dark."

She leaned forward, "But I see better in the light."

Elliot slid his chair back and swiveled it around to pull a weirdly familiar book out of his bookshelf. Laying it on his desk, he spun it around to face her. Eden examined the intricate cover with the hand-tooled leather and gold leaf embossed title.

It trickled over her slowly, a frozen memory melting back into place. Eden stopped her hands from reaching out and slowly withdrew them. To keep them steady, because she found the sudden need to strangle Elliot, Eden sat on them.

He passed a hand over the book and Eden swore she saw it glow for a moment then fade. She raised blazing eyes to his. Glancing down at the book, she could read that title that had been gibberish just moments before. "You sonofabitch!"

"Indeed."

Eden still didn't touch the book. Instead, she gripped the edges of her chair until her knuckles went white. Rage was an interesting emotion but when you combined that with the other complex emotions revolving around Elliot, well, that stirred the pot into full rolling boil.

She lunged. By rights, she should've been over the top of the desk and her hands around Elliot's throat before he could blink. She'd forgotten he was a freakin' Warlock. "Damnit!" He simply waved his hand and instantly suspended her in mid-air in a goddamn Spiderman pose. "You rotten, sonofabitch!"

"Now Eden," Elliot got to his feet and moved around the desk. He smiled coolly as he motioned with his hand and turned her slowly to face. "Are you going to play nice?"

Every ounce of her being went to the movement of her middle finger. When she had it raised in the perfect gesture of flipping him off, she manage to gasp, "Fuck you."

He folded his arms, "That's what I thought."

Elliot glanced at his watch. "I have all day. What are your plans like?"

She plotted his demise. With every breath she took, hanging in mid-air like a stupid spider, she would get back at him. The longer she hung there, the more the anger dispersed into embarrassment as she realized her hot dream from the other night actually happened. Heat bloomed bright red on her cheeks and she tried to growl at Elliot.

"You asked for it, Eden. Since when do you come snooping in my study?"

"Since we started playing these stupid games with each other."

Elliot raised a brow. "Are you ready to conduct a reasonable conversation now?"

She nodded. He returned to his chair and spun her body a hundred and eighty degrees before depositing her back into the chair. She swallowed her stomach. "Thanks so much."

He flashed white teeth at her. "Oh my pleasure."

Eden drew in a slow, calming breath. It didn't calm her, but she stayed in her chair. "So let's go back to the study the other night."

"All right."

She smoothed a strand of hair behind her ear. "The owl. Was that you?"

Elliot nodded. His eyes glimmered with the same color as the owl's.

Her lips pursed and she blew out a puff of air. "Okay, okay. In a normal world, this is weird. But, my world is anything but normal." She waved a hand as if she sorted through her thoughts like a physical file system. "And you were going to tell me *when* exactly?" He started to speak and she held up her hand again. "Never wouldn't be the right answer here, Elliot."

"I wanted to tell you—"

"That's nice. When?" She drew her seat closer.

"You weren't ready." Elliot drummed his fingers on the edge of the desk. "You're blatant hatred of magic was pretty obvious. You refused to learn anything about it. When would've been the best time to tell you?"

She shrugged, "I don't know. You could've tried."

"Probably." His lips twisted. "I should've told you when I became your guardian. But I didn't and as time went on, it was easier to let you think I was just a boring British stiff."

Her jaw hurt from gritting her teeth. "Swell."

"Maybe it was a bad choice. But what do you think your reaction would've been?" Elliot leaned forward and rubbed his temple with his index finger. "Think about it, Eden. Would you've accepted me?"

She thought. Took a long moment and thought about how she felt about a guardian when she was sixteen and had just lost her parents. It'd taken her nearly a year to trust the man in charge of her care. After that, they'd had a kind of formal arrangement. He was like an uncle or something not really familiar but not really like best friends.

Shifting in her seat, Eden wondered when this all changed. And last night just complicated the issue even more.

"Okay, you're right. I wouldn't have been too receptive toward it." She sighed and rubbed the back of her neck. "So you're a big magic guy?"

His lips curled. "Something like that."

"I didn't know you guys could shapeshift."

"Most can't."

She sniffed. Interesting. So she had the hots for a Warlock with some giddy up. Okay, she could deal. She would deal. In fact, she would find whatever advantage there was to having a magic lover. "So you can do this stuff, uh easily, right?"

Elliot's eyes narrowed, assessing her carefully. So carefully, that it made Eden wonder if reading minds was in his bag of tricks. "Easily enough."

"How long you been doing this?"

Elliot smiled, "Long before you realized you were a demon slayer."

"Wow, that long, huh?" Eden lips pressed together as a nervous giggle bubble up through her throat. She'd first thought something was up with her when she was eight years old. She wondered if magic had been the same burden/gift for Elliot as slaying was to her.

"That long."

Eden let her hands uncurl from the arms of the chair. She wanted to brush that stray lock from his forehead. A heavy golden curl fell forward making him seem vulnerable when she knew from experience that he was anything but. She licked her lips. "Well, the way I see it, you owe me."

"What?"

Her tongue ran over her lips. "That was one hell of a hot dream you gave me. If you can do that, then you owe me the real thing. Instead of just getting me all worked up for nothin'."

"I do?"

"Yeah, that's only fair."

"Eden, you need to read the book. Specifically, the part about the prophecy."

Her eyes went to the book then back to Elliot. Everyone was really interested in this prophecy thing. Way too interested from her point of view. "Is this thing going to flatten me against the wall again?"

He nearly laughed. "No, you're perfectly safe this time."

"Uh huh." She flipped open the cover with a lightning move. When she wasn't plastered against the wall like a fly on flypaper, she was a bit more at ease. "So what am I reading?"

"Obviously, you realize that that just isn't a tattoo on your hip now." When she nodded, he reached across the desk and flipped open the book. He evidently, had the spot bookmarked cause big and bold were their tattoos. "They signify a Guardian/Slayer prophecy where each is bond and a great power is unleashed."

"Great, back to that whole power thing again."

She started reading the words on the page. It took only a moment for things like *bond for eternity* and an *enormous power unleashed* to register in her brain. It was a lot to assimilate anyway when you added both she and Elliot into the mix, things started getting a bit dicey.

That brought things like *love* into the equation. Eden wasn't sure she was ready for that. It hadn't been long enough. They'd barely recognized each other. She wasn't sure they'd really done that yet. Last night might've been a fluke for all she knew. Eden didn't like that much, but she was a realist beyond all. And God, as much as she wanted it to be real, it could've just been that damn magic shit.

This smacked of finality. Shit that was carved in stone on a mountain side and she could not imagine Elliot giving into to it either.

Something shifted in her eyes. He felt the flare in his own spark and fade at her words. The word power seemed to trouble her. He wasn't certain why, but it did.

"So this unleashed power stuff, what do *you* do with it?"

Elliot rubbed his eyes and picked up his reading glasses off the side of the desk. He placed them on his nose and leaned over the book. "What are you talking about?"

"All this power you snatched up by us *joining*. What are you going to do with it?"

He raised his head and found the concern

darkening her eyes. He smiled. "Our joining? Eden, isn't that a bit formal for you?"

"Hey, I'm just trying to make sense of it all. I mean if somebody said to me fuck me and you'll win the lottery, I probably would. Hell, I can't blame you. It's like you just won the magic lottery, right?"

"Are you insane?" He flattened his hands on the desk and pushed up to his feet. Was that what was blowing around in her brain? She thought he'd used last night as a method to seal the prophecy. Elliot wasn't sure if furious was a harsh enough word for what he experienced when he got up. It seemed much to bloody mild a word for the acidic burning in his stomach and his lungs.

"I just said I wouldn't mind." She formed an odd smile on her full lips. "I might do the same, you know."

She must really think him a bastard. "Would you?" He advanced around the desk toward her.

"Yeah, like I said, if the stakes were high enough. And the Vampires sure seemed to think they were." Eden leaned back in the chair and Elliot could see the unease on her face. "They were real interested in the tattoo and the big prophecy thing but you beat them to it. Good on you." She slid out of the chair and pasted a strange smile on her face. "I'd rather be tied to you than one of the bloodsuckers anyway."

"Tied to me?"

She shrugged. "Well bound, I guess that's the

official term. She turned her back on him then. "I don't really like the whole slave terminology."

"Is that so?" He whispered menacingly soft. He was well past furious. Now, he wanted to take her and shake some bloody sense into that suddenly blonde brain of hers. He put his hands on her shoulders and bent his head close to her ear. "So what type of bastard do you imagine me to be, Eden?"

Eden stiffened under his touch. "Look Elliot, I'm trying to tell you that I don't blame you for doing what the Vampires wanted to do. You just took the upper hand when it was given to you, okay? I accept that and I just want you to tell me what's next. Where does it go from here?"

Touching her could so easily become his one and only addiction. The fury inside him instantly doused by a more primitive heat and it made Elliot hesitate. "You let that Vampire touch you, I could feel the infection on you. Why did you do that? Why would you let a beast like that near you?"

Eden swallowed. "You said it yourself. It was that Absinthe." It was a crutch and a weak one at best and it irritated him even more that he recognized it. But she played it because Eden was good at playing the cards she was dealt. "I could've fucked the room of them and not know it."

"Did you?"

She jerked out of his grasp. "Did I want, Elliot?"

"Fuck them."

"I can't believe you'd ask that!" There it was. The temper that he'd come to know and expect blazed to life in Eden's eyes.

He took a step forward. "Why not?" Then another. "You seem so bent on claiming me as a bastard slave trader. Why couldn't I think you'd fuck a Vampire just to get back at me?" He had a hold of her then and jerked her forward. Her body crashed rigidly into his and her breasts flattened against the muscled wall of his chest.

"Fuck you."

Elliot's arms slid around her waist and anchored at the bass of her spine. "There seems to be a lot of that going around all of a sudden. Why shouldn't I get my bloody share?" She struggled in his arms and he tightened his grip. "Not so friendly now. Why is that, Eden? Is it because with your own stupidity and hard headedness you fucked the Vampire responsible for killing your parents?"

"*What?*" Her skin went clammy and her entire became limp in his arms.

"You heard me. That Master Vampire you were screwing around with last night is the creature responsible for the death of your parents." He adjusted his grip, taking more of her weight.

"You're lying." She spat at him viciously. "They said you'd do anything for this prophecy – say anything." She struggled with a renewed sense of strength, kicking and punching at him. Her short nails dug hard into his chest trying to claw the skin away with the fabric. "Let me go, you bastard!" She slammed her foot into his instep and Elliot lost his grip. "You're fucking lying!"

"Why would I lie about something like that?" Elliot ignored the dull pain in his foot. "Tell me, what would be the reason behind that?"

"I don't know but you're lying. And the only person I fucked last night was you and obviously, that was a mistake!"

She wrenched open the door. Elliot slammed it shut nearly catching her hand in the door. He locked the door and swung her around to face him. "You think it's that easy. Not this time. You won't cut and run here." With his fingers locked around her wrist, he jerked her up to the desk and pointed at his spell book. "Look at this."

"Let go of me." Eden tried his patience on most occasions. She acted like an immature child. And it was quite probably his fault. "I might not have a choice in this –"

His hands went to her face and moved it. "Look at the goddamn bloody picture in the book, Eden!" He pointed at the illustration of their tattoos once the spell activated. The dark blue ink turned to a royal purple and the black ink faded to blue. The blade turned gold.

When he was certain he had her attention and that she'd studied the photograph, he pulled up her shirt even as she slapped at his hands. "If you won't behave, I'll restrain you." Her hands stilled and he opened the front of her slacks. "Look at your tattoo."

She did. For a long moment. "It's not the same."

Elliot yanked up his shirt so she could see his tattoo. "And mine."

"It doesn't look like the one in the book either." He saw realization dawn in her eyes. With it came a certain amount of shame that he knew Eden would loathe to admit. Elliot made a point of retucking his shirt into his waistband. "I don't understand. Last night, at the rave, you touched it and then we…" She trailed off and this time it was Elliot's turn to walk away. "Why didn't you?"

"Because I'm not the goddamned bastard you seem to think I am."

"Elliot—"

"So what do you want to do here, Eden? Cut and run or just fight your way through it?"

She held up a hand trying to stop the barrage. "I didn't mean—"

"What?" He ran a hand through his hair and walked to the study door. He didn't know what to do. The anger simmered. Inside it, hope melted and faded. A small part of him had been allowed to hope that she might accept him for what he was. Amazing how hope could snap in two almost as easily as a dried stick. He wanted it for them, a small piece of normalcy – a life together. He'd wanted her to love him. Fall so inescapably in love with him that neither would ever forget nor want more than each other.

He'd seen how she looked at him. The hatred

blazed in her eyes. He opened the door and with it a part of his heart closed off. Elliot suddenly felt very old and very tired. "I'll see you later at the casino." He gestured for her to leave.

At first, he thought she wouldn't go. That she'd stay and argue. That she'd stay and fight. Then, he would've known it matter as much to her as it did to him. Fight for them, what they could've become. But he caught the glimmer of tears in her eyes and Eden hurried out the door.

Anger growled and reared its head against the jealously brought on by the memories of her with those bloodsuckers. It fueled a rage in Elliot he'd never experienced. He needed a release. An outlet for his anger. Elliot ran for the door leading to the balcony and slammed it open. The sun was already hot and bright in the sky. Smog blistered along the Las Vegas skyline but Elliot paid no attention as he unbuttoned his shirt.

He stripped off his shirt and his hands unbuttoned his belt. Stress brought the hawk. It circled lazily in the sky waiting to take him away from the anger, the heat and helped him regain his focus. He let go of his sadness, of the anger and the hawk came for him.

She was halfway down the hall to her room. Halfway packed in her head and out of Elliot Warwick's life for good when she drew up on her heels, she skidded to a stop. Eden was stronger than this. She knew that. Deep in the depths of her heart, she knew you just didn't walk away from something like this.

Whatever the hell *this* was.

She couldn't begin to define it. Lust, desire, hunger, love all seemed way too tame for what she felt. It rocked her entire being when she thought about what he did to her. Eden turned around and opened the door to the study.

Air caught in her throat and turned to ice. Stars with colors of gemstones danced around the room and swirled in a mini tornado. In the center of the tornado stood Elliot. At least, Eden thought it was Elliot. Naked and gorgeous with his arms outstretched, Eden watched the astonishing transformation.

"Elliot?" She breathed his name on little more than a sigh.

It was magnificent and frightening all at once. Eden's arms went around her waist, holding herself in place. His limbs folded and reconstituted themselves into the shape of a bird. Feathers appeared over skin and his head shifted, ears shrank while a sharp beak formed in place of his mouth. She watched talons grow where his feet were and his body conformed to the shape of a Red-tailed hawk.

"Elliot, wait! Please."

He didn't look back. His large wings flapped effortlessly and he flew off into the morning sky.

She worked her shift at the Desert Mirage

without seeing hide nor feather of Elliot. She figured he was around. Some of her co-workers mentioned seeing him several times. He was avoiding her, she got that part. Eden didn't blame him. She'd had six hours to think about the fucking tattoo on her side and all the implications.

Eden watched a few cocktail waitresses cruise through the sports book on her way outside to take a break. She couldn't begin to assess the big galactic picture that seemed to come from a slayer and a guardian gettin' their groove on. Hundreds of years this prophecy had been around and it just had to come to pass during her slaying schedule. What kind of crap luck was that?

Hers.

Eden grabbed her cell phone out of her back pocket as she walked out into the hot afternoon. She'd already called Maya three times. Absinthe probably left you with a nasty hangover. Knowing she had Elliot to thank again for saving her ass made Eden all the more grouchy.

When Maya didn't pick up and she got her machine again, Eden worried her pal wasn't in a good state. She hung up and dialed Roland. The ever astute butler answered on the first ring. "Tell me you took Maya home last night, Roland."

"Good afternoon to you too, Ms. Camden."

"I'm not screwing around here. Is she okay?" Eden tapped her foot against a wall wondering why she didn't smoke cigarettes with all this tension hanging on her like a damn thundercloud.

"She's fine. Mr. Warwick gave me a remedy for her and she's sleeping off the effects of your party last night."

"Thanks, Roland. You're a jewel."

"Hmm."

She hung up the phone and decided as soon as the sun went down. She'd go looking for a bit of Vamp ass. Starting with that freak Titan and by the time the night was over, Mr. Master Vamp and his Renegade friends would wish they'd never heard the word slayer because she was about to redefine it for them in the most interesting way.

CHAPTER TWELVE

She got off work at eleven. Famished, she pulled into a fast food joint and ordered up a heart attack and a Pepsi. Then she found the nearest Old Navy. Screw the whole sexy image – she wasn't in the mood to be cute tonight. She picked up a white tank and a pair of painter style jeans and wore them out of the store. She still had her tennis shoes in her Nissan so that was no problem.

It bothered her a bit she still hadn't heard from Maya. After she took care of business, she'd go check on Maya. Maybe she could figure out what do about Elliot. Because Eden didn't have a clue. She'd screwed it up and it felt as if every move she made just dug a bigger hole as far as Elliot was concerned.

She cruised down Paradise and then headed south on Fremont. Titan and his crew usually took in anything seedy for an appetizer before moving on to bigger game. She pulled into the parking lot of Molly's Tattoos 4U figuring this was as good a place as any to start.

Molly catered to the Goth crowd. Her specialty was dark creepy Celtic designs that all the wannabe Vamps went for. Eden jumped out of her SUV and clicked the lock on her keychain before dumping her keys in her pocket. She really, really hoped that Titan was in there.

The door jingled when she walked in and, as luck would have it there were a half dozen Goths hanging out, picking out tatts. Eden smiled to herself. Where there were Goths, Vamps weren't far behind. She strolled through the parlor wondering who decorated the place. It looked like Mortisha threw up in a biker bar. Then she got a whiff, the rotted flesh combined with the damp earth smell was a dead giveaway.

Titan leaned across the scarred up counter and examined a new earring in a round mirror. Eden swallowed a snicker after getting a look at the giant Vampire's new bauble. Any gaudier and Eden would suggest Titan get with Elton John's old costume designer. She slid in on his blind side and shoved to young Vampires out of the way. "Hey Titan," she slapped him on the back. Hard. "what's up?"

"Shit!" Titan turned slowly.

When he faced her, Eden's hand snaked out and took hold of his ear by that pretty, little earring. "Cute earring. Didn't know you were so flamboyant." He tried to move away and she didn't let go of the earring. "Come on, Titan. Let's go have a chat. Just you and me." Her eyes flashed hard at the four Vampires angling position on her. "You wanna tell them to buzz off or should I?"

Titan sighed forlornly. It was long a pitiful,

kind of like him. Three female Vampires took up position and Titan waved them off. "Easy girls. Eden and I are old pals. We'll be back in a second."

She led him out the door aware that they had the interest of the Goths. His crew of Vamp pals followed closely. "Got some new buddies, eh?"

He sniffed, "Well since you killed the last bunch…"

"Technically, they were already dead." She spun him around in the parking lot by his ear.

Rubbing the torn flesh, Titan scowled at her, "What do you want?"

"A little information."

"What do I look like? Some search engine?"

Eden smiled wishing she had her own fangs to bare. "You were there last night.

He snickered, "Yeah, you looked really hot last night."

"I'll bet. So what was that little rave all about?"

He stuffed his hands in his pockets and the chains on his belt loops jiggled like a wind chime. "Just a party."

Eden's lips twisted. She took a step forward. "Let me ask this again. What was that party about?"

Titan glanced over his shoulder. The group seemed to accept that Eden wasn't there to kill everyone and most migrated back into the tattoo parlor. Titan leaned forward, "Look are you trying to get me killed?"

"The thought crossed my mind."

He reached for Eden's shoulder and she rotated

it out of the way. "Geez, aren't you testy. Over here, out of range of prying ears."

He walked closer to her SUV, which was a good thing because she always kept one of her bags full of Vampire slaying tricks in the backseat. "Start talking."

Titan glanced back one more time. "Okay, look the plan was to get you smashed on the Absinthe and then Carlos could fuck your brains out."

Eden folded her arms. "Lovely image. Why would he want to?"

He looked at her with the impatience of someone trying to train a puppy. "Hello? Slayer under the thrall of big evil Vampire – evil rules the world. Duh!"

"Is it the earring that's turning you into a flame or you just trying to be smart with me?"

Titan bent from his considerable height to whisper at her, "They were trying to fuck with you. You were the ultimate goal last night. The Renegades want you gone and hired Mr. Master Vamp to come do the deed. The fact that you didn't play along and fall under his spell of magnificent sensuality really pissed the son of a bitch off. They want you dead, Eden and since I've developed some weird sort of fondness for you, I'm telling you now watch you back." Titan moved back a bit when a couple of his cronies looked like they were going to make a move. "I'm supposed to be keeping an eye on you and when I find you –"

"What?"

Titan chuckled, "Eden darling, say hello to Lacey and Snake." His eyes gestured wildly at her as two Vampires strolled bravely forward. "Oh and Anna and Victoria."

Eden got the hint and slid her feet back so she had a clear jump to the SUV. "Greetings and whatever the hell you all say." Eden waved. Damn, this bunch stank. Her stomach turned wondering which one of them slept in sewage today. "Snake and Lacey huh? Well, at least that's got the big Goth thing going with it." Her mouth rounded into a perfect "O" and Eden put her fingers to her lips. "I get it. You guys were Goths." She pointed at them and chuckled. "Oh that's priceless."

It wasn't bad these Goths were such wannabes. But Snake, well, he reminded her of Spike from Buffy and a weak imitation at that. Lacey was just a Goth slut all black lace and a big tattoo of a black widow blooming out from her hefty cleavage.

Eden giggled. It was a snarfy irritating sound but well, she was in kind of a pissy mood. "You guys really suck." She moved assessing the two other Vamp chicks. "Oh yeah, you do! Ha! Ha!"

"This is the slayer were supposed to worry about?" Lacey smiled seductively.

Titan tugged on his earring and scratched his goatee. "Yeah, this is her."

"We should take her back to the cemetery. Carlos will want to have her." Snake rubbed his flexed bicep.

"Or she could just kill us and now she knows

when he is you moron." Anna sneered at the little hisser.

"She can't take on six of us at once."

"Snake, shut up." Titan looked at Eden's eyes trying to read what reflected back at him.

"Hey, I'm—"

"I said, shut the hell up."

Eden's hand went to her pocket and she triggered the lock on the SUV. "Now Titan, you know how anxious these young guys get to prove themselves."

"Oh hell…"

Lacey looked around as Eden's hand went to the door handle of her Nissan. "What? What?"

"She's going to kill us."

Snake flexed. "That girl? Nah, I don't think so." He flew at her with the kind of speed you only saw on a supernatural being. Hard, fast like a rocket out of control, he slammed into her stomach propelling Eden hard against the side of her vehicle. Then his fist went up and caught her in the chin with a vicious right.

Eden heard something crack. Angling her jaw, she knew it wasn't her teeth. She hoped it was her ribs rather than the side panel of her door. Down on her knees, she inhaled and the pain radiating up her body made her want to change her mind. Her head snapped back with Snake's next strike and Eden's teeth caught the edge of her lip. The little snake was fast and if she wasn't careful, he could become deadly. Blood dripped off her lip and she spat it out of her mouth.

She dove for his ankles, hit him open palmed and rolled as he fell face first. Eden was on her feet by the time Snake ate a face full of dirt. Her head darted around to catch a look at the other Vampires and to make sure they stayed put until she could get her hands on her goodie bag in the Nissan.

"Bitch!" Snake spat dirt and rock out as he stood up.

"Yeah, I hear that a lot."

Snake spat again. "You want to hear what it sounds like when bone breaks?"

Eden didn't see Lacey move. Later, she'd give herself hell about it but when the buxom bitch launched her shoulder into Eden's back, there was a sharp moment of agony. For just one second, Eden's vision went black. Then Snake dragged her up by her armpits and his eyes glowed red down at her. "What's it like to suck a slayer dry, Titan?" Snake's fangs dropped in a sinister mockery of a smile.

Eden slammed her right foot in his balls and used the leverage to walk up the front of Snake's hideous face before flipping over backwards and landing on her knees. She glanced back at Titan. He wasn't helping the Vamps and he wasn't hindering her – what was up with that?

She was breathing hard. Her body seemed to enjoy the torture. She wasn't exactly having such a good time. Later, she'd wonder if she needed x-rays or a dentist. Running her tongue over her lips, she didn't notice any jagged edges. But battling demons did wonders for her mood. Her anger had evaporated. She wiped her lip and smiled at the snake. "He hasn't tasted a slayer, little one." Eden moved to a prone stance where she could keep her eyes on all of them. "Now I advise you and your little group to shuffle back into Molly's and pick out a nice tattoo or something."

Lacey laughed, "Oh please! We've got you surrounded." She sniffed the air, "You're bleeding. Why on earth would we quit now? Not that you're much more than a morsel." She winked one of the heavily shadowed eyes at Titan. "Come on now, tell me the truth. This bitch is really a boy." Lacey smiled back at Eden. "So why should I listen to you?"

"Because I've given you the opportunity to save those big ass boobs of yours. The next tattoo you get, honey is going right through your heart." Eden dabbed at her lip once more. The flow of blood still ran from the cut.

Every nerve bristled at attention. There was a shift in the air. A shimmer. The hot summer night, which laid on you like a wool blanket suddenly, lifted on a breeze as cool and refreshing as the spray from the ocean. She straightened slowly. Oh man, she hoped she was right about this.

Lacey shifted her ample hips and dropped a hand to one. "You and what army, *honey*?"

Eden grinned wondering if her teeth were stained with dried blood. "No army." She turned her body a mere fraction so that she could pick up more range with her peripheral vision. Relief flooded her veins and her heart picked up a beat when she saw Elliot standing ten feet behind her. "Just him."

Titan threw up his hands. "Shit, shit, shit!"

Lacey laughed, "Oooh, I'm scared."

This time Titan moved. He backhanded her into a Cadillac. "Shut the hell up, would you? Unless you want to take your next breath as a fucking shish kabob."

"Hey, don't hit her!" Snake moved to pull Lacey up to her feet. "What the hell's the problem anyway? You don't think you can take on a damn librarian?"

"Not that damn librarian." Titan looked back at Eden as Elliot stepped up to her. He shook his head slightly and his lips pursed in disappointment. "Don't kill them because their stupid."

"I was kicking the girl's ass. How's the skinny dude going to do anything?"

Eden had to hand it to Snake. He was definitely determined. And it would get him killed, maybe not tonight, but he really was too stupid to be a Vampire. Eden jerked her hand at Elliot. "The skinny dude here, Snake, can turn you to ash without ever touching you."

It was fun when the light bulb went on. It was a bit dim at first, but as realization dawned Eden watched it turn to abject fear in the eyes of four other Vampires. She tried not to chuckle but she couldn't help it. She glanced at Elliot. He wasn't smiling or laughing. She could see him considering turning all of them into fireballs.

"Holy shit," Snake breathed, "He's that fuckin' Warlock."   The taste of fear was nearly palpable now.

Titan smacked him in the forehead. "Yes, you moron. He's the Warlock. Now how fast do you all think you can run?"

Lacey sauntered forward up to Titan. "Honey, if you think I'm scared of this little bitch and her boney assed pet, well, baby, you've got another think coming."

Titan moved aside as if he knew what was coming. Lacey thundered past him like a rabid lineman and crashed into Eden with teeth snapping. Eden managed to absorb most of the blow figuring she'd dodge the flying Lacey and her gargantuan boobs, but she'd been shocked the bimbo actually tried something this dumb.

They landed in a heap on the asphalt as Eden managed to smash her fist into Lacey pouty lips and shove her off. Eden didn't look back at Elliot or the other Vampires figuring she had enough to contend with at the moment. Snake was a threat, but she'd deal with him in a second.

"I'm going to snap your skinny ass in two then I'm going to suck your pet wizard dry."   Lacey snarled as she pushed to her knees. "Maybe he'd like a woman for a change," she adjusted her boobs giving herself more cleavage, "instead fucking a boy." She winked. "Or maybe he likes that sort of thing anyway."

Eden's foot accelerated through the air and connected with Lacey's chin. The end result was a satisfying crack that had Lacey bending back in a move Eden figured she practiced a lot. "Come on Lacey, no screwing around. You want to take me in to Carlos, you're going to have to put a little effort into it."

Out of the corner of her eye, she saw Titan put his hands on his hips. "I'm surrounded by fucking idiots."

Lacey swung and connected, raking her claws over Eden's shoulder and halfway across her chest. She grinned viciously as blood bloomed from the wound. "See? No tits." Lacey looked back at her group laughing furiously. "Your slayer is just a little boy."

Eden swung her legs on a whirling kick that caught Lacey's head and forced it to the ground in a direct ninety-degree turn. "Get a good whiff, Lacey. It's pussy." Eden slammed Lacey's head down hard. "And you're screwed."

She shifted and glanced at Elliot, "Something sharp and pointy would be nice." Eden held out her right hand as a stake materialized in it. She slammed it straight into Lacey's heart and watched as the bitch turned to back to the dust she belonged to.

Dusting her hands off, Eden sniffed and rose slowly to her feet. "Next?" She knew it was a bit clichéd. But hey, she was worth it. She sauntered up next to Elliot and actually took a real good look at him.

Holy hell, he was magnificent!   Like an avenging wizard from a fantasy novel, Elliot's dark seemed almost a golden halo around his shadowed face. Eden's system shut down. Air shuddered out of her lungs and rattled past her lips. This was no fantasy wizard ripped from an author's pages, this was full tilt urban Warlock.

He wore all black. Black jeans – Elliot didn't wear jeans. Tight, fitted over his muscled thighs that held her attention until Elliot shifted and turned his body. His dark shirt was open wide revealing perfectly sculpted pectorals and gorgeous, hard abdominals, which seemed more rock star than Elliot. Then the long black leather coat with all the pockets in it, reminded her if he'd been from another time, it would've been the robe a magic user wore.

She had to pinch her arm to keep from jumping him right then. She wondered if she could get him to wear this later.

His eyes examined her with a ferocity he'd never felt before. He wanted to tear each of these beasts apart with his bare hands instead of relying on magic. Elliot shuttered his eyes conducting a careful assessment of Eden. She was hurt, undoubtedly. But if he made any indication that she should let him take over, she would shun his efforts to aid her immediately.

It looked like the end result of a gang fight.

Her clothes torn to shreds laid limply on her shoulders. It wasn't lost on him that she'd switched back to the old jeans and tank – Eden's work clothes. Her hair was a matted mess of dust and trash. Dirt streaked down her face and arms mingling with the blood. She looked like hell and she grinned as if she'd never had so much fun in her life. The gleam in her eyes was frankly predatory.

Well, enough was enough. He needed to get her home and tend to her injuries regardless what she thought. He was a bit curious about Titan's part in this mess. The large Vampire seemed more than eager to leave with no bloodshed – especially his own.

She moved slow, almost stiffly as she came to stand next to him. "Thanks for the stake."

He inclined his head, "Magic has its uses."

She rotated her shoulder slightly and Elliot thought he heard it pop. "I'm learnin'."

"Eden, now that you've turned Lacey into potting soil," Titan put on a big pearly smile, "can the rest of us slink back into the tattoo parlor?"

"But things were just beginning to get interesting." Elliot stepped in front of her before she could answer. His left hand slid into his pocket and scooped up the contents. "And I do so wish to continue our little chat from the other day."

Titan swallowed. Hard.

Snake snarled and the two female Vampires hissed at him and Eden. She chuckled under her breath and folded her arms gingerly. "Where do you *find* these losers?"

Titan shrugged. "They find me."

"*Vala nya,*" Elliot gestured slowly with his right hand, palm downward. His left hand he lifted from his pocket and let the fine white sand slip gently through his fingers. All the Vampires save Titan slipped to the earth in a deep, dreamless sleep.

"You're gonna kill me, aren't you?" Titan's head swiveled around as if it were a meatball on a stick.

"Well that depends," Elliot put his arm carefully behind Eden's and urged her forward.

"On?"

"How well you cooperate now that your friends are sedated."

Titan nodded, "Look I told Eden everything I know."

Eden sniffed, "Wasn't much."

His eyes shifted to Eden for a moment then back to Titan. "You didn't pass on my warning." It wasn't a question.

"I did," the giant Vampire screeched. "That's what I was trying to tell you and Eden but you weren't getting it."

"So what is it, *precisely*, that we aren't getting?"

"He doesn't care." Titan sighed, obviously exasperated by their lack of vision. "*He does not care.*" Titan twisted his new earring. He tapped his foot and licked the corner of his lips. "Okay, let's try this. The only thing the Master is interested in is the Master and whatever gives him the biggest jolt—"

"The prophecy," Eden whispered.   Titan touched his index finger to his nose. "Shit."

Titan turned his full height on Elliot.   It surprised Elliot that he sensed indignation from the Renegade. "She means the mother lode of power to him and he is going to do anything to get it." He looked at Elliot but pointed at Eden. "You're going to need help protecting her."

Eden bristled, "I don't need protecting."

"Honey, you needed it the other night.   You don't think Carlos would try something like that again?"

It was a barb, Elliot recognized it and applied a cynical gleam to his expression. "And the reason you've decided to assist us is?"   Elliot continued to smile. He moved slowly over to Titan. "Because as amusing as you are, I have an innate distrust of your kind."

"Yeah, whatever." Titan held up a hand as if it didn't matter. "You care about her though."

Elliot's eyes narrowed.   "You haven't said anything useful to me yet." He produced a six inch burst of flame by idly snapping his fingers.

Titan's eyes widened in alarm. "Okay look, I can get you inside the Renegades. Seraphina is so in awe of Carlos and everyone else is too stupid to notice."

Eden huffed and folded her arms. "Titan, you are so full of shit. How stupid do you think we are? Nobody's walking into the Renegade lair like that. Especially not a slayer and a Warlock."

Titan shrugged, "Well hey, you gotta try. He wants her, you know?"

Elliot pointed his index finger and encircled Titan's feet with a ring of fire. "It's late and we're tired of playing games. Speak up or you can stand in the ring of flame until dawn."

"Carlos is looking for a way to lure Eden back to him. The jackass has enough ego to think no woman can resist him. He's pretty sure he can bind her to him and then he'll be unstoppable. He's having an initiation for the fledglings at the Voodoo lounge tomorrow. It's black tie. Masks, the whole Goth get up." Titan shrugged, "Beats the hell out of me why."

"And we're supposed to attend this ball?"

Titan snickered, "Well yeah, if you want to get killed." At Elliot's frown, the circle of fire turned up a notch. "Before the ceremony, is the party. No one will notice you all. Especially if you're dressed like the rest of the Goths." He pointed at Elliot. "You've got a good start there. Add an earring, some makeup, you'd be good to go."

"Funny. I didn't know Vampires had such a sense a humor." Elliot turned to Eden. "Who would've thought?" He hooked his hand around her arm. "Let's go."

"You don't believe him?" Eden looked as if she actually entertained the idea that the Vampire wasn't lying.

"Not at all." Elliot turned with Eden and began walking toward her SUV.

"Hey, uh wait a second! Did you guys forget something?"

Elliot glanced over his shoulder. "I don't believe so."

Titan jumped up and down and pointed furiously at the ring of fire surrounding him. "Yeah, I think you did, Mr. Warlock! I told you what I know, no sense leaving me with a hotfoot."

Elliot pointed a finger back at Titan. The flame vanished and he could hear Titan's sigh of relief. He didn't turn back again, simply angled Eden to her vehicle. He noticed she leaned against him a bit heavily. "Give me your keys, I'll drive." She dug around into one of those baggy pockets of hers and came up with a set of keys. "No arguments?" Elliot arched a brow at her and took the keys. "Now I know you're hurt."

She shook her head as he unlocked the door. "Nah, figured I would let you feel manly."

He settled her into the seat. "That doesn't do it for me, I'm afraid." Elliot walked around the side of the vehicle and climbed into the driver's seat. After adjusting the seat, he started the engine, put it in gear, and drove off into the night.

Titan watched them go, waiting until the taillights of the SUV were no longer visible. The he turned slowly and walked to the entrance of the tattoo parlor. The door swung open and Kristov stepped out into the night. Titan pointed a long index finger at him. "This had better work."

Kristov stared at the Vampires in a heap in the parking lot. "It will."

Not convinced, Titan bared his teeth.   "It'd better."

"You worry too much."

"When it's my skin on the line, yeah I do."

CHAPTER THIRTEEN

"Would you let go of me? It's not like I haven't had the crap kicked out of me before." Eden tried to shed Elliot's hold on her but he wasn't letting go.

He walked her into her room and closed the door. "You're hurt."

"Yeah and? I'll take a shower and go to bed. I'll be fine in the morning." Her complexion had turned pasty. Her eyes slightly dilated. Elliot watched closely. Not liking what he saw at all. Even her breathing seemed a bit shallow, but when she lost her balance, he stepped forward and caught her as she fell.

"Eden, listen to me," Elliot scooped her up into his arms and moved to her bed. "I need to tend to those wounds. You don't know what that beast had on her fingernails." He laid her down and he thought she mumbled something as her head hit the pillow.

He went into her bath and found a washcloth. Running some tap water, he soaked the cloth and went back to Eden. She'd managed to tug her torn shirt off, leaving naked flesh. Elliot winced at the wounds and knelt across her on the bed.

Magic flowed through him as he summoned

the healing glow of the moon. Silver sparks danced along his arm and into the cloth. Eden backed up in alarm. "It won't hurt you. I wouldn't hurt you."

Her curious dark eyes watched him. Her lips pursed as he gently applied the cloth. She started to hiss, then must've realized there was no pain. Only warmth as the cloth soaked up the wound. "I'm sorry about what I said."

Elliot nodded. He knew her temper well enough. "I know."

She grimaced. "And just forget about that love stuff, okay? We both know I didn't mean it."

"I see." If she'd plunged a stake right through his heart, it couldn't have hurt any worse. Elliot swallowed. He lifted the washcloth to test his ministrations. The wounds closed up nicely. He'd pretended last night that he hadn't heard her tell him she loved him mostly because it shocked the bloody hell out of him.

He hadn't expected it. Never thought either of them would teeter on this delicate staircase together. And now, she'd just yanked the banister out from under his feet. He withdrew the cloth and examined his handiwork. It looked good, a bit pink, but very good all in all.

His eyes darkened as his gaze swept over her dusky nipples. It blistered through his body with a tingling of acid and a sharp stab of lust. He licked his lips wanting a taste. "You can shower now, it's closed up. I'll leave you to it." Elliot slid to the edge of the bed and began to stand.

Eden took hold of his hand. "Do you want to stay?"

He closed his eyes for a moment. "You wanted to get some rest." Her hand ran over his in a move that Elliot had never considered sexy before.

She moved into a sitting position. "I think you owe me."

He tilted his head. Confused, trying to keep his mind off how sexy Eden looked in those damn jeans. Elliot twisted his body back to her. "You need to spell this out for me, Eden. This morning, I thought you were leaving for good." He lifted his hand out of hers and tossed the washcloth into the sink. "Now we appear to be back where we were last night and I don't know if that's what you truly want." Elliot sat beside her and put his hands on both sides of her hips. Deliberately, he kept his fingers on the fabric of her jeans. Her skin was too much of a temptation.

"You are a bit dense aren't you?" She smiled, "Is that a British thing or a Warlock thing?"

Maybe he was dense. He certainly seemed to have trouble sorting through the maze of emotions when it came to Eden Camden. It was navigating a minefield in a hurricane most of the time.

His body reacted to her in a way he'd never experience. The lava settling into his balls only reminded him how hot she made him. Elliot sighed letting his hands go to the button on her jeans. "It must be a Warlock thing."

She laughed, a deliberate, delicious sound.

"You have great hands."

He shifted off the bed then bent to lift her into his arms. "Come with me."

Her expression was a delightful mix of shock and excitement. "Okay. Looks like I've got know choice."

"There's always a choice, Eden." He walked with her in his arms across the hall into his room. He rotated his body and closed the door with his shoulder. "If you want to make it."

"What are you saying?" She stroked her fingers though his hair. Elliot couldn't remember that ever being an erotic gesture.

It was now.

He sat her gently on the settee in front of his bed. "Give me a minute."

If he'd planned this, he would've done the entire seduction in the good ol' fashioned way. But since he had no way knowing this would happen, he'd have to rely on his magic and a bit of imagination. In the bath, he created a picture in his mind. Warm scented water filled with florals and healing herbs filled the oversized tub. Candles flickered about the bath and soft, sensuous music lit the air assembling the perfect fantasy.

Examining his handiwork, Elliot smiled. He rarely used magic to create fantasy, but this was – well done indeed! He'd worry later about how much energy he'd expended and how long it would take the magic to replenish.

"Hey, do you want me to bring you a magazine or a newspaper or something?" The tone dripped with sarcasm, but Eden pulled it off with flair. Well at least she managed to not sound totally snotty. She'd been run over by a speeding locomotive or a speeding nutball Vampire two hours ago and her entire body already started to stiffen up. If Elliot wasn't going to loosen her up in a sexy way, she was heading for the shower.

Eden stuck her head inside the bathroom and gasped. She never gasped, nothing ever surprised her that much so the sound wasn't so much a burst of air more like a squeaky balloon. She blinked, rubbed her eyes, then blinked again.

On her next breath, the scent of jasmine, gardenia drifted across the steamy air of what *looked* like some enchanted garden. Eden wondered if smacking her head against her SUV was responsible for the delusion. Exotic plants spilled from what used to be walls in a lush tropical invitation while the tub had turned into a mystical pool. Candles laced the edges of the pool with a golden halo flickering in the moonlight.

"Oh my God…"

If this was what magic could do, well damn, she'd sign up in a heartbeat.

"Do you like it?"

"It looks like you captured the garden in the Bellagio and half of a Hawaiian island and stuffed it in here." The surface of the pool had petals of roses and other flowers she couldn't begin to name. And the water, appeared golden in the light from the candles.

"I take that as a yes." He smiled and the flash of white teeth was so amazingly sexy, it stole Eden's breath away.

"Oh yeah. Most definitely a yes in all categories."

"The water has healing herbs and other soothing properties it ought to make a big difference." Elliot started past her and she took hold of his arm. "Where do you think you're going?"

He tilted his head, "I was going to give you some privacy."

"Elliot, I'm standing in here topless. How much privacy do you think I need?" She grimaced and her hands went to her jeans. She shimmied out of them and used Elliot as a brace while she dipped a toe in the pool.

The water was warm like a hot springs but refreshing. She slid into the pool and leaned her head back against the edge. Petals from a wild orchid tickled her ear. "You're not leaving."

His lips twitched. "I wouldn't dream of it."

Elliot picked up a pitcher off what used to be the counter in the bath and knelt behind her. "Lean you head back for me."

"What are you going to do?" Eden was game, but forever curious.

Elliot scooped the hair off the back of her neck and fanned it out. He tipped her head back gently. Then he raised the pitcher and trickled warm water onto her scalp. "I'm going to wash your hair."

"Okay." She'd never had a guy wash her hair before. Kind of weird, but who knew?

He picked up another jar and opened it pouring the gel into his palms. The scent of mint and green tea combined with cloves filled her nostrils as he began working the shampoo through her hair. The aroma combined with the delicious massaging of his fingers was one of the most sensual experiences she'd ever had.

In seconds, he'd lulled her into a sleepy cat-like state. "You know, if this Warlock thing goes south, you've got a helluva career as a shampooer."

Elliot laughed, a darkly sexy sound. "Thanks."

"Just stating the facts."

His fingers massaged the back of her scalp and down her neck. "Is that so?"

"Mmm-hmm."

"Feel good?"

"Oh yeah…"

He chuckled again and rinsed her hair with the remainder of the water from the pitcher. Eden's entire body relaxed, the stiffness draining away into the herbal soak. She wouldn't be surprised if later all traces of the night's activities disappeared. Magic was getting more and more interesting by the moment.

"Are you going to join me?"

Elliot got to his feet and moved around to face her. With a wry smile toying about his lips, he answered, "I'd love to."

She watched him strip with an eager fascination. People said women looked good by candlelight. Elliot looked like a freakin' Greek god as he pulled his shirt from his broad golden shoulders. Muscles rippled when he bent to remove his shoes and Eden smiled smugly. "How tall are you anyway?"

He seemed surprised by the question and shrugged. "Around six two I suppose, give or take an inch." His hand went to the button on his jeans and Eden shifted in the pool as a ribbon of fire twined through her body. She lifted a hand to brush back her hair and sensed the effervescence in the water. If it weren't warm and with the scent of an English garden in full summer bloom, Eden would've sworn she was bathing in champagne.

Elliot slipped out of his jeans and her eyes followed the trail of deep golden hair from his navel to the apex of his shaft. She knew what that magic rod of his could do and it made her hot and hungry for more. She crossed her legs tightly under the water for a minute trying to choke off that wild appetite. Her eyes continued over his sculpted thighs dusted lightly with the same golden hair. His calves reminded her of a runner and it occurred to her that she really needed to find out more about this man.

Last night, she'd said she loved him. In a roundabout way, but she'd said it. Eden didn't say things she didn't mean. She was a fly by the seat of your pants kind of gal and her big mouth generally found a way of getting her in trouble. She said what she meant whether in anger or in fun. This was different. Harder. The more she looked at him the more things got clearer in her head and that just messed things up again.

Eden wasn't used to vulnerability. She spent her entire life walling herself behind defense mechanism to keep from hurting the way she did when her parents thought she was insane. As painful as it was to lose them, it hurt so much more knowing they didn't believe her when she tried to tell them about her abilities.

Elliot did. Her steady, staid, boring guardian had become a man she couldn't imagine living her life without. And with each admission, another lock to her fortress fell open. She raised her eyes to his as he stepped closer to the pool. "What happens if this prophecy comes true?"

He moved with the grace of a tiger. She watched the confident, rhythmic stride and another thought popped into her head. "Can you turn into a cat?"

"What kind of cat?" He entered the pool and slid in up to his chest across from her. "And what about the prophecy?"

"I don't know…say a domestic cat."

"Yes."

She pressed her lips together. "Really? How about bigger?"

"Much." Water sluiced off his hand as he ran it through his hair. "Do you want to know about the prophecy or not?"

She sniffed and tried to pretend not to care. "Sure."

"We have to do the spell together. It doesn't work with just one person because it binds us –"

"Yeah for all eternity, blah, blah. Got that part." Eden wasn't sure she was comfortable with the entire eternity. Not that she didn't believe in it, she did, she wanted to know how he felt about that *bound for eternity business*. "What does it do for you?"

He trailed his finger across the petal of an exotic lily. "I'm not sure. I never thought it would come to this."

"*This*?" Eden tried to draw him out with her gaze. Trouble was with a Warlock, they could still look at you without showing emotion.

"I never believed we'd be in this sort of position."

"In a tub together?" She smiled, raising her leg seductively under the guise of checking her bruises.

"Mmm, that and the fact that a Master Vampire wants you for his sex slave."

Eden inhaled. She wasn't especially proud of that. Not one of her finer moments, but she also was under the influence. "I'm as sorry about that as you are."

He turned his head. "Are you truly?"

She gritted her teeth. "Are you trying to spoil this moment? Or are you just not good at the whole romance thing?" She cupped water into her palm and poured it on her tender shoulder. "I'm thinking it's the first one because so far, it looks like you'd excel in the romance department."

"I didn't think you'd want that."

She huffed at him. "How would you know what I'd want? You never asked."

This time, he threaded wet fingers through his entire head of hair. Interesting, Eden had never noticed how gold his hair was or how many muscles rippled when a guy did that simple motion. "I didn't think you wanted this. Us."

"How was I to know that? Hmm? My whole life has been fighting demons in various forms. When exactly did I get a sex life?"

Elliot flashed a sexy grin. "Last night."

She splashed water at him, pleased that it ran down his face. "Exactly. You know I don't like change. I like things the same nice and steady so I know how to deal with it. You go and give me the hottest night of my entire life after I find out about the whole magic biz it's bound to make me a bit crazy."

"And that's why I didn't press you into learning about the prophecy or magic."

"Or about us." Eden's lips turned into a frown. "What does this prophecy do for us?"

"The spell that ties us together gives us greater access to more abilities. Your skills would enhance so would mine because we'd be able to draw on each other if we needed." She waited as he gauged her reaction. "You know we're different. Our lifespan will be much longer, we're stronger physically. We'll always be tied to each other if we enact the prophecy."

"Whether we want it or not?"

"It needs to be mutual, Eden. I couldn't hold you anymore if you didn't wish it than you could hold me."

Eden rubbed her face with her hands. She couldn't believe they were having this kind of conversation in this sexy pool made for seduction. She ought to riding that cock of his so hard and fast they splashed all the water out of the pool. "You were making me crazy, you know? I couldn't figure out if you liked me, hated me or just wanted to fuck my brains out."

"Depends on the day."

"You're a funny man." She moved her legs so they tangled with his. "Too bad I'm not laughing."

"I couldn't push this on you, Eden. I always thought it was for you to choose. How much you wanted to know about your ancestry and the prophecy. I couldn't demand your future." He slid sideways so his palms could run up and down her thighs.

That didn't seem entirely fair to her. She knew he'd sacrificed a lot taking on a bitter sixteen year old. A normal teenager isn't a lot of fun to deal with, a teenage slayer only adds to the glorious picnic. "What about you? You've given up a lot."

"It was my choice to become a guardian. I knew what could be asked of me."

"Still." She lost track of her train of the thought when he shifted her legs so they laid across the top of his. "What brought you to magic? I mean, I knew when I was five there was something seriously different about me."

"It's the same with magic." Elliot's hands rubbed over her legs under the water. She held onto the greenery outside the pool trying to concentrate. It was an amazing sensation almost like dragging your body over warm velvet. "Magic finds you as a youth. Then you spend many years in school and apprenticing."

"Like Harry Potter?"

Elliot smiled, "Something like that. You learn your craft. How to write spells, create potions, to channel energy and you make mistakes."

Eden chuckled. She'd made tons of mistakes. "Blow things up did you?"

"I'm surprised my family and the magic school are still in tact."

"So how long does it take?"

"What?"

"To get to your level."

He considered a moment and his hands stopped their massaging motion. "Years. Some never achieve it. It's a difficult task and a tremendous balance of power."

She moved her legs so that she was beside him. Her hand trailed droplets of water across his shoulder before she leaned her chin on it. "And that's the trigger word, isn't it?"

"Power? No, not for someone as immersed in magic as I am. There's a balance, Eden. A balance created by good and evil. Slayers and guardians are here to protect the world from being overrun by darkness." He turned his head to look at her. "I couldn't do that if all I thought about was power. And just for your information, Eden," he took hold her by her waist and lifted her up, "I have all the power I need."

Elliot entered her from behind with a strong forceful stroke that made Eden gasp in a mix of pleasure and surprise. He used his hands to bend her knees before his fingers came around to rub her clit while his hips set her in a forward rocking motion. Easing in and out of her pussy, Eden clenched her fingers into his knees. "Gawd, that's wicked."

"Isn't it?"

Sitting on his lap, he fucked her with slow tantalizing strokes. The combination of his rod and that warm water moving in a wave motion in and out of her pussy was enough to send Eden over the edge. Her nails dug in as she rocked back in forth in a feverish motion. Elliot took hold of her ass and pinched. "Shit Elliot, you're going to make me come."

He used his hands to rock faster. "Come then, Eden."

She slammed into him and clung while her pussy contracted and sent her into orbit. "Damn it," she shouted, "that was too quick!"

"We're not done." Elliot held her panting body close to him and whispered in the back of her ear. "Come on Eden, turn around. I want to kiss you." He rotated her easily at a ninety-degree angle. "Get that leg up or you'll kick me in the jaw." He shouted on a sharp hiss of breath.

"I didn't know we were playing Twister here." She leaned forward and her pussy swallowed more of his thick cock. Lifting her leg, she rotated it and her body until she lay in his lap still managing to keep them joined. "Damn. That little move nearly made me go off again."

Elliot bent over and Eden yelped. Heat. It spun over her thick as boiling sugar. She opened her mouth only to have it captured by Elliot's.

He couldn't get close enough. Buried deep inside her, Elliot still wanted to get closer. She consumed him. Totally, utterly consumed him beyond any reasonable measure and Elliot's control became tenuous. His mouth crushed hers. Hard and fast as teeth nipped and tongues danced, he wanted to fuck her until neither of them could think beyond the moment. He tasted the fiery determination in Eden flamed by need and Elliot was more determined to devour her.

"Put your legs around me." Their chests heaved as he sucked in air. His mouth went down her chin to her neck, using his tongue to taste and tease.

"What do you think I am?"

"Oh, I know exactly what you are. Now put your legs around me." He moved his body, splashing water up over the rim of the pool. But his cock went deeper into her warm pussy and Eden accommodated further by locking her legs around his waist. "How does that feel?"

He watched as Eden's eyes nearly rolled back into her head. "Oh it's good, real good."

Wrapping one arm around her waist, he pulled his legs up and pushed off. "Hang on to me."

She sank her fingers into his shoulders and her teeth into his neck in a playful bite. "How's this?"

"Nice." Her sharp teeth stung, but it was nothing compared to the deep plunge his cock made as he straightened to his feet with Eden wrapped around him. Water drained off them and he nearly lost his grip as that pussy closed tightly around him like an octopus.

"We're getting out?" She licked the spot she'd just bit. "That's a shame."

"Need more traction." Elliot carried her over to the thick trunk of a banana tree. He leaned her back against it. "Comfy."

She glanced around at the dipping banana leaves. "You're going to fuck me against the tree?"

He nodded. "Any objections."

"You're not going to rip the flesh off my back are you?"

He planted his feet in the thick sand, his arms tightened around her. "Maybe."

"Cool." She sucked his lower lip into her

mouth.

With his arms around her, Elliot absorbed the sensation of her breasts rubbing up and down his chest as he fucked her. His cock had a mind of its own and Elliot did everything he could to oblige. He pumped her up and down on his rod hard and fast. The scent of banana surrounded them as her back slid up and down the slick trunk.

Their wet bodies soon turned slick with sweat and Elliot. His head rested in the crook of her neck inhaling the sweet herbal scent that mingling with the dark fragrance that was only Eden. "I don't want to stop, Eden."

She used his shoulders now to brace as she jerked her hips up and down. Her sweet pussy swallowing him, caressing him until Elliot's vision blurred. "Who said you had to?" She fucked him faster and somehow slid her legs tighter around him. "Oh shit!"

He used his chin to push one of her tits into his mouth and sucked fiercely. "What?" Elliot breathed hotly over her nipple. Her head snapped back and she shouted. Her pussy tightened relentlessly on his cock fucking him into mindless oblivion.

*****

"Let me get this straight," Maya poured herself another glass of orange juice and scratched the back of her head. "I get shit faced by some damn Vampire drug, try to sleep off the whammy but get called out to take crime scene photos while you and

Elliot are doing the nasty?" Maya took her orange juice and sat opposite Eden at her breakfast bar.

Eden stirred caramel flavored cream into her coffee. She was glad to finally catch Maya at home. Even though it was too damned early for anyone to be up. "Yeah."

"How the hell did this happen?" Maya took a drink of the orange juice. "I've been working sixteen friggin' hours and you get all the sex? That just isn't right." She nibbled a piece of toast. "Here I was thinking I had a good night getting groped by Vampires. And you're telling me that Elliot is some sex god in hiding." Maya sighed, "Not right. My life hasn't been this pathetic in years."

"You're picky."

"*I'm picky?* And the last time you had sex was?" Maya waited. "My point exactly." She stuck her lower lip out and Eden grinned. "I want a sex god."

Eden lifted her coffee cup to her lips. "How was I to know he was a sex god? I mean, sheesh, you'd think he'd just bore you to tears. How was I to know he had a secret life and an amazing cock."

"Excuse me?" Maya held up her hand, gazing at her with an accusatory gleam. "We'll get to his cock in a minute. What secret life? He's not married is he?"

"If he is, he's real good at concealing that one." She couldn't imagine Elliot married unless it was to her. She took a gulp of coffee and squeaked in alarm as the hot caffeine sizzled its way down her throat. When had she started thinking of marriage? Especially since she had a hard time getting over the prophecy thing.

She wasn't sure why either.

"Okay, let's just back up a second. What happened at that Rave that I don't know about?" Eden feigned interest in her coffee. "Something happened. Come on, you owe me. I'm the one who transformed you into the hot piece of ass Elliot was drooling over."

"That Absinthe is like the ultimate date-rape drug." Eden shuddered at the memory. She couldn't believe she let a damned Vampire go down on her. "You're lucky Roland took you home."

"Yeah whatever, what happened?" Maya twisted the crust off her toast. "And was Elliot involved?"

"He was involved. He found me staggering out a room with my pants practically around my knees."

"No shit?"

Eden nodded, "No shit. I had a Master Vampire licking my pussy trying to get me come over to the dark side."

Concern sped across Maya's pretty features. "Are you okay? I mean, *eeeewwww*, are you okay?"

"Yeah, I'm okay."

"And Elliot knows?" Eden nodded and Maya rubbed her hand across his brow. "Wow, I'm surprised he didn't blow a gasket or something. Course in a room full of Vampires, you guys would've ended up on the buffet table."

Eden waggled a finger at her. "Not necessarily."

Maya's brownish eyes narrowed. "What do you mean, not necessarily?"

"Let's just say it goes with the secret life thing. No way Elliot and I would've been brunch." Eden got up, walked into Maya's small kitchen, and poured herself another cup of coffee. "If anything, those dudes would've been ash."

"Now I'm confused."

"Yeah well, join the club. I'm barely getting used to it." Eden sat back down and reached for the cream.

"So are you gonna tease me or tell me what the big secret life is." Maya turned out of her chair and took her plate to the range. She picked up a frying pan and dumped the rest of her eggs into it.

"Elliot's a Warlock."

"Elliot's afraid of wedlock?" Maya sat down and forked a piece of egg. "Well that's typical. Guys have a hard time committing even when they find the right girl."

"That's not what I said. Eden tapped her finger on Maya's plate until she had her attention. "He's a Warlock."

Maya frowned her face scrunching up. Her eyes gleamed. "A Warlock?" Eden nodded watching as Maya's brain continued to process. "A Warlock like Uncle Arthur in *Bewitched*? Or one of those hottie guys always exploding on *Charmed*?"

Laughter bubbled out of Eden's lip. "Wasn't

Uncle Arthur gay?   Cause Elliot is definitely swinging my way."

"Oh my God, you're serious? Shit I thought you were kidding."   Maya laid her fork down. "Well, why the hell not? We've got every beasty imaginable in Vegas. Why not a good guy for a change?" She frowned staring hard at Eden, "He is a good guy, right?"

"He's very good," Eden purred, tracing her finger over the rim of her coffee cup.

Maya picked up her toast. "I thought you hated magic."

"I did." Eden spent a lot of time mulling over that issue. A lot of time. Now, she began to realize that her prejudice toward magic was really ignorance. She didn't know what it was or what it was about until Elliot. "I've changed my mind."

"Or Elliot changed it for you?"

"Mmm, maybe."

Maya grinned, "So what's next? You two off to protect Las Vegas from all the demons?"

Eden didn't think she could explain it. The prophecy was too damn complicated. "Something like that."

Maya cleared her breakfast dishes and dumped them in the sink behind her. "Hey I forgot to tell you. That Rave did produce one good thing. I've got a date tomorrow night."

Eden's eyes narrowed slightly. It wasn't that Maya couldn't get a date. Maya could have half the men in Las Vegas at her feet if she really wanted. It was the location where the date appeared. Vampireville was not a good place to pick up men. "Really? Who is he?"

"Oh relax, he's not a Vampire. I met him at the crime scene from the other night."

"Cop?"

"Nah, are you kidding? Why would I want to date a cop?" Maya made a face of disgust. "No, I think he's a doctor or something. Gorgeous thick hair, with the most sinful coppery highlights." She gestured emphatically. "I wonder where he gets it done."

Elliot's hair reminded her of molten gold. Silky soft with a wave that most women would kill for and Eden loved running her hands in it. She loved running her hands over his skin feeling his muscles contract at her touch. When his cock slid deep inside her, it made every fiber of her being collapse in on itself and the only two people in the universe were them.

Eden snapped herself out of her sexy daydream as the walls of her pussy contracted instinctively waiting. Great, she about creamed her jeans just thinking about the guy's hair. She was seriously a lost cause.

"So where are you going on this date, Maya?"

CHAPTER FOURTEEN

Analyzing the month's receipts from the casino portion of the Desert Mirage, Elliot's brain waded through the mire of numbers. He didn't think he could show enough gratitude when Roland brought him his afternoon tea. Elliot tossed his glasses aside and took the proffered cup. "Ah, I needed a break."

Roland hummed a tune from some musical as he sat the cream and sugar in front of Elliot. "There you are sure. All is right with the world I take it?"

"We're up eighteen percent from last year. It's a good increase."

"I was referring to Ms. Camden." Roland smiled as Elliot added a spot of cream and a spoonful of sugar. "Now that the prophecy is fulfilled—"

"The prophecy has not been fulfilled."

Roland paused in collecting the tea items. "Pardon me?" The tea tray clattered onto Elliot's desk and Roland sank slowly into a chair. "But I saw the two of you…"

"Leave it be, Roland." Elliot stirred his tea determined to avoid this conversation with his butler.

"I'm terribly confused, sir. I thought you and

Ms. Camden, well I assumed after finding you together that the spell had been completed."

"I said leave it be." Elliot used a firmer tone. His butler was more like a bulldog with a new bone than a Brit.

"But sir — how could you take advantage of the girl?"

Elliot dropped his spoon on the side of the saucer. "She isn't a girl, Roland and she's capable of making her own decisions." That's what Elliot kept telling himself. The twinge of guilt, he stamped down as like a weed. Eden would assure him she was more than capable of making her own decisions including sleeping with him. He wasn't going to let the pleasure they'd found together come under any criticism.

Roland seemed positively crestfallen. "You're her guardian, she's the slayer. It was understood by the Order that your union would unlock the prophecy."

Elliot raised his eyes to Roland. His expression particularly bland. "I won't let politics and ancient lore push Eden into something she isn't ready for."

His butler opened his mouth, then closed it appearing to rethink something. Elliot waited. He knew something was afoot. Roland fixed him with a stare that appeared a bit judgmental. "Something Ms. Camden isn't ready for, sir or would it be something you're not ready for?"

Sipping at his tea, Elliot lifted a brow, "I'm sure you don't know what you mean."

"I think you do, sir. That girl's been half in love with you for years." Roland had enough sense to pick up his tray and start to withdraw from the study. "Now you've put her in danger by standing out on a fencepost. I'd say it's time to step up, Mr. Warwick." Roland walked hastily out of the room and closed the door on a sharp note.

A disturbing thought. Elliot frowned. How could Roland possibly know something like that? Eden masked her feelings from everyone. How on earth would the butler know?

Elliot shot to his feet and rounded the desk. His bloody butler knew everything and made it a practice to stick his nose into everyone's business. He took hold of the door handle and yanked it open. "Roland!"

Roland paused halfway down the short staircase. "Yes, sir."

"Explain to me how you're such an expert on Eden's feelings." Elliot came down the stairs with the deliberation of a panther stalking.

"You're not the only one who knows things." Roland hurried around the corner into the kitchen.

"Obviously not." Elliot followed him, not in the least bit fooled by Roland's sudden interest in polishing the backsplash of the granite counter top. "Start talking," his voice raised several notches in volume, "and I don't mean about how you're running low on silver polish."

Roland tossed his cleaning towel onto the cupboard. "Please tell me you aren't that blind."

"Excuse me?"

"Have you actually looked at the girl? I mean truly looked at her until this last month." Roland's voice took on a defensive almost fatherly tone. "When she first came to us, she fought it, kept her feelings hidden. But over the years, even a fool could see how she felt like you, how she waited for you."

Part of Elliot, a small part, was intrigued that Eden had a crush on him. That this crush bloomed over time into something deeper and that struck him sharply in the chest. Appalled that he hadn't recognized the signs, Elliot sighed. "How long?"

"I noticed a few years ago." Roland picked up the towel and folded it. "She was anxious for your attention. If you noticed anything different, if you'd commented on something she'd done. She was always especially pleased if she thought you might be proud of her skills as a slayer. Ms. Camden needed your approval and attention."

"And I never made a comment either way. I wanted her to set her own pace, find her way and not need me as a crunch." Elliot rolled his eyes. "I'm an idiot."

"Indeed."

"You don't have to sound so happy about it." He took the jibe. He deserved it. Foolish, foolish man, how didn't he see Eden falling for him?

"I assume her recent makeover was one last attempt to get you to notice her as a woman."

"I noticed," Elliot mumbled under his breath.

He'd thought she was irritated and trying to torture him again for some mysterious reason.

"But you didn't do anything about it, did you?" Roland chastised waving a finger at him. "Instead you let her go to that Vampire party after ripping her heart out." He sighed dramatically, "It's a wonder both she and Maya survived."

Guilt drove straight through to his heart. It festered making him wonder how much time they'd lost over the years. "That's true. The stench of Vampire reeked on her."

"That's your own fault. You were in the position to change that and you choice not to." Roland tilted his head. "How long do you think it will be before she looks for someone who will worship the ground she walks on?"

Elliot's lips twisted into an easy smile. "You're half in love with her yourself, Roland."

His butler sniffed, "Perhaps. The question is, are you?"

"What?"

"Are you ready? You know as well as I do that tomorrow night that Master Vampire will be prepared. He will come at Ms. Camden with all his charms and if you aren't ready for a commitment, then she could easily be taken from you."

He found Eden ready to clock out from her shift that night. His fingers wrapped around her upper arm. "We need to talk."

She turned. He noticed the change instantly as

if a light switch had been flicked into the 'on' position. She leaned into him. Before, she'd automatically pull away. "Okay. I was just going shopping for my party outfit."

"What?"

"You know, black leather. To match your sexy outfit from last night." Eden moved to the side of him and grinned. "We can go as matched Goths." Slipping her time key into her pocket, she linked her arm in his. "You hungry? I haven't eaten all day and I'm starving."

"What would you like?"

"Steak. I'm in the mood."

Elliot chuckled, enjoying the sensation of her body against his. "Then steak it is."

He took her to the most exclusive steakhouse in Las Vegas. In a secluded table over a bottle of good Cabernet, he watched her talk about Maya and her day job over candlelight. It warmed his heart in a way he never expected and it made him realize as their waiter served dinner that he would have a hard time letting her go.

Eden examined the steak and petite lobster in a manner he could only classify as predatory. She slid her knife through the filet and forked herself a healthy bite. "Mmm, delicious."

He speared a piece of asparagus. "You were hungry."

"Maya was already eating when I got there so I missed breakfast. I got involved with a whale this afternoon at the tables and missed my lunch break."

She chewed the steak thoughtfully. "So what do we need to talk about?"

"Tomorrow night. We need a game plan in case things go bad." Elliot cut into his steak. He wanted to broach the subject carefully. Eden exhibited skittish behavior on occasion. That's why he'd never figured out her feelings for him. Her tendency to fight usually discouraged serious conversation.

"Understandable." She nodded, digging into her salad. "I want this to go off without a hitch. And I want Carlos Venturi's head on a stick."

Elliot's mouth thinned into a line. "Don't put yourself in a no win position."

"That fucker started this by killing my parents." She paused for a moment, her fork in mid-air. "My parents thought I was going insane. They were going to send me to a treatment center. Their daughter was abnormal. It killed me." She inhaled and took a sip of wine. "I never wanted to see them hurt, but you are the best thing that ever happened to me." She shrugged it off, "Maybe I ought to thank him instead of forking him."

Leaning his elbow on the table, Elliot's thumb rested on his cheek while his fingers covered his mouth. He could see the weight that admission brought. The guilt, the inevitable sadness, and it twisted inside him. "Eden, I know it was hard. I'm sorry I wasn't there for you more."

"Ah, is that was this is about?" Eden raised her wine glass examining the dark cranberry colored wine. "You gave me everything I would accept at the time and more. It took me a long time to realize that what you offered was more than anyone ever gave me. You challenged me to become better. And more importantly, you never gave up. Even when I did."

"How do you want to handle tomorrow?" Elliot swirled his wine. The lump in his throat felt as if he'd swallowed a boulder. He wanted her. More and more, with an addiction he didn't see slacking in the coming years.

"That depends on how many Vamps attend this little get together. At last count, I had five hundred active in Vegas."

"There's twice that many."

She examined a piece of **asparagus**. "Okay, aren't they going to recognize us? **I mean,** even if we go in Goth, they've still got **to notice us.**" Eden committed to the vegetable **and stuck it** in her mouth. "I can smell them, you **know? They** stink like rot. So I figure they've got **to sense us.**"

"They know me by **reputation.** They can't sense a Warlock. But some can **sense** magic. A slayer is different. It's like a tiger stalking zebra, their hackles stand up but generally by the time it occurs it's too late." Elliot paid a bit more attention to his dinner, knowing he would need his strength tomorrow night.

"Can you conceal us?"

Elliot measured the idea. "I could make us appear *more* Vampire if that's what you're asking."

He raised his eyes to hers and searched her face for signs of regret or fear. There wasn't any. "You realize, that this is all likely a trap."

"But we know that going in." She cut up more of her steak. "So that means, we're ahead again. Even if Titan is lying, we *think* he is already, so we're still one up."

"I want us prepared."

Eden bit into a piece of meat. "Bring a big bag of spells." She twirled her fork at him. "And I'll bring stakes. Ha! I made a joke." She snickered at her brilliance making Elliot smile.

It was time to get down and dirty. They needed to remain likeminded when it came to the prophecy. If things went wrong, the spell linking them would remain as a failsafe. "We have to decide. If it's not Carlos Venturi, someday, someone will come along that holds the capacity to turn you. You'll need to learn the spell."

"Why is it always me that can be corrupted? Aren't there other slayers out there?"

"Of course there are." Elliot finished his glass of wine. "But none of them are at the crossroads as we are."

"Goodie."

"It's for you to decide, Eden."

Eden shoved her plate aside. "Why is it always me? Aren't Warlocks corruptible? Or vulnerable?"

"We have vulnerabilities." The conversation seemed to leap away from him and into the middle of Eden's temper. "Just like anyone. Vampires aren't generally one of them though." He wanted to broach this gently. It wasn't going well. Elliot considered ordering a whiskey. "If you want to discuss my faults, we can do that another time. But I need to know that you are ready for this, if need be." His tongue seemed thick and he tripped over the words. He used to believe he was quite eloquent. He was tempted to just say *sod off* to the whole works and take Eden to a Caribbean island. "If you want to do this." He shook his head slightly in an effort to clear the fog from his brain. Thick, gray rolling into his mind as if it were the hazy streets of London, Elliot found it difficult to think straight. "We need this to be right." The quizzical look on Eden's face gave him his answer, he rambled like a bloody idiot. "I'll get the check."

She'd waited. On the drive home, she'd waited for him to say the words. Eden watched lights from the MGM and New York, New York hotels pass in a blur as they turned off Tropicana and headed up to the Desert Mirage.

Why couldn't he say the words? Eden dragged her fingers through her long, black hair. And what *were* those words? They approached a giant yawning precipice. The big one. Before she bound herself to her guardian for all eternity, she wanted the words. It was silly maybe. Coming from a slayer, it was girlie. But damn it, she was a girl. She knew she'd drawn them closer with her complete makeover – she'd wanted him to finally notice her, see her as a woman. She'd gotten her wish and now she was greedy. She wanted it all.

Staring with Elliot Warwick.

"So what are we doing, Elliot?"

"Hmm?" Eden saw his eyes framed by gold wire rim glasses. He studied the newspaper as if he'd find the Fountain of Youth in it. It reminded her just how great he was at hiding his feelings. He ought to play poker cause he was the king of the emotionless gaze.

"I want the words, Elliot."

Their limo pulled into the underground parking garage of the Desert Mirage. Elliot seemed distracted. "What words?"

"You know, for a smart man, you're a thick-headed son of a bitch at times." She didn't let the flare of temper takeover. Instead, she remained cool. Eden was damn proud of herself. She could control her temper when it was important. "This prophecy thing is messing with our lives and I've got a right to know where you stand in this. Because I'm positive, even you, could realize that I've laid all my cards out on the table a long time ago."

Elliot folded his newspaper as limo pulled up to the valet parking. An elevator off to the left led to the residence. "I'm sorry, what?"

Eden's fingers went to the door handle. She nearly squeezed it back into liquid form. Temper seethed and she wondered if his deliberate avoidance was because he was emotionally inept or he just wanted to fuckin' irritate her. "Forget about it." She opened the door and climbed out of the limo. "I'll learn the spell tonight." She slammed the door closed as he got out of the limo.

"That's a good idea."

She waited for him to slide a keycard into the elevator entrance. She leaned against the wall and glared. "You keep Vampires out of the hotel because of magic, don't you?" Changing the subject was one way to keep from strangling him when they stepped into the elevator.

The doors whispered shut. "Yes."

"I wonder why I never put that together." Eden tsked herself loudly. "Amazing isn't it? How something could be standing right in front you? Practically smacking you right in the forehead," she pressed the heel of her hand into her forehead, "and still, you've got no freakin' clue what's going on."

If she hadn't known it was a disguise, Eden would've shit her pants right then and there. His gold hair was jet black. No, make that blue black pushed away from his ears to reveal rings of silver hoops. Leather, black, ripped open t-shirt and tattoos visible crawled out from under the collar and up the side of his face. Eden gasped, "You look disgusting!"

"Excellent." He walked over to her and held out a silver stud. "This is for you."

Eden held out her hand and Elliot dropped it into her palm. "For what?" She twisted the stud between her thumb and index finger.

"It's for your tongue."

Her eyes widened. "No way."

"I've heard it's a great stimulus."

"For who? Because it doesn't do jack for me." She handed the stud back to him. No way was she piercing her tongue. Ack! She couldn't begin to imagine the pain and gory details of that little trifle. "I'll go along with this costume thing and the fact that you look like a monster, but I'm not piercing anything that isn't already pierced."

He laughed. More than a chuckle, it was rich, and so sensual Eden wanted to wrap herself up in it and roll around. He didn't laugh like that a lot. Not in front of her anyway. She smiled and the warm sensation curled her toes.

"It's a mirage. Just like your appearance will be." Elliot continued to chuckle as he grasped her upper arms and walked her over to a large mirror in the hall.

He walked her over to the hall mirror and Eden howled. "Oh God, I look like hell." Her hair had white streaks in it. Tattoos littered her skin wherever it showed and a lot of it showed. She wore black leather, skintight pants and a black leather vest that shoved her minimal boobs into respectable cleavage. "What's up with this?" she pointed at her boobs.

"I thought you might have fun with it."

Eden snickered. "Or you." She examined the myriad of artwork over her body. Everything from roses to dragons and motorcycles all to conceal the guardian/slayer mark on her hip. "This is just bizarre."

"Consider it a costume party." Elliot glanced at his watch. "It's eleven. We should get going."

Eden turned into him. A spasm of something close to fear stuck her in the back. She wouldn't let anything happen to them tonight. No matter what it took, how many Vampires she fried. She and Elliot were walking out of there alive. "I'm ready."

She glanced away suddenly unwilling to meet his eyes. So much to say, so little time. They'd get to it later. Eden let her hands fall where they'd been at his shoulders.

Elliot held the door up and affected a Cockney accent, "Let's go, babe."

CHAPTER FIFTEEN

Designed to accommodate three hundred people, Eden was positive there were at least that many in the lounge overlooking the Las Vegas Strip. They squeezed out of the elevator and walked into the chaos called a party. Music rocked the windows and the walls as a band, Eden used the term loosely, played their guts out.

"This is hideous." Several people shoved by them on their way to what looked like a blood bar in the corner near the entrance. She leaned across Elliot and gestured with her head, "Tell me that isn't what I think it is."

Elliot turned his head slowly. "Oh it is."

"You know, they really are a bunch of sick mother fuckers."

"Indeed."

"Let's go find something more like a martini." Eden took hold of his handcuffs hanging off the belt loop of his pants.

"You might find beer, love. Probably not a martini." She watched Elliot take in the room assessing the threat and filing it away.

Eden could barely hear above the din that the Vampire party called music. For a violent bunch, they were certainly party animals. It was a Goth-a-rama in the lounge at the Palms, a popular hotel for celebrities and those with serious cash. She wondered how much good ol' Carlos had to fork out to rent the place for the night.

Incense, a weird vanilla and floral mix combined with clove and imported tobacco to create a bluish haze in the air. Eden figured it was a way to mask the smell of the dead. It wasn't working, the joint stank. Eden tried breathing through her mouth as she followed Elliot into the center of the lounge. When he hung a left heading for a bar that actually sold alcohol, Eden was grateful. "I'd settle for a Pepsi about now."

"I'll see what I can do."

So far, so good. Everyone appeared to accept them for what their illusion painted them to be. Goths in training. Dancers gyrated in some bizarre sex act up near the band. Eden just looked away. It was too gross for words. Wannabes and fledglings exhibited no self-control. Obviously, they thought everyone wanted to see blue-veined asses and piercings du jour.

Eden scanned the crowd, checking access points and exits. If they needed to get out of Dodge, she wanted the easiest route through the least amount of Vampires.

Her eyes flitted across the room and with each breath she drew energy as Elliot had shown her last night. It had always been there, now she knew how to channel it. He revealed to her direct it the pull of green earth energy and harness it for slaying demons. The first time she touched it, her head swam as if she'd been dropped on a rollercoaster. Elliot steadied her, helped her gain focus and when she was ready taught her the spell that would bind them.

The prophecy spell was the midterm from hell. As Elliot read it to her, her eyes nearly rolled back in her head. Some bizarre foreign language Eden spent all night studying to get the pronunciation down properly. Elliot had remained adamant about her ability to recite the thing. So she'd spent half the night doing it.

Now, the dark shadows under eyes were half hers and the other half Goth makeup.

"Aren't you a honey?" A man with a mane of hair wrapped his arms around her and squeezed. He was gorgeous. Tall, muscled and moved like a freakin' lion. His eyes were an amazing greenish blue. She wondered how anyone so gorgeous could stumble into a place like this.

Oxygen drained out of Eden's lungs and all of a sudden she felt like a sardine in the black leather. "Get your hands of me, asshole." As cute as he was, she didn't need the dude caught in the crossfire tonight.

Elliot appeared at her side holding two drinks, "They had Jim Beam."

"Swell," Eden snarled. "You wanna tell this mother to get off me." Elliot shook his head and his eyes shimmered with something close to surprise.

Before Eden realized it, another man joined them who resembled the blonde but with harsher features.

All sharp angles, with long dark hair tied back in a ponytail, this man made you think of walks in the moonlight with eyes like a poet. Next to him was a tall woman of Hispanic decent and another couple. If she was paranoid, she'd think they were surrounded. Instinctively, she slid closer to Elliot and took her drink.

She hated whiskey, but it gave her time to check out the newcomers. Eden tilted her head trying to place the woman. But the guy, she'd seen him before. It was on the tip of her tongue. She sipped the drink. It burned all the down her throat and formed a pool of fire in her stomach.

"I wasn't expecting to see you tonight, Dr. Tennyson." Elliot offered his hand that the smaller woman accepted.

"You know these people?" Eden's head snapped around then back at the couple. Now, she recognized the man. Christian Blackthorne, artist extraordinaire who decided to make Las Vegas home a few years ago. She lowered her voice, "You might want to get the hell out of here tonight then. Not a good place to be tonight."

The blonde guy squeezed her cheek. "You're right, she's a pistol. I'll be she's a hot one in bed."

Stunned wasn't a good word. The shock of someone shoving a pole vaulting stick up your ass would've been the equivalent of what she experienced when this guy squeezed her cheek. "What the hell?"

A tall woman shoved the blonde in the arm hard enough to make him wince.

Elliot only chuckled. Eden decided she didn't like that anymore. It was irritating. Especially when it looked like she stumbled in on an inside joke. Elliot put an arm around her waist and pointed her at the blonde. "Draigon Blackthorne, this is Eden Camden."

The blonde man flashed dazzling bright teeth. "Pleasure." He reached behind him and pulled the tall woman forward. "This is Madison." The other woman nodded and mumbled greetings. "Honey, this is the slayer chick I told you about."

Eden froze. Her eyes dilated to saucers and she saw the angry glare from the dark haired man as Elliot introduced him. "This is Garridon Blackthorne." She heard the clicks of a combination lock tick into place in her mind as she sorted through this information at light speed. Eden didn't even pretend to conceal her shock. "And Christian, I'm sure you've heard of, and his lovely wife, Hillary."

"Wife?"

The smaller woman nodded and smiled. "We got married a few months ago."

She thought she heard Elliot say, "Congratulations."

Eden took a step up to the one Elliot said was Draigon. Man, he really was pretty up close. She sniffed. Nothing. She leaned in and inhaled deeply.

Draigon smiled, "Interesting custom."

"You don't stink."

Draigon shifted his body and raised his arm to sniff at his pit. "I hope not."

Eden inhaled again. Sage, citrus and a splash of spice, Draigon smelled positively edible. She looked back at Elliot. "Why doesn't he stink?"

"He isn't evil."

"But he's a freakin' Vampire," Eden hissed with the capacity of a viper.

"They all are save Ms. Reyes."

Eden fell back, "You're fucking kidding me. Why don't they smell? Seriously."

Garridon moved with the grace of jaguar. "I think it would be wise to lower your voice, Ms. Camden." He moved his brother away and separated him from Madison Reyes. "Your guardian is correct. It isn't the stench of a Vampire you can smell. It is evil."

She turned a vicious gaze onto Elliot. "Why didn't I know this?"

The Vampire slid his hand around her arm. "You didn't know it because you didn't want to, slayer." Garridon effectively insinuated himself between her and Elliot. "You believed all of my kind is evil."

Christian Blackthorne moved forward. "I suggest you open your mind, Eden. All Vampires aren't evil. Anymore than *all* humans."

"You're saying I'm prejudice."

He shook his head. "I'm simply asking you to do as your guardian and see beyond stereotypes." Christian put an arm around his wife. "We're here tonight to assist you. If you need it, we're here."

She turned her head smoothing he wild Goth hair away from her eyelashes. Eden swallowed. She'd lived her entire life chasing monsters and now the monsters were on their side. She drank the rest of the whiskey in one gulp. The fire bounced around her and splattered hotly against her sides. She pinched the bridge of her nose instead of rubbing her eyes, which she'd smeared with black liner.

"O...kay. I think."

Eden's eyes narrowed sharply. When the two Blackthornes touched her, their skin hadn't been chilly. Most Vampires blood flowed at a very slow pace. If they were Vampires, their skin should've been cool to the touch. And that was in the best of situations. Most of the time, they were clammy like snakes which Eden found very fitting.

She turned her attention to the dark one. "For Undead, you're skin is warm—too warm."

This time the one Elliot referred to as a doctor moved up next to her. "We're not dead, Eden. We simply function on a different level. It's an anomaly in the blood that allows a genetic alteration to occur."

"Yeah, whatever." She faced Elliot, "Goth boy, I need to talk to you—" She took hold of Elliot by one of his chains and yanked him forward.

"Not now," Elliot jerked her around the opposite direction. "The entertainment's started." He moved out of the way so she could see passed her. "Over there, the flaming Vampire."

Eden shifted back, glad she decided to where the biker boots instead of the spiked heels Elliot suggested. Because when she located Titan in the crowd, she nearly passed out as she saw who was with him. "Oh my God!" She glanced back at Elliot her eyes laced with fear. "Oh my God!"

"And there's the lure," murmured Elliot.

Across the bar, with Titan and Kristov looking much too blonde and stunning for this crew was Maya. Eden closed her eyes on a shudder, "Her blind date. Her freakin' blind date." Eden hissed as rage exploded in her. Why didn't she see this earlier? Put two and two together like a normal person?

"What's she doing with that big ugly?" The woman named Madison spit out. "I always thought the girl had better taste than that."

Eden turned, "You know her?"

"Yeah, she works in the crime lab downtown."

You could've blown Eden over with a feather. She wobbled. "You're a cop?" At Madison's nod, Eden shook her head, "And you hang out with Vampires?"

The tall woman shrugged as if it were no big deal. "Occasionally."

"Did I miss the sign on the door that said *entering an alternative reality*?" Eden's head swam with possibilities and none of them added up correctly. At least, not in her way of thinking.

"Hey Maya!" Madison roared above the crowd and waved her arms.

"That's my girl," Draigon smiled, flashing those teeth again.

Eden picked up on a gnashing of teeth coming from the dark one. It was gone as quickly as it appeared. Her attention drawn to Maya as she threaded her way toward them. Eden hoped she didn't bring Titan and Kristov along but the pair dragged behind her almost like eager puppies.

"Hey Detective, how's it going?"

Madison flashed Eden a brief look and fit it all together. If Maya didn't recognize Eden, then Titan and Kristov probably wouldn't either. "Great. See you've got plenty of entertainment tonight."

Maya grinned, "Yeah I didn't know I was getting a two-fer when Kris asked me out."

Eden blinked. So it wasn't Titan. The sneaky Warlock asked her out. Eden clenched her fists wanting to pound Mr. Cute and Magical into a bloody pulp. She growled under her breath.

Elliot put his lips to her ear. "Not a good idea. We need to get Maya and the good detective out of range first."

"I'm gonna kill them. Both of them. And when they're ash, I'm gonna stomp on them some more."

His eyes peered over the top of her head. "Watch yourself. Even in this noise, a Vampire's hearing is incredibly acute. You don't want to tip our hand."

"And I don't want my friend used as refills at the blood bar."

"Hey Maya, Hillary and I were just going to hit the oyster bar downstairs. Not much in the way of food up here."

That's because you guys are the food! Eden had to bite the inside of her cheek to keep from shouting at them.

"Ewww," Maya scowled, "I don't do raw oysters."

"Well, they've got other stuff down there. Mexican, I think." Madison did her best to nudge Maya forward. "I'm starved, we can come back and get the boys after the wet t-shirt contest."

"Oh I don't think so, we just got here, and it'd be rude for me to take off, you know?"

Now Eden wanted to pound Maya too. Something snapped and she strutted up to her best pal and snarled, "Are you trying to get killed?"

"Wh-what?" Maya jumped back landing solidly against the Warlock. "What the hell's your problem, lady?"

"Get out of here. Now." A hum of tension rippled along the air with enough force to tear out a wall.

"Who made you queen?" Maya angled her head. Her eyes glimmered with a weird kind of recollection and before Eden could get her own hands around Maya's mouth – "Eden? Is that you?"

Maya pushed off Kristov and grabbed Eden by

the arms. "What's with the get up? Geez, you look like hell." It was more an aside, but Eden frowned shaking her friend off. "I didn't know you were coming here tonight. We could've gone together."

Madison just looked down her nose and shook her head, "Party's about to get more interesting."

"I don't know what the fuck you're talking about, chick." Eden pointed an index finger at Maya's throat. "But get off me and take your ugly ass friends with you."

"Where's Elliot?" Maya put her hands on her hips and tapped her foot. "You two didn't have a fight again did you? That's why you're in such a pissy mood, isn't it? You guys had a fight."

The quiver in the air lasted only a second while the fight or flight reflex kicked in for six people that weren't flapping their big mouths wide. Eden knew she had an instant to get Maya out of the way.

Lunging forward, she gripped Maya around the wrist and yanked her out of the way of Titan and Kristov. Spinning them both around, she knew it wasn't a good idea to turn her back on Vampires, but she shoved Maya at Christian and Hillary Blackthorne. "Get jabber jaws out of here, please."

An icy hand embedded into her shoulder and squeezed. Eden winced, astonished at the strength. "You seriously want to let go of me."

"I don't think so." Kristov smirked, laying his chin on her shoulder. "You're the guest of honor, Eden." He snuggled up against her, "I want a shot at that pussy Carlos is so intoxicated with."

"That rips it!" Eden rammed her elbow into his stomach with enough force to cripple a buffalo. Kristov bent over gasping for air and Eden pointed at Draigon. "Anyone that's human, get them out of here. It's about to get nasty."

Draigon did as she requested. With a protective arm around Maya, he led her and Madison toward the exit while Christian and Hillary watched their back. Elliot came around to the side of her as Titan decided to take point.

"They won't let them leave."

Eden folded her arms across her chest. "They'd better."

"Your friend's not getting out of here."

Eden lifted her foot and kicked it into Kristov's shoulder to the time of the wild drumbeat. He landed on his ass. Then she turned to Titan, "I'm pretty sure you know who those Blackthorne boys are." She grinned back at Garridon then over at Titan. Jerking her thumb back toward Garridon, she continued to smile, "This one doesn't look real friendly."

Titan bent down to snatch Kristov up off the ground. "Not too worried, Eden. You're in a room of about two hundred against you. I'd be a bit more polite."

"You know me, Titan. Since when am I polite." Eden figured they'd delayed this long enough. She took a quick look over her shoulder and sure enough, some Goths were trying to keep Maya and the troupe from leaving. But she noticed Christian explaining the situation and when the doors opened, Eden let loose. "Where's Carlos?"

She jumped, her feet snapping forward in sharp movements to connect with Titan's ribcage and chin. She landed in front of him on a bounce as he staggered backward. "Don't screw with me, Titan. I'm really sick of your shit."

The music died down and the crowd turned their attention toward the fight. Eden figured this would bring Carlos out in the open.

Titan rubbed his chin. "Ouch!"

"Where's Carlos?"

He popped his jaw. "I've got know idea."

"And you're a lying sack of shit."

Swinging his arm, Titan connected with the side of her cheek. The force was enough to spin Eden off balance and into a group of fledglings eager for a tumble. Claws raked down her arms and legs as they pinned her to the floor. Eden's jaw tightened, fighting against the pain while searching for her center of focus. Three eager little Vamps snapped teeth at her and Eden flexed her arms straining each muscle. She managed to bend her arms then snap them forward into the jaws of two Vamps. Eden threw herself forward into low crouch.

Kenpo karate was all about circular motion. Eden maintained a Zone of Protection and with it effectively blocked enemy attacks. Even if she got hit from behind on a cheap shot, she still kept from being vitally damaged. Her moves were well timed and focused. Her chi drawing on the earth's green energy, Eden dispatched her young aggressors by creating a bit of a fight club in the Vamp's party.

These guys were aggressive by nature. She just incited them. Eden rotated and danced away so they could occupy themselves. She swiped her hands together appreciating her handiwork.

A hand reached out and wrenched Eden forward by the only real earring she had on. The hoop tore out of her lobe and Eden slammed her jaw shut to keep from screaming in rage. She raised her fingers to her earlobe and when she came away with blood, the rage turned to steam and blew out her ears.

Two blonde Goth chicks laughed over their new found earring. Goths might be human, in some aspects and Eden strode up to them and pointed mildly at the hoop earring. "Give it back."

"What?"

"The earring was a gift." Eden moved closer. "I *want it* back."

"Fuck off."

The lobe throbbed as if someone stepped on it. Eden shook her head, "See now? Here we are at this party and you're startin' trouble." Eden shoved the first blonde backward and snagged the earring from the other one. She stuffed the earring into her pocket and reared back. She slammed her fist into the Goth's nose and heard a satisfactory crunch.

Sniffing slightly, Eden smiled, "My work here is done." Eden turned back to find Elliot and a fist connected with her jaw. Her head reeled like a slot machine. In fact, she was sure little cherries flashed in front of her eyes. "Shit!" Eden jerked her neck and jaw back into place with a loud crack. Her eyes scanned the crowd as brawls burst out around the lounge. If she wasn't in a hurry, she'd jump into the center of it all.

Elliot made sure the two girls were out the door before he turned his attention back to Eden. To add to the distraction, Elliot hurled a small fireball at one of the guitar speakers. It exploded, a roman candle showering the crowd with sparks. Cover blown, so to speak and it appeared that things might get messy. A pair of Vampires tackled him hard into a crowd and Elliot shoved off another pair to try and right his balance. Chaos erupted while Vampires, Goths and the scattered human screamed and dove for either cover or jumped right into the fray.

Moving with determination, Elliot began to push his way back through the crowd toward Eden. He could see her punch some blonde Goth in the nose. A smile of appreciation lit his lips. As good as she was, he didn't want them separated for any length of time. Tonight, they needed to stick like glue to avoid a hazardous situation. A blast of hot air next to him made Elliot turn his head.

He recognized the mistake the second it occurred. The Vinquant herb dispersed in a mist at his face. Even with lightning reflexes, he couldn't avoid the spray. It hit his face and the effects of the vicious poison were instant.

Fire seemed to ravage his face. Warlocks of his level had very few Achilles' heels. Two things could stop a Warlock in action. Binding their hands kept a Warlock from spilling spell components or directing a spell toward the desired target. The other was to hinder eyesight.

One of the quickest ways to do that was ancient root harvested by dark witches of druid times. To become blinded by the Vinquant herb was an incredibly devious and rare method and only another Warlock would know this.

Elliot's eyes burned, raw, and stinging as the acidic herb ran down his face. Tears burned his eyes. He knew there was no use in wiping the herb from his eyes. His vision blurred and Elliot yanked every ounce of control he had to pull a spell together before he couldn't see. He shoved a hand in his pocket and whispered the words to the sleep spell he'd used the other night. It didn't matter that he could see the target. This time, the only thing he wanted was a wide dispersion.

Elliot completed the spell tossing a handful of sand in the air. The last thing he saw was Kristov's smile.

He could hear Vampires and Goths passing out around him and crumbling to the floor. Elliot knew there were only seconds left for him to pull defensive shields up and keep the throngs from assaulting him. He pulled a light shield around his perimeter right before someone threw a bat into the back of his knees.

CHAPTER SIXTEEN

Snapping and growling, followed wild barking forced Eden to turn around. Somehow she didn't thing the owners of the hotel planned on this when they allowed the Vamps to throw their little party. Eden's feet practically dug into the ground with spurs as she watched the Vampire called Garridon shift into a large black wolf. Before he didn't have human lips he turned his beautifully dark face and shouted, "They've surrounded you guardian! Get to him." Then his body folded and manipulated into the wolf and he launched himself into the fray.

It was hard to concentrate. The noise, the chaos and above it all, Eden forced herself to keep that damn prophecy spell in her head. Eden walked passed the blood bar and reached behind the icy display to pick up a few chunks to put on her ear. She wondered how long it would take for her ear to heal when Garridon's words finally permeated her thick skull.

"Goddammit!" Eden bulldozed her way around the blood bar only to have some weenie assed Vampire try to bite her on the ankle. She jerked her foot forward trailing the skinny bloodsucker after her. He had the bite of a freakin' terrier. Eden bent down to smack the little shit in the head when some other brawl rammed into her like a goddamn semi.

Somehow, she manipulated her body into a twist avoiding the gang tackle into the blood bar. Eden rolled off three men losing her ankle biter and climbed to her knees as the blood bar tumbled its main beverage onto a good dozen Vampires and Goths who suddenly looked like they were in a scene from *Carrie*. Blood poured from the punch bowl and martini glasses into a macabre type of scene that Eden turned from.

She needed to find Elliot. Now.

"Over here, my sweet."

The words whispered through Eden. Making her shudder with awareness in a very eerie oily kind of way, Eden tilted her head and tried not to squirm with Carlos so close. She didn't inhale, just kept her body stiff as a pole. "Carlos, I was just looking for you."

"Were you, my delicious one?" Carlos put an arm around her waist.

It grossed her out having him touch her but until she could get close to Elliot and get one of his magic stakes to appear in her hand, she was shit out of luck. "Yeah, I was. How come you didn't invite me?" She flashed her best pouty look at the Vampire. "I'm kind of hurt. Especially after our last fling."

"Fling?" Carlos laughed. "You are charming. A breath of fresh air in this world."

"Yeah, I'm just freakin' Doris Day," Eden half snarled. Never in a million years would she admit that she dug watching old Doris Day movies with a giant bowl of popcorn.

"I didn't think you'd find this sort of entertainment stimulating."

This time, her smile was real. "You'd be surprised what I find stimulating."

Carlos rubbed up against her and Eden's skin crawled. Amazing what a Vampire drink would do for you. She didn't find Carlos the least bit attractive. Repulsive maybe, but so not attractive.

"Well after we've concluded the ceremony, we should stimulate each other."

Vampire thrall, Carlos laid it on so slick and heavy Eden could only classify it as ooze. Green, nasty snot of Vampire sexuality. Her stomach pitched and rolled and Eden sucked in air through her nose.

It was nasty deviate shit and Eden caught herself in mid thought. These Vampires were different from the one she'd seen launch himself into a ten to one fight. Eden hoped the black wolf found his way to the door. His brothers had appeared so honorable it made Eden uncomfortable. But now she knew, this was the difference.

The Blackthornes were day.

Carlos Venturi an endless night.

"First we'll take care of a bit of business and then we can get back to the celebration." Carlos maneuvered her through the broken glass and furniture and strewn bodies to the center of the lounge where the band had simply given up.

"What's that?" Eden's booted foot crunched on the glass as she stepped around one of the blonde's she'd punched out earlier.

"Just a bit of inconvenience. We'll dispose of it and have the rest of the evening together."

Eden smirked. "Well Carlos, that's great but you're going to have to send out for some ribs or burgers or pizza or maybe a nice stake or something cause that blood thing just isn't happening."

Carlos gripped her upper arm and rotated her around to face Kristov and Titan. A good handful of other eager Vampires surrounded them. Eden flexed her arm and Carlos released his grip just as the group of Vampires parted. She watched as Kristov bent over and pulled a slack body forward.

Eden closed her eyes. *Not dead, not dead, please, don't let him be dead.* The rage was instant and suddenly so was the ability to clamp it down and hold the pure bloodlust at bay. Eden opened her eyes slowly and bit the inside of her jaw. It was the only thing she could think of to keep a look of stone on her face.

Kristov eyed her cautiously. "Do you want to get this done?

Eden raised a brow and looked at Carlos. "What's that?"

Carlos brushed a hand through her hair and leaned closer. "The only thing keeping us from being together, my sweet, is that troublesome

Warlock."

Elliot was face down. His hands tied behind his back and his mouth gagged. His head lolled to one side and she saw what looked like grape juice stained across his face and neck. Her hands fisted and her muscles flexed to readiness, but she moved slowly like a mama lion, not yet ready to pounce.

The Vampires backed up to give her some space. Only Kristov remained nearby. "Don't touch him."

She was really going to enjoy snapping this one in half. "Why? He doesn't look like much of a threat to anyone at the moment?" She ignored Kristov and bent down on one knee next to Elliot. She couldn't tell if he was even conscious.

"Step away from him." Kristov's accent became more pronounced and Eden figured it had a little agitation to it.

Eden stood up but didn't move away. Instead, she nudged Elliot with the tip of her boot. His arms shifted and his head moved slightly. "So what'd you guys do to him?"

Kristov moved around to face her. "Get away from him."

Looking passed the irritated Warlock, Eden found Carlos. The Vampire was way too confident. No, he was just cocky. Eden didn't appreciate cocky. Especially not in a Vampire. "What's his problem anyway? I just asked a question."

"Warlocks like this one are very dangerous, Eden. They threaten to undermine the very existence of our kind." Carlos walked closer and the group fanned out. Eden sensed the ripple of evil hovering over them like a black, oozing haze.

"Really? Huh," she folded her arms and clicked her tongue, "I never realized that." She inched closer to Elliot. All she had to do was touch him. "What's all over his face?"

Carlos flipped his long wavy hair back. "A concoction made by Kristov. Something to temporarily blind him."

Eden tried not to smirk. The trouble with cocky was you thought everyone was stupid. They'd never catch on to your tricks or your plans. You had free reign to do whatever you chose. *That* was a huge mistake.

The blaze of anger in Kristov's eyes was enough to let Eden know Mr. Wizard didn't want the general public telling his secrets out of school. Interesting. She turned her attention on the Warlock. Wasn't this the be all end all of movie themes? The Warlock pretended to serve Carlos until he could take control. It locked into place like a puzzle piece. Titan and Kristov never intended to assist them. They needed them here to help get rid of Carlos.

Eden's eyes flittered across the crowd. She could spot the giant redhead anywhere. Probably bailed, the big chicken. She shifted her weight gingerly so as not to attract any attention. The brawls among the fledglings and other party folk died down to a dull roar.

Elliot groaned and tried to move. Two brave Goths surged forward only to receive a piercing glare from Eden. They backed off. "So what's the deal here, Kristov? Why blind him?" Man, she was going to slit this fucker wide when she got a chance. "I thought all you Warlock dudes had a code or something."

"We need to start this. Before he gets to lucid." Kristov directed his comments at Carlos avoiding Eden's eyes.

"My sweet, in order to take your rightful place of me. You must dispose of your guardian." Carlos didn't move any closer but she the tentacles of that Vampire thrall wrapped around her feet and tried to pull her under.

Eden pursed her lips and waited. On Kristov, she could practically taste the fear. Raw, nervous and the pungent odor of onion assaulted her nose. He didn't play as good a game as he pretended. She took a step toward him and sniffed. "Wow Kristov, you *stink*."

"Wwh—wassh's going on?" The booming voice slurred from behind them. Titan stumbled forward holding a large shot glass of tequila and a half empty bottle. "I leave for two minutes and you all start without me?" He glared accusingly at Kristov and pointed his tequila with shaky fingers. Titan slurped on the tequila and then sucked on the ice cube. "Who says Vampires can't hold their alcohol?"

He staggered over a broken bottle amidst the

snickers of some of the younger Vampires. Titan shooed them away until he came to a swerving stop in front of Eden, Kristov and Carlos.

"You're drunk!"

Titan snorted, "Ya think?"

"Have you lost your mind?" Kristov hissed leaning forward as much as he dared.

Wreaking of tequila, Eden was sure that Titan spilled more of the Reposado than he drank. The sweat steaming off Kristov clued her in that Titan was part of the plot. Too bad, Titan didn't hold his alcohol. Eden slid closer to Elliot as Titan poured himself another shot. The alcohol sloshed over the rim and Titan bent his head to lick the excess off the rim. He licked his fingers and tilted the glass, "Aww, damn…"

"You idiot." Kristov lunged for the bottle of tequila.

Eden stepped back again as Titan jumped, frightened by the big blurry shape moving for him. He did a weird juggling act with the tequila bottle and the glass before managing to get his legs tangled over some imaginary object. The glass and bottle fell at Kristov's feet shattering. Tequila splashed across the Warlock.

"You stupid son of a bitch!"

Titan fell against Eden hard. He knocked her up against Elliot and it took a good shove of strength to maintain her balance and keep from tumbling down on top of him. She wrapped her arms around the waist of the big Vamp, trying to straighten him. She felt his chin, heavily on her shoulder and his face turned toward her ear. "This is the best I could come up with, babe. So if you've got a plan, now's a good time."

Her ears strained to pick up the soft words he'd mumbled. She twisted her head and his eyes shut. He snored softly. Eden's body jerked as if she'd been electrocuted by his words. Whatever his intent, she was touching Elliot. "Get off me you big boob!" Eden shoved hard and Titan tipped over like a giant redwood. "The bigger they are." He hit the floor hard, an echo reverbed through the floor, without breaking a snore.

Eden fell to her knees, placing a hand in the middle of his back and the other clutched his bound hands. There wasn't time for a mistake. She needed to do this right the first time cause she knew there wouldn't be a second opportunity. Circle. *Cerchio magico.* He'd taught it to her in Italian because she could wrap her mind around something that sounded like a pasta dinner.

Kristov made some weird spreading motion with his hands and Eden could see the shimmer of a bubble wiggle around her and Elliot. An arc of energy sizzled around the circle and when Kristov tried to damage it, the energy swirling around reached out and caught him in the chest. The scent of burning flesh permeated the air and Kristov whirled on Carlos. "*I warned you.* I warned you this could happen. Now you'll have to deal with the consequences."

Carlos folded his arms and looked at Eden. "You're worried about a girl? The Warlock is unconscious. She won't be able to sustain the shield for long."

Eden ignored the river of ice trailing down her spine. She inhaled slowly through her nostrils paying no attention to the stink of rotten flesh suffocating the lounge. The only thing she concentrated on was Elliot. She snapped the plastic binds on his wrists and untied the gag. "Elliot, if you can hear me, now's a good time to tell me."

Careful not to broach the shield's barriers, Eden rotated Elliot around onto his back. She figured without him, they had about ten minutes of power to the shield. His eyes were swollen shut and some nasty looking crap oozed out of them. Eden tore off part of his shirt and blotted the crusty stuff away. "Come on, Elliot. A little help here."

"Eden, I can't see. I'm no good to you if I can't see anything," his voice rasped out weakly.

"What can we do? Tell me, how to heal you."

Elliot shook his head, "You can't."

She refused to believe that. Giving up wasn't her nature. "So we should just wait for this shieldy thing to collapse and let the fuckers eat us?" Eden bent over him and her breath mingled with his, "Bullshit."

Ripping the remnants of his torn shirt away, Eden placed her right hand on the tattoo. She took hold of his thumb and guided his hand to her mark right above her hipbone. A tingling sensation almost like static cling spread up her body. "Say the words, Elliot."

He opened his eyes, bloodshot and blurry. "Not like this."

"Yeah." She touched her lips to his, "exactly like this."

The shield acted like a soundproof bubble and she could barely hear Kristov shouting outside. "See, what did I tell you? They're going to fulfill the prophecy."

Yeah, we so fuckin are! She wanted to shout it but couldn't afford losing the concentration she had on the spell.

"I can't do this to you. It isn't right."

"You know how I feel about you, Elliot. You're not *that* blind!" She placed her lips on the lids of his eyes. "Oops, sorry about that. You know what I mean. Now say the words."

Eden could see the shield begin to sparkle and pop, a sure sign its power would soon fade away. Leaving them in a really bad situation. Her palm began to warm against the tattoo on Elliot's chest while hers emanated a deep orange warmth all the way through her body.

The words flowed from him, soft as a petal with the rhythm of poetry in a language Elliot said originated with Elves. Elliot spoke the first part of the spell that would bind them. It drifted over her warm as a summer wind caressing her body. Rapture shuddered through her and Eden nearly forgot her part when it was time. She never heard the fizzle and pop as the circle lost power. She said the words of the spell as if they were written as a vow. A solemn promise which Eden intended to be alive to keep.

On a loud pop, the circle collapsed. Eden started to move into a defensive stance only to find her body locked in position. Flames of gold licked across her skin as threads of icy blue wove an intricate web around them. The edges of their tattoos turned white hot and burned inward by the magical brand. Eden watched, because she couldn't move as the transformation began on Elliot.

His eyes opened and the whites that were an awful blood red were brilliant white once more. The summer green of his corneas sparkled in something close to amazement. The stain across his face faded. The clarity returned and she never felt more relief than when he inhaled a deep cleansing breath.

The tide of energy rose. Swirling around them, it blew hot and cold with rocketed speed. It absorbed them, redefined them into something stronger. An entity composed of two strong willed people forced to recognize fate and meet it head on.

A thunderous roar echoed through the lounge as a cloud of silver energy billowed from where Elliot and Eden were. Goths ran for cover. Fledglings screamed as the silvery mist exploded across them with the effect of a back burn.

Elliot's entire body tingled with reaction. The hair on his arms and neck stood up. It was almost like being in a sauna then leaping into the icy Thames on a winter day. Elliot lifted Eden's hand to his lips. "We need a distraction."

"You're okay?"

He nodded, "I'm fine." He wasn't exactly fine, but close enough. His eyes blurred in and out, but that would correct itself once he shifted. Certainly enough to finish this off, Elliot held his palm up. A blue sphere appeared and he bounced it slowly in the air. "You wanted a distraction, hmm?"

Eden looked at the glowing ball. "Yeah, I think that will work." She shifted around the back of Elliot putting her hands on his hips. "You okay?"

"Let's get this finished." Elliot raised the ball and hurled it into the crowd. It exploded like a sun on fire. Vampires of all ages shrieked in alarm and went into instinctive mode. Sunlight turned Vampires into dust. Some of the Master's could fight it off but the first reaction was to shift into bat form and flee. "Hold your arm up, Eden." She raised her arm high as he'd taught her and Elliot called for the Red tail hawk.

He changed at his leisure on most occasions. Tonight, he needed speed. Elliot drew the energy in and pictured the bird of prey. An immense power surged through his veins like molten gold. His skeletal composition altered as he jumped and his eyesight became sharper. He was in midair, flapping easily to land on Eden's arm before he realized it. His vision cleared and sharpened to even finer degrees. He let out a triumphant screech knowing they made an imposing sight together.

Eden tossed him in the air and he sailed easily after the fledgling bats huddling in the corner of the lounge. He was across the lounge in a blink of an eye and talons raised, he smashed into a dozen or so bats. His goal was to slice through as many as possible to clear the way for Eden. He hit one in the back of the head and it fell to the floor into its original form. His hearing beyond acute now, he sensed a group approaching him. Elliot dove sharply just before he smacked into the massive window overlooking the night sky of Las Vegas. Four bats turned into smudges on the glass as Elliot circled back over the lounge.

In the center of the lounge, Eden took on seven burly Vampires. They sparred and danced over the comatose body of Titan. She never ceased to astound him. Eden took off at a dead run and launched her body into the air, flying over the top of Titan. She extended her legs, twisted her body, and landed a solid kick in the center of on Vampire's chest. She spun, bending her elbow and cocking it. The next Vampire coming up behind her got a vicious surprise.

Elliot angled and soared past Eden settling on the remains of the blood bar. He lifted one talon, avoiding the spilled blood to search another set of bats out for the taking. His eyes dilated and he found them on one search. A group huddled by the door hoping to flee if anyone opened the lounge up. On another sweep, he found Kristov.

There was never any choice in the matter who to pursue. Elliot had a duty to the Warlock contingent. For a Warlock to align with Renegades, the punishment was severe. It was a shame to waste the hawk form so quickly. Especially when there were such easy pickings, the instinct of the hawk was to hunt and Elliot wanted to hunt this night. He wanted to clear the room of this stench.

Elliot scanned the lounge searching for Carlos. The Master Vampire wasn't anywhere in sight. He didn't believe for one instant that Carlos had fled the building. He wanted the slayer too badly to give up the perfect opportunity.

Kristov thought he could rally the Vampires into fighting for him. He'd managed to beguile the Goths that weren't dead or unconscious along with a handful of young Vampires. Elliot assumed the man believed that was all he needed to begin a coupe on the Renegades. It was a foolish mistake on his behalf.

Magic was an every ending cycle of energy that Warlocks tapped in to. The amount of power the magician personally wielded came to them based on skill level, and how well the body managed the force flowing in and around them. It too years to control and manage to cast more than one spell a sitting. Magicians conserved power by limiting their spell selection. Elliot didn't have the luxury.

He transformed back into his regular form and Kristov saw him. The younger Warlock had his hands together and his lips moving as he formed a defensive spell. Elliot's fingers rubbed together and drew a mystical line straight to Kristov.

Time sped forward crazily and Elliot stood face to face with his opponent. Elliot cocked the heal of his hand and slammed it into Kristov's nose. Blood spattered and the Warlock fell back smashing into an overturned table, his spell fizzling.

"You've betrayed your contingent."

Kristov spat blood, "Fuck them." Kristov tossed shards of glass in the air shouting the phrase to turn them into shards of metal hurling toward Elliot.

Elliot's arms windmilled backward as his body bent to avoid contact with the missile. One shard nicked him on the chin drawing blood but the remainder embedded in the back of an unsuspecting Vampire. Going up onto his knees, Elliot lifted a brow. "Not a terribly controlled attack."

"Try this!" Kristov hurled a fireball at him.

Deflecting with one outstretched palm, Elliot pushed it into an unsuspecting Vampire. "That's no way to make friends and influence Vampires now is it?" He straightened, glancing around at the Vampires figuring out that standing next to the Warlock firefight wasn't a brilliant idea nearly leaped out of their own skin trying to get out of the way.

"I deserve the power. Not a weak romantic fool like you." Sweat poured off Kristov in buckets. The man was so far out of his element he had no idea had to retire gracefully from the battle. Elliot saw no remorse or willingness to reform in the other man.

He hated to see a magician turn. He knew there was evil. It made its presence known everywhere, infiltrating and corrupting. While the Warlocks prided themselves on honor, perhaps it was the pride that led them down the path to what Kristov became. Elliot sighed. He wasn't the law enforcement wing of the contingent. "I will give you one opportunity, Kristov. That's all."

He saw the Warlock plant his feet and pull energy from the earth. Manipulating it into a ball of blue energy, Kristov threw it at Elliot with all his strength.

"*Ta-daiaz.*" A full-length shield appeared in front Elliot, hard with the crest of Warwick emblazoned on it. Blue with three lions, the crest held a warrior in the center raising a mighty battle-axe. As the lightning crashed into the shield, the lions erupted forth along with the warrior. They were on Kristov within seconds.

Elliot folded his arms and turned his back on the carnage. There was more work this evening.

He strode through the bodies of the wounded and frightened walking to the door of the lounge. Elliot opened the door. "Pass now, those that remain will meet the dawn in a new form." He saw the prone form of Garridon Blackthorne under pile of what he could only assume were body parts. Elliot went to him and pulled the Vampire up to a sitting position, "Up you go, ol' boy, time to leave this party."

Garridon shook his head. "I'm fine. Just give me a minute." Garridon started to stand and Elliot shouldered most of the weight. "Not tonight, chum. We can take it from here." He maneuvered Garridon out the door. He hated going all out British on things but sometimes that received the greatest attention.

A wave of Goths vacated. Followed by what he now termed clever Vampires. Elliot then closed the door once more and locked it magically.

As a hotelier, he hated the mess. Tables and chairs overturned. Blood splashed on the carpet and walls. Glass broken and spread across the floor glittering like diamonds in the fiber crunched under his feet as he pushed his way to the surreal fight club with Eden in the center.

"Need any assistance?" He shouted over the roar of Vampires caught in a bloodlust. Their eyes a wild glowing red and the musculature and bone structure in their faces hideously altered.

Eden executed a perfect aerial kick by taking a few steps forward then turned her body sideways with her left foot in front. She put your right hand over her head and swung it forward as she jumped off her front leg. The momentum carried her and Eden whipped her body around letting the second leg take her over. The resounding smack of a female caught hard enough in the jaw to shove her back into the crowd. "Something sharp and pointed might be nice." She fell to a crouch and spun in a helicopter motion with one leg hopping her arms as she rotated.

It was a bit ostentatious, Elliot knew but achieved the desired effect when Eden knocked five of her remaining opponents flat on their backs. Elliot smiled. "Ready for the stake?"

"Anytime," she panted, "anytime." Eden extended her hand like a relay runner and Elliot provided the stake. He watched as Eden dispatched the remaining Vampires in the fight club ring.

"Where's Kristov?" Eden tossed the used stake away in the pile of ash.

"Cat food."

She looked at him quizzically. Her head tilted, eyes narrowed and she dusted her hands off her leather pants leaving prints of blood and ash. "Wanna explain?"

He sniffed, the place wreaked of death. "Later."

"Okay, well that just leaves Mr. Big Stuff."

Elliot arched a brow. "Do you mean that literally or figuratively?" Eden smacked her tongue loudly. A surge of jealously ran through his veins and Elliot forced it down into his stomach to lodge against whatever other ulcers ate at his digestive tract.

Eden turned and put her hands flat on his chest. "I'm kidding, asshole. Lighten up, Warwick, I wouldn't have done that whole prophecy thing if I didn't plan on spending my life with you."

"I had no idea what a charming couple the two

of you made." Carlos Venturi applauded loudly. The sound echoed off the walls of the room creating an eerie effect. "I applaud your effort, but I have no intention letting you out of here alive."

Eden pointed a finger at Carlos. "You've got this mixed up, Carlos. In the morning, I'm planting your remains in my new veggie garden."

Carlos threaded his fingers through his long hair and grinned. "Oh Eden, I do enjoy your sense of humor."

She shifted away. Elliot interpreted the move easily enough. Glancing at him, she winked. "I thought when you got to be a Master, you were smarter."

"Anyone who drank the Absinthe the other night belongs to me."

Elliot smiled with a sinister twist to his lips. "I'm afraid you would be mistaken." Elliot put a hand on Eden's shoulder and squeezed it. "She belongs to me."

"That can be remedied." Carlos vanished. In less than a second, he reappeared behind Elliot. "In a blink of the eye." Wrapping an arm around his head, Carlos raised a wickedly twisted dagger to Elliot's throat and with a motion faster than lightning, he slit Elliot's throat wide.

CHAPTER SEVENTEEN

Mirror Image was the name of the spell. Elliot described it as a holographic type image but the image remained solid until the image was touched. They'd *recorded* it earlier to use for this purpose. Eden had to admit she'd felt kind of dumb acting for an answering machine on steroids.

It still creeped Eden out. Seriously creeped her out to the point it sent icy wet shudders down her spine. Watching a pretend version of her react in horror as Carlos slit his throat just made her stomach tangle into a vine around her intestines.

The image of Elliot and Eden shimmered and faded leaving Carlos standing empty handed with the wicked dagger. Before he could move or react, Eden sprinted at him at a dead run. Her arms pumping, blood roaring in her ears, she knew she had one chance at this and needed to make it good.

Seven feet from Carlos, she planted her foot hard like taking off on the long jump. She launched into the air. The switchblade kick was something Eden wanted to try out. Carlos was the perfect outlet for this. On the jump, Eden executed a spinning crescent kick hitting Carlos in the chest and followed it with a front kick to his jaw, with the opposite leg, before landing

Obviously, Carlos' instinct to look up at the swoosh of air wasn't a good one. The dagger fell to the floor. Eden tucked and rolled, her hand extending for the dagger. She was on her feet in one motion spinning around and leaping for Carlos.

"Let's see how you like it." She drove the blade into the side of Carlos' neck. Blood oozed from the wound. Not the typical arterial spray you'd see on humans, Vampire blood was thicker and flowed a lot slower. More like red syrup.

Blood dripped over Carlos' hand as he reached for the handle of the dagger. His fangs lengthened and his brow bone extended. "You will be sorry for that." He yanked the dagger out and hurled it in her direction.

Eden twisted as the blade zinged past. It slid across her upper arm and Eden hissed at the pain. She smiled at Carlos. "And you'll regret that." Eden glanced at Elliot. "Your turn."

An arc of blue lightning flashed. It crackled across the room and into the chest of the Master Vampire. Fire crackled and popped as the blue electricity surrounded him. Followed by a sonic boom that leveled the Vampire, Eden figured it was some weird invisible punch.

Eden straddled him, "I know you killed my parents."

"They were going to institutionalize you," Carlos coughed, blood oozing from his mouth. "I did you a favor."

"You thought with them dead, I'd be out of your way." He grabbed hold of her ankles and forced her down. Eden's knees hit his chest. He tried to jerk her forward, his teeth bared. "You were meant to be mine, you know."

"The idea of that just makes me want to puke, you know?" Eden shoved his head back when he tried to bite her. "That so isn't happening."

His arms reached up and crushed her to him as he rolled. Carlos flattened her into a bed of broken glass. "I'm going to enjoy this." He lowered his head, using his weight and the superior strength to angle her head to one side.

Eden's stomach bounced hard against her intestines and God knew what else on its way back down from her throat. Rotten garbage combine with decaying flesh was never her first choice for cologne. Carlos was an abomination and Eden knew how to deal with that. Her knee slammed up into his heavy crotch. Carlos howled in rage as his body went slack. She pressed her hand on his chest and rolled him off her. Kneeling across him, her eyes flashed. "You made a mistake coming here, Carlos. You made a mistake trying to screw with me."

The stake appeared in her hand. Eden raised it around six inches from his chest. "It's too bad that Seraphina missed the big party." Carlos moved his hands reaching for her and she slammed the stake through his heart. Carlos erupted in a ball of flame. Elliot jerked her back out of the way before the fiery ball gasped and crumbled in mound of ash. Eden leaned heavily against Elliot. "Can we leave this mess for Seraphina? I think she deserves a treat from the party."

They returned to the Desert Mirage and after one helluva wild fuck, Eden showered and went to get a sandwich while Elliot dosed. She didn't blame him for crashing – hell, he'd gone from blind to nearly dead this evening all in a few hours. She'd made Elliot a sandwich, just in case, and as she passed the study door decided she wanted to check out one of the latest mystery novels Elliot had on his shelves.

The view from Elliot's study looked out high above Las Vegas at night catching just a third of the Strip from where the Desert Mirage sat. It was easy to see why Elliot liked this room with all the lights glittering like diamonds among neon.

She sat their late night snack down on the desk and flicked on the desk lamp. A soft warm glow filled the room and Eden's eyes fell on the spellbook containing the prophecy. "Well, we don't you out anymore." She picked the book up, her fingers curling around the leather binding. She should've known better.

Chalk it up to such a wild night, Eden sighed when the gale force wind blew into the room and whirled around her in a wild hurricane of magic. She dropped the book just as the wind lifted her off the ground and flattened her against the wall.

"Son of a bitch!" It was her fault. She knew it.

In her crash course in magic of the bazillionth degree last night, Elliot warned her that some books and items might have protective wards place on them. That didn't make her any less pissed that her roast beef and horseradish cheddar sandwich was six feet away and she was starving. "Damn, damn, damn." She wiggled against the wall only succeeded to work her boy cut, pajama shorts half way down her hips. "Elliot!" With her arms pinned back next to her head, who the fuck knew how she'd managed that one, she looked like some damn centerfold pinned to his wall. "Elliot!"

The door opened. "Well this is an interesting sight." He walked into the study wearing a pair of black pajama bottoms that she had to admit looked really sexy right now. "I wondered where my sandwich had gone."

Eden growled as he picked up one of the sandwiches and raised it to his lips. "If you take one bite of that, I will so kick your ass when I get down from here."

Elliot's eyes glistened reminding her of a cat toying with its prey. "What would you have me eat then?" He moved silently across the floor to where she was. Placing one hand on her hip and the other on her waist, he skimmed his mouth across her stomach.

Muscles tightened instinctively as the scrape of his beard did amazing things. "Well," Eden coughed as on of Elliot's fingers tucked under the waistband of her shorts, "we didn't finish this last time."

"No, we didn't." Elliot's eyes flickered. "I owe you, don't I?"

Eden's lips twisted, okay she could go for having her pussy eaten while she hung on a wall. Not like they hadn't started this before. Fire blazed a trail from her belly into her pussy as she anticipated Elliot's tongue. Her body tensed as he dragged the shorts over her hips and down over her feet, each nerve ending stimulated by the scrape of fabric.

She slid a bit lower on the wall and he brought her legs by waving a hand. "I did warn you about touching certain items."

"Yeah, yeah," she mumbled as two fingers moved over her mound and then parted her wet lips. He teased her clit and Eden's nervous system jerked to complete awareness.

Elliot shook his head. "Tsk, tsk, Eden, what am I going to do with you?"

"Oh I could think of several things." His fingers toyed with her clit, pinching, massaging and driving her insane in the most delicious way.

Elliot's tongue scraped across her inner thigh and Eden needed to fight back the raging wave threatening to pull her under. It was way too fast. She was too hot for him, too quick and she didn't want it over this soon. He dipped one finger deep inside testing her readiness. "You've given me one hell of a hard on, Eden."

"If I could bend my head, I'd love to see."

He used his fingers to frame her pussy and then lowered his face. Elliot's tongue licked, and stroked across her clit then nibbled gently. Eden thought for sure she couldn't hold back. That tidal wave gained ground on her. Shuddering as his tongue slid deep inside her warm hole, Eden knew that Warlock's had magical ability in all areas. He fucked her with his tongue, driving it hard and fast so deep inside her that Eden began to come completely undone by it.

He lapped her honeyed juices, as she searched for something to hold onto. Something to break her fall when she fell. Her body tensed, nerve endings totally scorched as the wave built to a crescendo. Eden reached out for anything, her body and mind disoriented as her fingers found their way to Elliot's hair. "Oh my gawd!" Her blurry vision noticed they were now in his bed and he ate her pussy like a man feasting on a buffet.

The orgasm hit her so hard it knocked the air right out of her lungs. Her body bucked and surged, her legs wrapping around Elliot's shoulders while her fingers pulled at his hair. It rolled her back, one hot wave after another until all she could do was gasp for air. "You're trying to kill me!" He hadn't stopped yet and she knew any second she'd die a fabulous death. "Put your cock inside me, Elliot. Now!"

He was quick to oblige. A shuffling of fabric and Eden cracked her lids open as he parted her legs farther. He wiped her juice from his face, positioned himself and drove his long thick cock deep in her shaft.   Her pussy instantly tightened, greedily accepting him and anxious to send her rocketing into orbit once more.

"Oh hell, this is so good." Elliot pumped with hard strokes going deeper inside her each time. "Your pussy is so tight and wet, it swallows me." His balls slapped against the back of her pussy and Eden wiggled forward so she could give them a good squeeze. Elliot's body jerked and she wrapped her legs tighter around him. "You're going to make me come."

"Good." She could practically see the wave of fire bearing down on her as it was. "I'll be lucky if I last much longer."

He increased the pace. Sliding in and out with that hard shaft that her pussy adored, Eden wished it could last hours but there was too much here. Emotions swirling around them over what had happened this night along with unused energy and it roared to life between them.

The wave appeared in over her, her pussy surged with slick heat. Sweat dripped off his hair as he pumped harder and faster. There wasn't much time. And for once, she needed to hear the words no matter how old-fashioned they were. "Say the words, Elliot." Her nails dug into his shoulders, and she angled her hips giving him even deeper access. "Say the words."

His eyes glazed with something beyond passion. "I do love you, you know."

His arms went around her tight and fast as he fucked her. Locked together, he managed to raise his head as the wave crashed over the top of them. Hot seed poured into her receptive pussy. Eden knew the world slipped away as thousands of stars danced across her vision. Tiny frissons of current spun off around them. Eden shut her eyes and enjoyed the ride.

And now for a special sneak peek at

TORMENT AT MIDNIGHT

By EPPIE & CAPA nominee
Elaine Charton

Coming to a bookseller near you in
October 2006

Catch the fever at

Triskelion Publishing
<u>www.triskelionpublishing.net</u>
All about women. All about extraordinary.

Orlando stood, glad to stretch after his long flight from Poland. He'd been in Eastern Europe for the past six months visiting friends, doing research for his latest book, and teaching the occasional class. He'd accepted a new teaching position at Massachusetts College. It would allow him time to see his sister and brother-in-law. Pulling his case out of the overhead compartment, he walked out the airplane and into the terminal. All he wanted was to get in a cab and head for Angie's house. It would be good to see his sister and brother-in-law again. Lost deep in thought he almost didn't see his sister waiting in the baggage area for him.

"Lando!" She flung herself into his arms.

"Angelina!" He hugged his sister and set her back on her feet, holding her at arms length. "Look at you!" He laid his hands on her burgeoning belly. "When are you due? Why didn't you tell me?"

"She insisted on surprising you." A deep male voice spoke from behind him. "You know what she's like once she gets an idea in her head."

Orlando turned and hugged his brother-in-law. "Hello, Simon. Yes, I do know what she's like. However, that's ok. We love her anyway."

"That we do. I'm going to get the car, meet me

outside once you get your bags." He kissed his wife. "Try not to overwhelm your brother on his first day home, sweetheart."

With an arm around his sister, Orlando steered her toward the luggage carousal. "So baby sister, when are you due?"

"In about three months. I was going to write you and then you called to tell me you were offered a position at the college, so I decided to wait and surprise you."

"That you did. Do you feel all right? Is everything ok?"

"Couldn't be better. The doctor is pleased with the way things are going and we know it's going to be a girl. We're going to name her Rosa Angelina, after Mom."

He hugged his sister. "Momma would have liked that."

"I know. I told Aunt Millie and I thought she would never stop crying."

"How is Millie?" His aunt had taken them in after their mother's death and taken care of them both, regardless of the fact it had been her brother, Orlando's father who had committed the murder.

"She's fine. She'll be over tomorrow for dinner."

He glanced down and found his sister was biting her lower lip. "What's wrong, Angie?"

"Nothing? Why should anything be wrong."

He stopped walking and turned his sister to look at him, keeping his hands on her shoulders.

"Angelina, I know that look on your face. You're afraid of something, so tell me now. It's not Simon, is it? If he hurt you?"

"No! Lando, Simon would never hurt me, you know that. No, its just Millie reminded me that '*he*' was released earlier this week."

Lando didn't have to ask who '*he*' was, the date had been marked on his mental calendar for months. Truth be told it had been one of the reasons he came back home. "As long as he stays away from us, he can do whatever he wants."

"Millie and I have both talked to his lawyer and told him the same thing." Instinctively, she began rubbing her belly.

He hugged her and placed his hands over hers, rubbing her belly. "You and the little one are not to worry, ok?"

She nodded, "I'm so glad you're home, I've missed you."

"I've missed you as well, little sister." The lights on the carousel began flashing, ending their conversation as the luggage began unloading. He grabbed his bags off the carousal and followed Angie out the door. Simon had parked right at the curb. After stowing his bags in the trunk of the car, they were on their way.

"Did you find a place to stay yet?" Angie asked.

Orlando shook his head. "I hope you don't mind me imposing on you for a few weeks until I can find a decent place."

"We told you, stay as long as you like," his brother-in-law said. "But we do have a place you might want to look at. My brother-in-law owns a triple-decker around the corner from us. The third floor apartment is available. Let me know when you want to look at it and I'll give him a call."

"Sounds good." Orlando stifled a yawn. Jet lag was finally catching up to him. He knew Angie and Simon would understand if he just closed his eyes until they got home, but he didn't want to. He hadn't been back in so long. He was curious to see how much had changed. His body however, had other ideas and before they were out of the airport he was sound asleep. He woke with a start as they pulled in front of the house. That's when he felt it.

Getting out of the car he stopped, his senses on alert. He looked around. They lived directly across from a park and the boulevard leading to Dark Fort Isle. It all looked so peaceful and idyllic, nothing like what he felt. In the distance, he could see the Fort and lights from several cars, more than would normally be there at this time of night. Something seemed to be happening out there. Whatever it was, it wasn't good. It had to be extremely evil if he could feel it out here.